T0283334

Praise for Matthew FitzSimmons

The Slate

"Matthew FitzSimmons breaks out of the pack of DC novels of politics and crime with *The Slate*, a sobering ticking-clock(s) screen of Washington power beyond mere election fraud—and he does so with strong twenty-first-century kick-ass women. While FitzSimmons spotlights evils like political corruption, human trafficking, and murder, what makes *The Slate* stand out is its climax core: redemption."

—James Grady, creator of *Condor* and author of *The Smoke in Our Eyes*

Chance

"FitzSimmons hooks readers with the clone angle and then expertly mixes SF and mystery tropes till he's implicated every party in sight in some sort of crime or cover-up. A seriously playful novel of ideas."

—*Kirkus Reviews*

Constance

An Amazon Best Book of the Month: Science Fiction & Fantasy

"Maybe what we need most as this bewildering summer winds down is a diverting story about an interesting futuristic topic that injects no new anxiety into our nervous brains . . . [*Constance*] shines in its interstitial moments . . . In between the sleuthing and the schemes for world domination and the eluding of people with guns, we are invited to grapple with genuinely thoughtful questions about the philosophical, legal, and ethical implications of cloning and scientific innovation in general . . . The debates around cloning in *Constance* echo many of our contemporary preoccupations—skepticism of science, radical mistrust of those with opposing views, conspiracy theories."

—Sarah Lyall, critic, *The New York Times*

"Full of technological surprises and ethical dilemmas, this inventive thriller hums with the electric excitement of the best 1950s science fiction."

—Tom Nolan, critic, *The Wall Street Journal*

"In this timely thriller, tantalizing clues, complex motives, and shifting views of the truth flow around such issues as the relationship between money and power, the right to life, and the definition of self. FitzSimmons has upped his game with this one."

—*Publishers Weekly* (starred review)

"A super-brainy high-concept dystopian tale guaranteed to reward anyone who's in the mood."

—*Kirkus Reviews*

"A propulsive sci-fi thriller that questions the very nature of what makes us human."

—POPSUGAR

"What a book! Like all the best speculative fiction, FitzSimmons's compelling thriller *Constance* takes elements of real science and spins them up into a novel and terrifying premise."

—Blake Crouch, *New York Times* bestselling author of *Dark Matter* and *Recursion*

"*Constance* is a blistering, balletic read—silky-smooth world-building that effortlessly grounds a wonderful, harrowing tale of mystery, suspense, identity, friendship, and redemption. This is, for all its twists, turns, and tricks, a novel that does what a novel should do: examine what makes us human after all. Genuinely one of the best books I have read in a long, long time."

—Greg Rucka, *New York Times* bestselling author and creator of *The Old Guard*

Origami Man

"FitzSimmons brings Gibson Vaughn and an old enemy full circle in *Origami Man*—an intricately plotted, rapid-fire thriller guaranteed to hook you from page one. Easily the best Gibson Vaughn installment to date."

—Steven Konkoly, *Wall Street Journal* bestselling author

"Matthew FitzSimmons's rapid-fire novels are loaded with twisted plots, explosive action, and dialogue that crackles with wit and emotion. His bighearted characters keep me coming back, book after book. Grab this thriller with both hands because *Origami Man* is a total blast."

—Nick Petrie, bestselling author of *The Drifter*

Debris Line

"Matthew FitzSimmons writes the kinds of thrillers I love to read: smart, character driven, and brimming with creative action sequences. If you're not yet a fan of FitzSimmons's Gibson Vaughn series, strap in, because you soon will be. *Debris Line* is tense, twisty, and always ten steps ahead. Don't miss it."

—Chris Holm, Anthony Award–winning author of *The Killing Kind*

"Matt FitzSimmons continues his amazing literary feat of creating an ensemble cast of troubled heroes and shooting them through page-turning thrillers with his latest, *Debris Line*, continuing the fast-paced adventures of Gibson Vaughn and his crew as they battle to stay alive and find some measure of justice in this unforgiving world. The Gibson Vaughn series is on its way to being a classic franchise of thriller fiction, with a unique voice and an unusual approach that keep the stories as appealing as they are entertaining. Highly recommended."

—James Grady, author of *Six Days of the Condor*

"*Debris Line* . . . doesn't waste a word or miss a twist. It's always smart, always entertaining, and populated top to bottom with fascinating and unforgettable characters."

—Lou Berney, author of *November Road*

Cold Harbor

"In FitzSimmons's action-packed third Gibson Vaughn thriller . . . fans of deep, dark government conspiracies will keep turning the pages to see how it all turns out."

—*Publishers Weekly*

"*Cold Harbor* interweaves two classic American tropes: the solitary prisoner imprisoned for who knows what and the American loner determined to rectify the injustices perpetrated on him. It's a page-turner that keeps the reader wondering—and looking forward to Gibson Vaughn number four."

—Criminal Element

"There are so many layers and twists to *Cold Harbor* . . . FitzSimmons masterfully fits together the myriad pieces of Gibson Vaughn's past like a high-quality Springbok puzzle."

—*Crimespree Magazine*

Poisonfeather

An Amazon Best Book of the Month: Mystery, Thriller & Suspense Category

"FitzSimmons's complicated hero leaps off the page with intensity and good intentions while a byzantine plot hums along, ensnaring characters into a tightening web of greed, betrayal, and violent death."

—*Publishers Weekly*

"[FitzSimmons] has knocked it out of the park, as they say. The characters' layers are being peeled back further and further, allowing readers to really root for the good guys! FitzSimmons has put together a great plot that doesn't let you rest for even a minute."

—*Suspense Magazine*

The Short Drop

"FitzSimmons has come up with a doozy of a sociopath."

—*The Washington Post*

"This live-wire debut begins with a promising lead in the long-ago disappearance of the vice president's daughter, then doubles down with tangled conspiracies, duplicitous politicians, and a disgraced hacker hankering for redemption . . . Hang on and enjoy the ride."

—*People*

"Writing with swift efficiency, FitzSimmons shows why the stakes are high, the heroes suitably tarnished, and the bad guys a pleasure to foil."

—*Kirkus Reviews*

"With a complex plot layered on top of unexpected emotional depth, *The Short Drop* is a wonderful surprise on every level . . . This is much more than a solid debut; it's proof that FitzSimmons has what it takes."

—Amazon.com, an Amazon Best Book of December 2015

"Beyond exceptional. Matthew FitzSimmons is the real deal."

—Andrew Peterson, author of the bestselling Nathan McBride series

"*The Short Drop* is an adrenaline-fueled thriller that has it all: political intrigue, murder, and suspense. Matthew FitzSimmons weaves a clever plot and deftly leads the reader on a rapid ride to an explosive end."

—Robert Dugoni, bestselling author of *My Sister's Grave*

THE
SLATE

OTHER TITLES BY
MATTHEW FITZSIMMONS

The Gibson Vaughn series

The Short Drop

Poisonfeather

Cold Harbor

Debris Line

Origami Man

The Constance series

Constance

Chance

THE
SLATE

MATTHEW
FITZSIMMONS

THOMAS & MERCER

Published by Thomas & Mercer, Seattle

www.apub.com

Amazon, the Amazon logo, and Thomas & Mercer are trademarks of Amazon.com, Inc., or its affiliates.

ISBN-13: 9781542009508 (hardcover)
ISBN-13: 9781542009515 (paperback)
ISBN-13: 9781542009492 (digital)

Cover design by David Drummond
Cover image: © Hoover Tung / Shutterstock; © jayk7 / Getty

Printed in the United States of America

First edition

For Eric

Whenever people tell you they are going to wipe the slate clean, it's your slate they mean to wipe.

—*P. J. O'Rourke*

July 13, 2001

Her phone rang shortly before midnight, or more accurately, one of them rang. She'd fallen asleep fully clothed, sitting upright in bed beside the stack of *Washington Post*s she hadn't gotten around to this week. On the television, David Letterman was interviewing Vince Vaughn about his new movie. Without opening her eyes, she muted the volume with the clicker and reached for the cordless on her nightstand.

"Yeah?" she said, stifling a yawn.

"Agatha," Paul Paxton stated as if she were an amnesiac needing a reminder. "I wake you?"

She appreciated the congressman's feigned concern, but it was Friday night, and that was personal. "What do you need, boss?"

"There's been an incident out at the Grey Horse in Middleburg."

Middleburg was a quaint little town in Virginia with a scenic main street boasting shops and restaurants where a certain segment of DC went antiquing on weekends. The Grey Horse was a historic inn that had been a fixture there since the eighteenth century. It wasn't the kind of place that had "incidents."

"Who?" she asked.

"Clark."

Agatha's eyes were open now. "Clark" would be Congressman Harrison Clark of the great state of Illinois. "Is he alone?"

"Of course not."

Congressman Clark's wandering eye had always been his Achilles' heel. That he was having a tryst hardly warranted a midnight phone call.

"So what happened?" she asked.

"There were drugs involved. Apparently they were having a little party. *She* overdosed." Paxton sounded almost excited, but it wouldn't be until much later that she stopped to contemplate what that meant.

"Who's the girl?" Agatha asked, although she already knew the answer.

"Yes," he said.

Agatha let out a breath she hadn't known she was holding and looked away to Letterman laughing silently, head back like a man possessed. Charlotte Haines was dead. Dead. That was a lot to take in, and Agatha didn't know how to feel about it.

"Is that going to be a problem?" Paxton asked, mistaking her silence for reticence.

"Just tell me what I need to do." She swung her feet off the bed and reached for a notepad.

"That's why you're my killer." He meant it as a compliment, but she would always wonder what it said about her that she took it as one.

"Why didn't Clark call his own people?"

"You know his chief of staff. The man's a damn Boy Scout. He overlooks the infidelities, but this falls too far outside his comfort zone."

Paxton carried on, laying it all out, while Agatha wrote everything down in her neat, economical script, making notes to herself as she went. In the top left corner, she wrote "COFFEE" in all caps and underlined it three times.

"So what's our play?" she asked.

"Be a knight in shining armor. Clean up his mess."

Neither said anything for a long moment, as if both knew a bright, uncrossable line was being crossed. They played plenty dirty but always just this side of legal. Helping Clark with his predicament was a whole other proposition. Right now, no crime had been committed. A young Hill staffer overdosing in a congressman's hotel room wasn't great, but it was only a career-ending scandal. What they were discussing now was a criminal conspiracy.

"Speak your mind," he said.

"Are we sure we want to do this?"

"I don't like it any more than you do. But this town is built on quid pro quo, and this is the mother of all favors. We do this for Clark, and I'm on the fast track. That much closer to accomplishing everything we came to Washington to do."

He wasn't wrong. Clark was the party's whip in the House, and his opinion carried weight. That was why Paxton had targeted him in the first place. If Agatha did this, the congressman would be in their back pocket. What might have taken years of networking and maneuvering could be done in the blink of an eye. Paul would jump to the front of the freshman class. Choice of committee assignments, a voice in the party—Paxton could write his own ticket. She told herself it was worth the risk.

"I'll get it done."

"I knew I could count on you," he said. "And Agatha? Get pictures. You understand?"

"On it."

"Good. How soon can you be there? I need to let the congressman know. He's understandably anxious."

"At least an hour. Probably two. I'll have to round up Darius."

"Is it wise bringing someone else into this?"

"I can't move a body *and* take pictures."

"Right. Right. Okay."

"Is there anything else?" she asked, itching to get moving. She had a little more than six hours of darkness remaining, and sunrise would not be her friend today.

"No. Call me when it's done."

"It'll be late."

"I won't be asleep," he said and hung up.

Agatha set aside the cordless and reached into the bag at her feet for one of the three Nokia cell phones she carried everywhere. She'd need to destroy it after tonight.

"What up, A?" Darius said when he finally answered on the fifth ring. It was loud wherever he was, and the music all but drowned him out.

She felt a little jealous. There was a time in her life when she would have been the one out on a Friday night.

"I've got a job. You want it?" she asked, kneeling to slip on her shoes.

"That depends on what it is."

"Does it?"

"Oh, it's like that?"

"It's definitely like that."

———

It was past 2:00 a.m. when they pulled into Middleburg. The town was dead, and that was a concern. A bored cop might get curious what a white woman and a Black man were doing cruising around his rustic hamlet in the middle of the night. They weren't breaking the law, not yet anyway, but this was still the South, and she didn't want their names in a deputy's log. When the press tried to reconstruct the events of tonight, and they would, there couldn't be anything placing them here.

She was happy to see so many DC plates in the parking lot of the Grey Horse Inn—guests who'd fled the city for the weekend. Easier to blend in. She found a spot around back and killed the engine.

"Clear on the plan?" she asked, handing Darius her keys.

"Wait here. Keep a lookout. Take pictures of Mr. Congressman with the girl when you bring her out."

"He can't see you."

"Nobody sees Darius till I let them," he answered with the characteristic swagger that had made him a legend at Saint John's College High School. Everyone had known Darius McDaniel back then, a five-star recruit at free safety and the starting point guard on the basketball team. His nickname had been Ninja for his uncanny ability to materialize out of nowhere at exactly the right time. He'd had a bright future ahead of him. No one doubted that.

He and Agatha had met in a photography class and had been friends for a spell. That had ended abruptly the first and only time she'd been invited to his house in Trinidad. Mrs. McDaniel had taken one look at the white girl with green hair and recognized trouble when she saw it. Her baby had a full ride to Auburn, and nothing and no one would stand in the way of it. That was until the Gonzaga game his senior year. Not even Mrs. McDaniel could protect her son from the 260-pound pulling guard who bent Darius's knee backward like a folding chair. There wasn't a soul in the stands that night who would ever forget his unholy screams. The injury put a pin in his scholarship, permanently, and after graduation he'd enlisted, serving two tours as an army photographer. Agatha ran into him at a reunion event after his discharge. He'd moved back in with his mom and was trying to catch on as a press stringer without much luck. He'd been working off the books for her ever since.

"What are we doing with the body after?"

That was a good question. Ideally Agatha would have liked to take Charlotte home and stage the scene there, but that wasn't realistic. Charlotte lived in an apartment building. The odds of carrying a body up six floors, sight unseen, even in the middle of the night, were too remote to risk.

"I'm thinking we take her car back to the city. Maybe Shaw. Leave her there."

"Oh, hell no. We're not dumping a rich white girl in a Black neighborhood. The police will lose their damn minds."

"Hey, easy, her name is Charlotte Haines." It was the first time tonight that Agatha had said her name out loud. It sounded like a blasphemy coming from her mouth.

"I know her name."

"So how about show a little respect?"

"Respect? Respect like you carrying her body out of a congressman's hotel room while I snap pictures? That the respect you want me to show her?"

Agatha put up her hands in surrender. "You're right. Forget Shaw. It was just a thought."

"Well, have another one. White girls might come downtown to score, but they ain't hanging around to do the shit."

He had a point. "So where would she go?"

"You think *I* know? You're the only white girl from DC in this car. Where would you've gone back in the day?"

That gave her an idea that would add an extra layer of misdirection onto any investigation. The more confusion around tonight, the better. Darius must have seen it on her face.

"Oh, I know that look. What you got?"

She told him, and Darius let out a laugh. "Man, you always were evil. Remind me never to get on that naughty list of yours."

Agatha had been told she thought like a felon. If so, it was only because her dad had been a detective with the MPD and her mom had been an English teacher at Saint John's. Surviving high school with any kind of freedom had meant staying one step ahead of her ever-vigilant parents.

"Alright, I'm going," she said. "Give a ring if you see anything."

"Eyes and ears," Darius replied and reached for his camera bag in the back seat.

The congressman's suite was located in the converted carriage house behind the inn's main building. Agatha pulled on a pair of latex gloves before knocking lightly. Harrison Clark answered as though he'd been waiting on the other side of the door. Tall, white, and patrician-handsome with a head of coal-black hair that defied his forty-eight years. Agatha would've bet good money it was getting help from a bottle, but word on the Hill was good genes. He wore a bathrobe over his suit as if he'd caught a chill. All things considered, he looked pretty good for a man whose career hung in the balance. He was accustomed to looking good under pressure, though, and there was a glow about him as if he were standing in different light than she.

"Congressman," she said. "I'm Agatha Cardiff."

He looked her up and down. "You're who Paxton sent?"

Agatha took his skepticism in stride. She knew what he saw, the same thing every man in Congress saw when they looked at her: a young woman better suited to fetching coffee, laughing at their jokes, and taking their clumsy advances as the compliments they thought they were. That was why her first job when entering a room was dispelling any doubt that she *belonged* as quickly as possible.

"I am, sir."

"How old are you?"

"I passed an old-folks home on the way into town," she suggested pleasantly. "I could swing back and rustle you up a senior if that'll put your mind at ease."

"It's a reasonable question," he insisted peevishly.

"I'm thirty-one, and this isn't a job interview. I already have one. You want to call for someone older, be my guest. I've got an hour drive back to DC either way." She turned to look toward the parking lot and her car.

"Wait. It's just . . . ," he started and stopped, searching for a word that would articulate while also minimizing the mess he was in. "Delicate."

"That's why I'm here, sir. We both want the same thing. So why don't you show me where she is."

Reluctantly, he let her in. She followed him back through the bedroom. The sheets were undisturbed. His night had never really had a chance to start, or maybe he found beds too mundane. In the bathroom, on the black-and-white-tile floor by the toilet, a woman lay motionless. She wore a colorful bra-and-panty set from Victoria's Secret that seemed far too festive under the circumstances.

Agatha crouched to take a closer look, but Charlotte remained just as dead up close. Eyes closed, her face looked oddly peaceful, as though she were only taking a quick catnap. Up until that moment, Charlotte's death had been an abstraction. An opportunity to be seized and exploited. But now, looking at her, Agatha remembered that Charlotte was only twenty-three.

Charlotte Bella Haines was the daughter of wealthy patrons of Agatha's boss. A campaign favor was the only reason she had a job in Paxton's office. The problem had been that Charlotte knew it. She arrived late, left early, and did little in the way of work in between. There was nothing quite so irritating to Agatha as someone who mistook parental connections for personal accomplishment. She'd disliked Charlotte on contact, writing her off as a dim, unserious party girl. It had proved an accurate assessment. Most days, Bad Charlotte—as Agatha dubbed her—turned up to work hungover. A fact she seemed oddly proud of, as if it were proof that she was the only one in the office truly living life.

As far as Agatha could tell, Charlotte's two most marketable talents had been her looks and her carbonated personality, for which she'd traded her common sense and anything resembling a work ethic. Among Agatha's responsibilities as Paxton's chief of staff, running interference and preventing Charlotte from embarrassing the congressman contended for the most frustrating and fruitless. Firing Charlotte was out of the question, so the next best option had been to compel her to quit. Charlotte had no spine, and Agatha had reckoned all it would take was turning the screws until she went scurrying home to Mommy and Daddy.

If there were a menial task or errand, it fell to Bad Charlotte. Make fifty copies of an amendment and deliver it to the floor of the House; clean the storage cages at the top of the Cannon House Office Building; collect the dry cleaning; update the holiday card list; run to the drugstore to pick up the congressman's Viagra. Agatha was relentless and publicly critical of everything Charlotte did. It was cruel but absolutely necessary to drive her out. Unexpectedly, though, she wouldn't quit. No matter how many times Agatha reduced her to tears, Charlotte turned up the next morning for more.

Agatha hadn't seen it until someone pointed it out, but inexplicably, Charlotte looked up to her. A misguided hero worship that might actually have been endearing if Charlotte hadn't been so fundamentally unsuited to the work. She was desperate for Agatha's approval but didn't know how to earn anything that wasn't freely given. She was a disaster, but she also wouldn't take the easy way out.

It had been Agatha's idea to introduce Charlotte to Clark. The congressman had a type, and that type was Charlotte Bella Haines—young, blissfully ignorant, and down for anything. The idea had been to aim Charlotte at him and let her natural chaos work its magic. Had Agatha known Charlotte would do it hoping to please her? There was a question to keep her up at night. She looked at Charlotte's face resting on the bathroom floor, and a black hole, the result of Agatha's guilt collapsing in on itself, began to form where a doctor might have expected to find her heart. She didn't know then, but it would live there for the rest of her life.

Not that guilt would stop her from doing what needed to be done. The way she looked at it, Charlotte was dead either way. Playing the saint wouldn't bring her back, and failing to take advantage of the situation would be like leaving house money on the table. Agatha might've argued against it on the phone earlier, but she had a gift for compartmentalization, and once the decision was made, that was that. It was the only way to get the job done, and the job was all there was.

She hadn't known Charlotte used drugs, but it didn't exactly shake her faith in humanity. Four vials of white powder were arranged carefully on the toilet seat like witnesses. Two had been emptied out on the cover of the May issue of *Town & Country*. Agatha could see contrails where cocaine had been arranged into lines before disappearing up Charlotte's nose. Was that really all it took to kill someone? Agatha didn't know a lot about drugs. They weren't among her vices.

"Jesus," Clark said behind her as if this were his first time seeing Charlotte this way. "She was so young."

Agatha was thinking the same thing but for different reasons. "Was she a regular user?"

"I have no idea. She just went into the bathroom with her purse the way you girls do."

Agatha let that go. "Did anyone see her with you tonight?"

"No, I had a fundraiser nearby this evening. Charlotte drove out and met me here afterward."

"Is there anyone she would have told about meeting you here?" Agatha asked, knowing the answer but needing to pose the question to keep up appearances. Clark had to believe he knew more about this situation than she did.

"No, she's always been very discreet."

Agatha inwardly rolled her eyes. *If only you knew.* "Good. Where's your wife? In DC?"

"No, Wilmette." He didn't sound pleased to have her dragged into this. Wilmette was a suburb of Chicago, where the congressman's family lived. A nice safe distance. Spouses tended to stay back in the home district, which made Washington an unchaperoned playground for husbands eager to explore the limits of their power.

In this instance, the fundraiser created a useful cover story, so Clark's wife was unlikely to ask questions about why he'd spent the night at an inn. That was something.

"How are you getting back to DC?" she asked.

"A car is picking me up at seven."

"Alright, keep that schedule. Everything like normal."

"Sure." He hadn't taken his eyes off Charlotte.

"Where are her clothes?"

It wasn't an easy thing to dress a dead body, and Agatha wasn't getting any help from the congressman. She was grateful to Charlotte for choosing a little black dress for her rendezvous. Not that it would matter in the end. She knew from her dad that a re-dressed body was one of the first things police looked for at a scene. It never looked right and was an immediate tip-off that a third party had been involved. That suited Agatha. She didn't want the congressman connected directly to Charlotte's death, but it wouldn't hurt if he stayed nervous and remembered who his friends were.

She swept the drugs back into the purse and wiped down all the surfaces in the bathroom until they sparkled. The magazine would come with her. Making a final pass through the suite, she picked up anything belonging to Charlotte.

"We have to move her now," she told Clark, who was sitting in an armchair staring blankly at the wall.

"We?" He sounded profoundly put out by the suggestion.

"Congressman, I can't carry her by myself. If you want, I can call a guy, but that's more eyes and ears and, most importantly, lips that will know what happened here."

The idea of more witnesses got him out of his seat, and he followed her back into the bathroom like a child who didn't want to do his chores. Agatha took Charlotte's legs, and the senator stood over her shoulders, unmoving. His Hi-Pro glow was gone, and he looked like he needed to be sick.

Agatha didn't have time for that. "What are your plans this weekend?"

"What?" he said numbly, the question catching him out, distracting him. That was the point, though, so she continued as conversationally as possible.

"Why is the car picking you up so early?"

"Oh, I'm playing golf with the vice president at noon."

Inclining her head, Agatha gestured casually to Charlotte, as if she were furniture he'd agreed to help move, and Clark gently scooped his hands under the shoulders and lifted the body. Progress.

"That sounds nice. Should be a beautiful day for it. Where are you playing?"

They navigated their way out of the bathroom and waddled through the bedroom. "At Andrews. Decent enough course, but security is the main thing."

"Of course," she agreed. "I hear the fairways are pretty hairy."

"No, it's not the best-maintained course I've ever played, that's for certain."

She kept him talking until they arrived at the front door, where they set Charlotte down. Agatha assured him she'd be right back and went out to Charlotte's little BMW M3 with the keys. The inside looked like an abandoned refugee camp, but she was careful not to disturb anything except the map of Virginia spread out on the passenger seat. That she folded up carefully and put away in the glove box. Starting the engine, she circled the parking lot, backed the car up to the room, and popped the trunk.

"Should we wrap her in something? A rug?" Clark asked when he answered the door. "What if someone sees us?"

"I don't want the staff wondering why a congressman stole a rug. Do you? It's only a few feet to the trunk. It's late, and there's no one out there. We move quickly, no one will see a thing," she said, lifting Charlotte's ankles.

"I don't know. Seems risky."

"Risky is every second this body stays in your hotel room."

Grudgingly, he nodded at the truth of it. "When this is all over, you should come work for me."

"I have a job, but I appreciate the offer."

"Well, Paul's lucky to have you."

Agatha opened the front door and took hold of Charlotte's ankles for a second time. She waited for the senator to be ready.

"Alright, on a count of three. One. Two . . ."

CHAPTER ONE

Twenty-One Years Later

Since mid-March, spring had been playing a coy game of "Will I? Won't I?" with the city, like a candidate teasing a run for office. One day was sunny and beautiful, with a breeze that made you believe in the possibility of miracles; then the next would hover in the low thirties with winds fresh off the Arctic Circle. Today was a good one, though, and the weather gods were feeling beneficent—seventy-four degrees beneath an iridescent sky dotted with cartoonishly perfect wisps of cloud. The Tidal Basin was a riot of pink-and-white cherry blossoms, gifts from the Japanese in 1912. Not that Felix Gallardo would be basking in the sunshine. He couldn't remember the last time his workday ended before sunset, and serving at the pleasure of the president of the United States didn't come with weekends off.

Not that Felix would have taken them if it had.

No, he thought, gazing out the pollen-stained window of his ride-share inching its way up Independence Avenue toward Capitol Hill, this was as close as he was likely to come to springtime this year. With the good weather had come thousands upon thousands of tourists, migrating from one monument or Smithsonian to the next in majestic herds. Traffic was a mess. Up ahead, the light turned yellow, but instead of accelerating through it, the driver braked. A chaotic mob of high schoolers in matching red T-shirts and lanyards streamed across the intersection.

Felix checked his watch. Just his luck to have hailed a ride from the only responsible driver in the District. He needed to be back at the White House, where a draft of the president's remarks for the Canadian prime minister's visit awaited a final polish. Then came the list of possible messaging responses to the new tax plan introduced by the House and reviewing the party's proposed travel schedule for the upcoming midterms. The list went on and on, all of it routine, day-in-the-life stuff for a senior White House aide.

What was really at stake was the Albert Northcott bombshell.

Justice Northcott had called the president on Sunday morning to say he would be retiring before the end of the current session. The administration had been praying for an opportunity to leave a mark on the Supreme Court but hadn't expected it to come this early in the first term. And certainly not in the guise of a sixty-four-year-old firebrand who'd been on the court for only twelve years. Northcott had agreed to forestall a public announcement until the beginning of next week to give the White House a head start on vetting his replacement.

Ordinarily these things dragged on for months, but the president was determined to fast-track the nomination. It had been all hands on deck ever since. A short list of potential candidates from the campaign already existed, so that had served as a starting point. Lawyers, each from a different top firm, had been assigned to scour the professional and personal lives of one candidate all the way back to grade school. A thorough review of judicial records was also underway for rulings that might prove controversial. Anything the other side could use to torpedo a nomination.

As far as Felix was concerned, this was why he had gotten into politics—the opportunity to help shape the Supreme Court for the next thirty years. The president was leaning toward Judge Raymond Bower from the Northern District of Texas but was willing to be convinced otherwise. Felix had his heart set on Judge Diana Millbrook from the Fourth Circuit Court of Appeals. She ticked all the boxes among the party's base and had a better record than Bower. Given time, Felix knew he could sway the president. But to do that, he needed to be at his desk in the West Wing, not in a rideshare watching his day go up in smoke.

He scrolled through his work phone, checking the most recent of his sixty-seven thousand unread emails. He mentally reshuffled his schedule, prioritizing what had to get done now over what could safely be pushed back. His meeting with Hoskins would have to wait until next week. It was like this most days, an endless stream of fires to be stamped out, but Felix felt particularly aggrieved to be running this errand—hand-holding a congressman with a sudden case of cold feet about a crime bill the president had gone out on a limb to champion.

This kind of thing was par for the course whenever legislation was important to a president. Add to it the party's narrow majority in the House, and the opportunists would always take the occasion to feed from the trough. The vote had been scheduled for tomorrow, and right on cue, thirteen firm yeas that had supported the bill from the start suddenly developed a crisis of conscience. It was all performative bullshit. There were no crises of conscience in Washington, only openings to be exploited. Felix knew the drill and had been ready—how many times had he pulled a similar stunt in his congressional-aide days?

Twelve of the fence-sitters had required straightforward horse-trading—an agreement to do a fundraiser, a photo op with the popular president, a minor appointment for a family member. But the thirteenth, Representative Paul Paxton, had dug in his heels and wouldn't budge. Never mind that he and the president both hailed from Illinois and were longtime allies. Never mind that Paxton was senior leadership and expected to model party unity. No, Prince Paul, as he was called behind his back, always put himself first.

The president was characteristically unperturbed. His nature was to remain circumspect and philosophical about such things. It was only politics. How many friends a president had on any given day depended on the latest polls. The only loyalty in Washington was to power, and to expect differently was naive. Those were the words the president had used to chide Felix last night when his temper got the better of him. Of course, right after that meeting, Steve Gilroy, the White House chief of staff, had taken Felix aside and told him the exact opposite.

"This son of a bitch needs to learn his place. Light the congressman on fire, Felix."

Felix would be more than happy to oblige. His job, as he saw it, was to be the designated asshole, allowing the president to remain above the fray. Well, he was pissed off and relishing the opportunity to play bad cop.

Felix spent much of his time angry about one thing or another. His stomach was constantly a knotted mess, and he'd lost twenty-five pounds in the last year. A friend outside the White House had suggested therapy, but when exactly was he expected to fit that in? One week bled into the next, like an ever-expanding ulcer. How was it already the beginning of May? His last distinct memory was attending the lighting of the National Christmas Tree in December. Probably because that was the last time Stephanie smiled at him. People had warned them that a wedding right after the election was madness. The White House was a jealous, demanding mistress, one that did not take kindly to rivals for its attention. But he and Stephanie had laughed off the well-intended advice. They were so in love, they knew they'd make it work.

Stephanie's final ultimatum—their marriage or the president— had come on the one-year anniversary of the inauguration. The White House was shuffling roles and responsibilities as the first wave of departures hit. Many were friends and colleagues Felix had worked with since the early days of the campaign. He understood burnout was real but couldn't comprehend their decision to step away. Was the work grueling? Absolutely. But wasn't this exactly what they'd all fought so hard for? Stephanie believed it was the perfect opportunity for him to give notice. After two years of campaigning and a year on the front lines, who knew the inner workings of the administration better than Felix

Gallardo? And with three years left in the president's first term, both K Street and the news networks would be lining up to secure his insights and connections. Wasn't it time to reap the rewards of his many sacrifices? Wasn't it finally time to start their life together?

She'd filed for divorce the following week. Felix hadn't fought her. To be honest, a drawn-out divorce was a distraction he could ill afford. There was too much on his plate as it was. Fortunately their marriage hadn't lasted long enough to become complicated. Stephanie made a hell of a lot more money, and they didn't own anything more valuable than one consistently bemused English bulldog named Gordy who adored Stephanie and mostly tolerated Felix. When her lawyer drew up the papers, Felix had signed everywhere he was told without reading a word. It had been a relief to be at her mercy.

They'd parted amicably, both melancholy never to know how this version of their lives might have turned out. He'd rented a one-bedroom in Penn Quarter, walking distance from the White House. Stephanie had moved home to Chicago and taken a job at a firm there. Honestly, the distance was a relief. DC could be a very small town exactly when you least expected it. The thought of running into her out with their friends, or worse, on a date, was too much to bear.

Ironically, his new place was in the same neighborhood as the studio apartment he'd rented when he first moved to DC after college with his one ill-fitting, off-the-rack suit, three dress shirts, and just enough neckties to make it through a week without wearing the same one twice. When he was feeling sorry for himself and allowed himself to miss his wife (*ex-wife, ex-wife*), he would marvel sardonically at how far he'd come: a whole block in just over a decade. More than once, after an especially long day, he'd gone home to the wrong building and felt foolish when it dawned on him why his fob didn't work.

But those had been good years too. Right out of college, cutting his teeth as a legislative assistant to Tom Huntsman, congressman from the Commonwealth of Pennsylvania. Home might have been a crappy studio apartment, but how much time had he really spent there? Maybe he hadn't been born on third base, but he could swing a bat and knew how to get the ball in play. He was always hustling in those days, doing the jobs no one else wanted and never saying no to more responsibility. That was how you made yourself indispensable by twenty-four and a congressional chief of staff by twenty-seven. That was how you got cherry-picked by a presidential campaign and became a trusted White House aide by thirty-four.

He was thirty-four years old, and his desk sat a scant twenty feet from the Oval Office. True, his office was little bigger than a closet, but anyone in Washington could tell you that proximity *was* power. The day he was banished across the street to the Eisenhower Executive Office Building and put in a big, cushy office with sweeping views of the Mall? That was the day he'd know he was finished. No, give him his stuffy closet that smelled faintly of mothballs any day. Only a handful of people in the world had the ear of the president. Felix Gallardo was one of them and everyone in town knew it. To this day he couldn't believe that Stephanie had expected him to give *this* up.

She hadn't been alone. Felix's love affair with politics had been met with bewilderment by his determinedly apolitical parents. The Gallardos had sacrificed much to send their son to Princeton, which often made them feel more like shareholders than parents. One thing they'd made painfully clear was that a career in the murky world of American politics did not constitute an adequate return on investment. Not even now that he worked at the other end of Pennsylvania Avenue.

Felix had hoped that introducing them to his boss—the president of the United States—would finally win them over. After all, President Clark had won thirty-seven states. Surely he could charm a plumber and a hairdresser from Pittsburgh. No such luck. If the electorate had been entirely composed of Hector and Felicia Gallardo, Harrison Clark wouldn't have been elected dogcatcher.

As the car crossed Third Street, the Capitol dome appeared on the left above the Botanical Garden. Felix told the driver to pull over in front of Rayburn, one of the House office buildings. Paxton's office was inside, although that wasn't where Felix was heading today. As senior leadership, Paxton had a cubbyhole in the Capitol building. Cubbyholes were prized second offices just off the House floor that gave ranking members a place to wait during votes rather than trek back and forth across Independence Avenue. There was no good reason to meet there; Prince Paul probably just wanted to remind Felix he was an important man. Fine. If Felix had been summoned to dance through hoops, then dance he would.

He jaywalked across to the Capitol. After passing through security, he made his way upstairs. Heads turned as Felix walked, a murmur of curiosity following him. This was his first time back in Congress since the election, and he'd be lying to say he wasn't thrilled at how much his star had risen.

Then he'd been just another chief of staff grinding away behind the scenes. He'd had a good reputation—otherwise the president wouldn't have poached him for his campaign—but he'd still been largely unknown. Now, though, now he was the president's man. A mainstay on cable news. The *Times* had dubbed him "the eloquent defender of the administration." These days, people he didn't know knew him. The name Felix Gallardo meant something. He didn't hate that, even if it made discretion much more challenging.

Felix rapped lightly on the congressman's office door, and the sound echoed in the hallway's high, vaulted ceilings. Paxton's chief of staff, Tina Lu, opened the door and shook his hand warmly. She didn't like him much, which he attributed to his passing her on the career ladder despite being twelve years her junior. He took her antipathy as a compliment, and besides, the feeling was mutual.

The thing about Tina Lu was that she was exceptionally good at her job. She stood a hair under five feet, but woe unto anyone foolish enough to take that as an invitation to underestimate her. She'd more than earned her reputation as one of the toughest backroom negotiators in Congress. What Tina Lu wanted, Tina Lu generally got. Coming up, Felix had been outmaneuvered by Tina time and again. Painful, hard-earned lessons. He would have been grateful to her if she hadn't made it a priority to kick him when he was down. Well, those days were over now, and he looked forward to reminding her and Prince Paul of the new pecking order.

Speaking of which, where was the congressman? Felix glanced around the empty office. Where was his staff? He hated surprise parties. Especially if he was the unsuspecting guest of honor.

"Is Paxton running late?" he asked.

"The congressman is in Boston," she said, ushering him inside and closing the door in a way that felt distinctly like a trap being sprung.

"As of when?" He'd spoken to Paxton less than two hours ago. The congressman hadn't mentioned anything about Massachusetts.

"He flew up yesterday afternoon."

Yesterday? Felix felt his temperature begin to rise but kept it out of his voice. For now. He'd come up the Hill this morning expecting gamesmanship, but now he wasn't clear what game they were playing.

"When's he due back?"

"Will you sit?" she suggested. "Let's sit."

He did not sit. If it got around that Paxton was holding the White House hostage at the eleventh hour, how many other reps would follow suit? Felix needed to nip this petty rebellion in the bud here and now. "The vote is tomorrow."

"And he has an early flight back in the morning," Tina said, as if comforting a child. "It's a good bill. Tell the president he can count on our vote."

"Then what am I doing here, Tina? Why've you got me trekking up the Hill on a Tuesday morning?"

"It's only a mile."

It was 1.7 miles as the crow flies, but that wasn't nearly the point. "Nothing is a mile in this city."

"Northcott is stepping down," she said.

His eyes narrowed, and he instantly regretted even that small indication of surprise. Albert Northcott's retirement from the court was supposedly a closely guarded secret. Felix racked his brain for who might've leaked the story. It wouldn't have been Northcott, would it? No, that didn't make sense. If the justice wanted the story out there, he would've done it last week instead of calling the president. Anyway, the blame wouldn't fall there. That left only the four people in the administration who knew—the president, Chief of Staff Steve Gilroy, White House Counsel Samantha Maddox, and Felix. It wouldn't be any of those first three. That left Felix holding the bag. *Damn.* He already had a reputation for being too chummy with the media and could feel himself being fitted for the noose. Hell, he'd have blamed *himself* if he didn't happen to know for a fact that it hadn't been him.

"Still with me?" she asked amiably.

Felix smiled and spread his hands. "Northcott is considering it. That's all. Nothing is set in stone yet."

"Cut the crap, Felix. The man has pancreatic cancer and is afraid his legacy will be dying on the bench and gifting his seat to the other side. He called the president personally on Sunday to tell him he wanted to walk away on his own terms."

"How the hell do you know all that?" The time for Felix's poker face had passed. The chief justice had used those exact words, "on my own terms," in his conversation with the president. Tina didn't merely want Felix to know she knew; she was rubbing his face in it.

"It's my job to know." She gestured to the chair opposite her. "Sit. Please."

Grudgingly, Felix lowered himself into the chair, trying to rediscover his lost poise, aware he was failing miserably. Tina reached for a glass of water, letting him sweat it out. He plucked lint from the sleeve of his jacket and waited her out in return.

"The congressman would like to be considered for Northcott's seat on the court."

Felix sat in stunned silence. That was *it*? This was Paxton's big play? If so, then Prince Paul had lost his mind. Instead of being angry, Felix almost felt sorry for Tina. They'd never been friends, but he'd always respected her strategic nous. How had she let herself be roped into this suicide mission while her boss hid out in Boston? When things went sideways—and they would the moment Felix reported back to the White House—there was a good chance she'd get thrown under the first bus headed out of town. She had to know that.

"You're joking," he said, trying to give her an easy out. The president had made promises during the campaign about whom he would nominate should a seat on the court become available. None of those promises involved Paul Paxton.

"That's not something I'm known for."

"Paxton isn't even a judge, Tina." He didn't know why he was letting himself get drawn into this debate, but Paxton's ask was so outrageous that he couldn't help himself. He *had* to know what the congressman was thinking. After all, he'd be telling this story at parties for decades.

"He went to law school," Tina said dismissively. "Besides, a judgeship is not a requirement of the court. Earl Warren was the governor of California when he was nominated."

Felix looked at her in disbelief. "Warren died in '72."

"Seventy-four," Tina corrected.

"Whatever. The point is, this is the twenty-first century. It doesn't happen anymore."

"Well, we believe the court is long overdue for a course correction. For too long it's been overrepresented by judges from the court of appeals. Nominating an experienced lawmaker to the bench would inject a valuable perspective," Tina replied, as if this were the most reasonable request in the world.

Felix stood to go. This had ceased being amusing and was becoming pathetic. For her sake, he hoped Tina had updated her résumé. "The president appreciates the congressman's support on the bill tomorrow."

She put out her hand, and he shook it. That proved a mistake, because her grip was like a python that had gone too long between meals. "Always a pleasure, Felix. We look forward to the president's swift reply."

With her free hand, she passed him a manila envelope. He took it. Anything to get out of here.

"What's this?" he asked, turning it over in his hands suspiciously. It was neither marked nor labeled, but the flap had been sealed with wax. "What are you, a medieval squire?"

She smiled at his joke. "For the president's eyes only. It should make clear our position."

For once Felix was at a loss for words. What was the old saying about messengers and bad news? He allowed Tina to usher him out of the office. In the hall he turned back to face her. She was smiling warmly—not at him, but for the benefit of staffers passing by.

"Always good to see you, Felix. Give the president our regards," she said and closed the door on him.

CHAPTER TWO

On weekends, Seventh Street Southeast between North Carolina and Pennsylvania Avenues closed to traffic along Eastern Market. Farmers, local artisans, and vendors of all stripes set up stalls, selling everything from handcrafted furniture to local artwork to artisan pickles. It was hard for transplants to imagine what DC had been thirty years ago—a small, sleepy government town. The population had more than doubled in that time, and so had the pace of life. But for a few hours on Saturday and Sunday morning, life slowed down, and Agatha caught a glimpse of the city of her childhood.

The street fair ran year-round, but there was something special about Eastern Market in the springtime. By noon Seventh Street overflowed with families and young couples out to enjoy the weather. That was why Agatha got her shopping done early—less chance of bumping into anyone who knew her from the old days. Besides, she told herself, that was all a long, long time ago. No one cared anymore. Two decades was ancient history on the hamster wheel of DC politics. It had been years since she'd run into anyone who remembered her.

Why would they? If she didn't recognize the face in the mirror, how would anyone else? Her jet-black hair, once a trademark of sorts, had turned silver in her forties. She was also twenty pounds lighter than she'd been in those days, and her face, once a deceptively innocent oval, was now all hard angles and aggressive cheekbones. And the best bedtime moisturizing routine in the world wouldn't erase the years of sun damage or the weary skin folds where her neck met her chin. Perhaps that was why she'd been lulled into a false sense of security and gotten such a late start this morning.

"Agatha?"

Her name spoken slowly and as a question, tinged with excitement as if she were a rare beetle spotted by someone sure they would win a prize for the find. She turned slowly to see a couple standing behind her and resisted the urge to feign ignorance. One of her great skills was names and faces. The man she'd never met, and she hadn't seen the woman in over twenty years. It took a moment for her mental Rolodex to match the face to a name.

"Kat!" she said, forcing a smile that said this was the most wonderful chance encounter of her life. Kat what, though? *Milbrandt*. Kat Milbrandt. She'd been on Congressman Park's staff back then. Their bosses had belonged to the same caucus, so they'd been on good terms.

"It's Katherine now. How are you? What's it been?"

"Fifteen years?" Agatha suggested, knowing full well it had been longer.

Katherine nodded in earnest agreement. "Fifteen years. Unbelievable. Do you still live on the Hill?"

"Aren't you going to introduce me?" Agatha said, meaning Katherine's husband. She didn't do personal questions, but it also didn't pay to be rude. Rude was much more memorable than friendly. She didn't spend a great deal of time on social media, but catching people being rude in their natural habitat appeared to be the internet's third-largest economy. She'd settled instead on what she referred to as early-onset vagueness. An old joke around Washington was that the best way to spot an employee at Langley was to ask them anything personal. If you ended up learning more about yourself than them, then they were likely CIA. Agatha had taken a page from the Agency's book and trained herself in the ancient art of conversational judo—take any incoming question, pivot smartly, and return it to the asker using the question's own momentum.

The supreme irony being that Agatha had been recruited by the Agency in college. Apparently she fit a certain profile, although they wouldn't say which one. The work intrigued her, but in the end, she'd turned them down for the simple reason that toiling away in anonymity held less than no appeal. At twenty, attention had been at the very tip-top of her hierarchy of needs, Maslow be damned. She would be a star, of that she'd been sure. She'd been sure of a great many things in those days.

Katherine clearly sensed she was being redirected but, unsure in the moment what to do about it, moved on awkwardly. "Oh, where are my manners? This is my husband. He's at Brookings," she said, mentioning the policy think tank where he worked without actually getting around to his name. It was a funny oversight and not an uncommon one. This was Washington, DC, after all, where your job and education counted for a hell of a lot more than who you were.

The man extended his hand politely. Agatha doubted that networking was how he'd envisioned his Saturday morning. "Gerald Smith."

"Oh, of course, I'm sorry," Katherine said with an embarrassed laugh. "Gerald. This is my Gerald."

Agatha and Gerald told each other how good it was to meet the other. Neither meant it, and that should have been that. Agatha had zucchini to sort, and Gerald had the glazed-over eyes of someone who would rather be literally anywhere else.

Katherine wasn't so easily put off. "This is Agatha Cardiff."

That wasn't precisely true anymore, but Agatha didn't correct her. "She was Paul Paxton's chief of staff back in the day."

"Oh?" Gerald said, perking up at the name.

"You used to scare the shit out of me," Katherine confessed.

Agatha already knew that and felt her old pride rekindle at the terror she'd once inspired. She feigned modesty. "I was more bark than bite."

"Well, it was one hell of a bark."

Before Katherine could dig for any more gossip, Agatha beat her to the punch with questions of her own. How long had she and Gerald been married? Did they live in the area? Any children? A tried-and-true technique for making a good impression was to ask questions and be fascinated by the answers. Most people preferred talking to listening, so offering someone the chance to wax rhapsodic about their life was like handing out free drugs. That was at least doubly true of Washington, a town full of professional talkers.

"Are you still with Park?" Agatha asked.

"No, he got primaried in '14," Katherine told her.

Gerald, who knew all these answers already, wandered away to a stall selling old vinyl LPs.

"Oh, I'm sorry. I didn't know. Don't really keep up with politics these days." Her first out-and-out lie—Park had lost to a Gulf War veteran by a bitterly contested ninety-one votes, requiring two recounts and a lawsuit.

"That's life in the big city. But I caught on with Tomlin. She's a good boss."

"You're on Senator Tomlin's staff?"

Donna Tomlin was the new chair of the Senate Judiciary Committee. A former law professor with a reputation as a serious, thoughtful politician, she had risen quickly through the ranks. Agatha was impressed and more than a little jealous.

"Yeah, you know how it is. I needed to get out of the House. Do something meaningful for a change."

"Good for you."

Katherine, sensing she was losing her window, said, "So what about you? *Do* you live on the Hill?"

"I'm actually just visiting friends. I'm out west now."

"Oh?" Katherine said. "California? Washington? Oregon?"

"Mm-hmm," Agatha confirmed.

"That must be nice. We keep talking about getting away from all this, but where would we go?"

Agatha often asked herself the same thing.

Katherine took her hand. "We should catch up before you go."

"I'd love that, but my flight's tomorrow morning. Last day." Katherine looked disappointed, so Agatha added, "Maybe next time?" She knew that was a mistake even as she said it.

"Still have a 202?"

"Till I die."

They traded numbers, and Agatha made her goodbyes, waving to Gerald's strategically turned back. All the way home, she kicked herself for being so careless. Kat Milbrandt. If loose lips sank ships, then Kat had sent entire fleets to the seabed. Whenever Agatha had wanted something to get around but didn't want to be the obvious source, she would whisper in Kat's ear and let nature run its course. And now the woman had a story to tell.

At least Kat's facts would be wrong. That was some comfort, although running into her at Eastern Market hadn't been ideal. It was only a few blocks from Agatha's house. Fortunately the happy couple lived up in Brentwood and were on the Hill only to meet friends for brunch. She was unlikely to bump into them again. But Kat would certainly be opening more than one conversation with, "You'll never guess who I ran into this weekend." Agatha's name would be back on people's lips, so she would need to lie low for a while. No more weekend shopping in Eastern Market, and she should keep an eye out for mentions online. Her social media accounts would need to be dusted off to see if anyone came sniffing around.

At the same time, she recognized how ridiculous she sounded. So what if Kat Milbrandt did gossip about running into her? It wasn't as if anyone gave a damn anymore. People had hardly cared the first time around. Of course, 9/11 had had a hand in that, effectively erasing every news story that had preceded it. The world had moved on. Agatha was like a child playing a lonely game of hide-and-seek, only no one was looking for her. Still, she'd feel better when she was home. She even picked up the pace when her row house came into sight. Almost back now. Almost safe.

A cheerful voice called out her name. She looked up from her thoughts to see her neighbor standing in his small front yard holding a shovel like an extra from *American Gothic*. Fucking Jim Talbot. Alright, that wasn't fair. He was a perfectly nice man, and she'd like him a whole lot more if he just stopped talking to her. That seemed unlikely given the considerable time and effort she'd already invested into giving him the cold shoulder. He'd moved in next door eight months ago and had been relentlessly charming and kind ever since, irritatingly so.

She knew far more about him than was wise. For example, he was a fifty-one-year-old law professor at Georgetown and had run most of the major marathons, but London was still on his bucket list. He was originally from Colorado, never married, although he'd come close twice. Parents were both deceased, but he had an older brother and sister. His thirteen-year-old corgi was named Regis, and for whatever reason, Agatha found the sight of Jim, rain or shine, patiently trailing the ancient dog up and down the block while it sniffed every tree indecently endearing. Jim also wore a tank top better than a man his age had any right to, but that was a separate issue.

He waved from the garden while Regis sunned himself at the top of the wrought-iron stairs.

"Hello, Jim."

"How'd you make out at the market? Bags look a little light."

This was why she didn't like to get chummy with neighbors. They started noticing things like how much she usually bought.

"It was fine. Just realized I was running late," she replied, indicating her front door, which was tantalizingly close.

"Well, I won't keep you."

"I appreciate it," she said and started up her stairs, keys at the ready.

"It's just that I bought too many of these flowers, and I realize now they won't all fit. Any chance you'd want them?"

She looked at the pallet of purple and white flowers at his feet. "I'm not really much of a gardener."

"I'll do it," he suggested gladly. "What do you say? Won't take any time, and I'm already dirty."

"I don't know. That sounds like a lot to ask." Not that she had.

"Come on, you'd be doing me a favor. This way I won't feel so guilty that Regis always pees on your fence," he said with a grin.

She should have been gracious about it and said yes. But running into Kat Milbrandt had rattled her, and she was in no mood.

"What're you doing, Jim?"

"I'm sorry?" he said, smile faltering.

Regis's head came up, sensing something amiss.

"The flowers. All of it. How do you know when I go to the market, or how much I usually buy? What was the plan? Stake me out until I come home, so you could drop this line about extra flowers? What do you want from me?"

"I just . . . I just thought it would be nice. We're neighbors."

He looked pained, and she knew she was over the line, but she couldn't stop herself. "Nice? Don't shit where you eat, Jim. Ever hear that expression?"

"What? Wait, what's going on? I . . . I'm sorry. Forget the flowers."

"Just don't. Okay?"

"I won't. I apologize."

"Thank you," she said and went in her front door. Inside, she turned the dead bolt definitively, put her back against the door, and breathed a sigh of relief. It was probably how astronauts felt returning to the airlock after a spacewalk—exhilarated at surviving the experience but aware they couldn't last out there for long. In the before times, home had been a pit stop on the way to somewhere else, her days populated by a revolving carousel of work, friends, parties, and social events. There'd been so much to do that a night at home felt shortsighted. She'd known everyone, and everyone had known her. Now her life was a cautionary tale of *never say never*. She worked and lived almost entirely at home, venturing out only in strategic bursts. How horrified would thirty-year-old Agatha Cardiff be if she could see herself now?

A white cat twined between her ankles.

"Riggins, what the hell's wrong with me?" she asked him.

The cat had nothing helpful to say on the matter and stalked off toward the kitchen when she didn't immediately stoop to pet him.

"Hey, I'm having a crisis here."

Riggins was entirely uninterested in her excuses. That seemed fair; she was pretty much over them herself.

CHAPTER THREE

Kicking off her shoes, Agatha followed the cat back through the house. Given her personality, she'd have expected her decor to gravitate toward bare-knuckle Scandinavian minimalism and had been surprised to discover she tended toward what could best be described as cluttered New England farmhouse. Every surface was piled with papers and books. The dining room table had been her grandparents', but Agatha had never sat there for a meal. It had long since become a staging area for various half-finished or half-forgotten projects. The only time she tidied up was if she needed to make room for something new. Housekeeping had never been a point of emphasis.

In the kitchen, Riggins leaped up onto a sunny windowsill while Agatha propped open the back door. Despite the downpour of pollen, she couldn't resist the fresh air. That was what allergy medicine was for. She was happy to suffer for springtime—the best time of year. Powering on a portable speaker, she scrolled through her playlists. She'd been on a local DC music kick of late and settled on Marvin Gaye's "In Our Lifetime." The singer had always claimed to hate his hometown, which he said filled him with hopelessness. That was alright. She still counted him. If you were from here, you could judge DC however you wanted. Everyone else could mind their business.

Unpacking, she realized just how right Jim had been. She'd fled Eastern Market without half the things on her list. Going back now wasn't an option, so she'd have to run to the store later. That was fine;

she tried to alternate between the gym and hot yoga. Today should be yoga, and her studio was on H Street near the Giant. She could kill two birds with one stone.

A tapping sound interrupted the mental rearranging of her day. She paused the music and listened—a shy, almost apologetic knocking was coming from the basement door. Agatha glanced over at the refrigerator calendar and frowned at the date. This couldn't go on, she reminded herself.

"Hi, Shelby," Agatha said, unlocking and opening the basement door. The young woman standing at the top of the stairs didn't have a check in her hand and looked monumentally sheepish about it. Instead, she held the note that Agatha had slipped under her front door on her way to the market. "It's the eighth."

"I know."

"We talked about this in February." *And again in March and April,* she thought.

"I know. I'm sorry. I just need a couple of days."

"Come on up," Agatha said and went back to the kitchen to finish putting away her groceries. She worried that if she answered now, it would get ugly, and she really didn't want that. This place was special to her, and she was very protective of it. The little two-story row house near Lincoln Park was the only thing she had to show from her old life. The only thing she was proud of, anyway. She'd bought it back in '97 at the dawn of gentrification, scraping together a down payment with a little help from her father. The plan had been to restore it herself—sweat equity, her father called it—but a fixer-upper it had remained. Even in the state it was in, there was no chance she could afford a property like this today, and truth was, between the mortgage and the constant upkeep of an aging house, it was a stretch even holding on to it. That was why she'd followed the neighborhood's lead and converted the basement into an apartment. She'd had nine tenants in the last fifteen years and was proud to say she didn't know a single salient detail of their lives other than names and credit scores.

But then along came Shelby Franklin, number ten. What made her so different? On paper, she was just another striver in a city full of strivers. Smart, passionate, overly serious, and heartbreakingly idealistic. Maybe it was the way she'd gotten here that endeared her to Agatha. Shelby's father wasn't in the picture, and her mother back in Arkansas had gotten pregnant at sixteen and dropped out of high school. Education wasn't the emphasis for the Franklins—survival was. Shelby had grown up the kind of poor that was impossible to understand unless you'd lived it. And yet, despite all that, she'd been the valedictorian of her class and the first Franklin to go to college. By twenty-four, she'd already finished graduate school and gone to work for the World Justice Initiative, a nonprofit think tank combating human trafficking.

So, yes, fair to say that Agatha admired her downstairs tenant, even if the rent was often late. DC was an expensive city, and nonprofits, even prestigious ones like the WJI, didn't pay twenty-five-year-olds enough to cover rent, living expenses, and student loans. The city's dirty little secret was that it was hard for someone starting out to survive without parents willing and able to make up the difference. Shelby certainly didn't and had made it this far on her own. Maybe that was why Agatha had been willing to take the rent late. But enough was enough. It was starting to feel like she was being played, and that didn't sit well with her.

Shelby had followed her into the kitchen like a dutiful child who knew she was in for it now. "Monday?"

What difference did two days make? Even if Agatha deposited the check today, it would just sit in the bank until then. She knew that, but it was the principle of the thing. Wasn't it? This would all be easier if Agatha didn't have so much affection for the young woman.

"Monday morning," Agatha said finally.

"I'll have the money by then. I promise. Thank you so much."

Maybe if she'd had her head a little less up her own ass, Agatha might have stopped to wonder how Shelby would come up with the rent over the weekend. She'd have plenty of time to kick herself about that later. For now, she was too busy playing the righteously aggrieved landlord to care. "It's fine. But I need you to hear me. This is the last time."

"I understand. It won't happen again."

"Good," Agatha said, unsure why Shelby was lingering in the kitchen. The chewing-out concluded, shouldn't she be heading back downstairs and not standing around like she'd been invited over for tea?

"Can I help with your groceries?" Shelby asked, reaching into a bag.

"I can put away my own things," Agatha snapped, more harshly than she'd meant, but honestly, what the hell?

Chastened, Shelby removed her hand and showed Agatha it was empty. "Sorry."

"It's just I know where everything goes."

"Sure, I'm the same way," Shelby agreed.

"Is there something else?"

"I was wondering. I know you're mad at me, and you should be. But could I make you dinner sometime?"

"You want to make *me* dinner?" Agatha said with the same surprise she reserved for people who confessed to being from the future.

"Yeah, as a thank-you. You cut me a lot of slack, and I just really appreciate it."

"That's very kind, but I'm busy tonight." She was not but didn't want to be any ruder than she'd already been.

"That's fine. I have a date tonight. How about Monday?" Shelby said, not taking the hint. "The weather is supposed to be nice. We could sit in the backyard."

Now Agatha was irritated. Was she going crazy? First Jim Talbot and now Shelby. When had reading the room become a lost art? Paying the rent late wasn't a pretext for inviting your landlord to dinner.

"I don't think it's a good idea."

"Oh," Shelby said in a tone that made Agatha feel like she'd just been caught kicking a puppy. "I'm sorry. I just wanted to make it up to you somehow."

"If you want to make it up to me, then get me a check on Monday and pay your rent on the first from now on."

"I will. I'm really sorry. Thank you," Shelby said, retreating back down the stairs.

After the door closed, Agatha put both hands on the kitchen counter and leaned against it heavily. Well, there it was—zero for three. When had she become so painfully inept at basic human interaction? Hard to believe there'd been a time when she would have considered people her strength. But that was what happened when you shut yourself away from the world for twenty years. Had she become the neighborhood kook and somehow not noticed? Was that how it happened? One day you were a normal person minding your own business, and the next you were making tinfoil hats and treating an old colleague like an enemy agent; yelling at the neighbors; being offended that someone offered to cook you dinner? Agatha looked warily at the stacks of magazines surrounding her dining room table, all carefully organized by date and periodical—the *Atlantic* here, the *Economist* there, *Forbes* and *Wired*, just so.

Hoarder, a voice whispered.

Why was she keeping them all? She'd already read them. What was she planning to do, start a library?

She got the garbage bags from under the sink and came back with every intention of recycling all of it. But the longer she stood there looking at it all, the more daunting it felt. She set the garbage bags on the corner of the dining room table next to all her other half-finished projects. Tomorrow . . . she'd stop being a crazy person tomorrow.

CHAPTER FOUR

"Bern, have you heard any chatter about Justice Northcott retiring?" a female voice asked.

Bernard Goff removed his bifocals and held them up before his eyes like a conductor hushing a waiting orchestra. He'd been lost in thought and required a moment to refocus his attention. It was becoming embarrassing, and he was suspicious that he had a reputation around the offices as befuddled. There'd been a time when his mind *had* been philharmonic, responding effortlessly to his direction. But since turning sixty-five, he'd become conscious of a gradual deterioration. The unpleasant awareness that his grasp on the baton was slipping. His orchestra, once a finely tuned mechanism, seemed now to be perpetually tuning up for a symphony it never quite got around to playing. He was beginning to wonder if he had any great performances left and whether his editors wondered the same.

It also occurred to him that, instead of gathering his thoughts, he'd gotten distracted with an unnecessarily elaborate metaphor about orchestras. This was exactly the kind of thing that was ruining his reputation around the newsroom. With his free hand, he rubbed at the corner of his tired eyes before looking up at the young, eager face peering down at him.

"Albert Northcott?" Bernard asked to clarify, although who else could she mean? He'd been covering the Supreme Court since before the Towers fell, since before one of the richest men in the world bought the newspaper, and before it moved from the decrepit but infinitely more charming offices to these new, soulless corporate digs on K Street. Bernard increasingly felt like a dinosaur in a Spielberg movie, but not one of the marquee dinosaurs that children loved. The only time the cubs ever spoke to him was when a case came before the court on an issue mattering dearly to their inscrutable millennial hearts.

This particular cub was the exception to the rule. Isha Roy had been with the paper for only two years after cutting her teeth at Politico and TPM, and Bernard had done his level best to find her as irritating as the rest. Unfortunately her competence, dogged determination, and dedication to the job had won him over against his better judgment. Isha had an old-school, fourth-estate fervor for journalism that made it seem as though she'd come of age during Watergate and then stubbornly ignored the unraveling of the profession in the intervening decades. Only warriors and true believers hung around the newsroom this late on a Sunday night. Honestly, Isha reminded him of himself at that age, although Bernard suspected she wouldn't take that as a compliment.

It had only recently dawned on him that she must have designs on his job. But even then, all he could muster was a token affront. Wasn't that how he'd gotten the position himself? Getting old didn't mean he had to become a hypocrite too. What use would she ever be if she wasn't ambitious?

And so Bernard had resolved to teach her everything she'd need to do his job. But that didn't mean he'd give up his desk without a fight. If she wanted it, she would have to earn the privilege, and he would do his best to be proud of her when she did. Still, it was a strange thing to mentor your own replacement.

"Albert Northcott," Isha confirmed.

"Retiring? No, and I wouldn't believe it if I had."

"Why not?"

"Because he's only sixty-four. And because he put the *lifetime* in *lifetime appointment*. He'll retire when they wheel him out in a body bag and not before," Bernard concluded, wincing at the uncomfortable parallel to his own situation.

"He's sick," she said, perching on the corner of his desk. "I don't know what with."

Bernard leaned back in his chair, trying to decide how he felt about her sitting there. *Good, maybe?* "Where are you getting this from?"

"A source."

Bernard knew better than to ask for a name. Probably someone she knew from Princeton. School ties were currency in this town. His guess was a clerk at the court. "On the record?"

She paused to think about it. "Off."

"Are you sure?"

"Well, it wasn't explicitly off the record, but they were pretty hammered."

He noted the leather jacket and the purse dangling from her shoulder. Where had she come from? "Well, that's their problem. There's no retroactive get-out-of-jail-free card because they can't handle their liquor."

She grimaced uncomfortably.

"Unless they're a friend, and you feel the need to protect them from themselves."

"Something like that."

"That's your call, but it might be smart, long term. You can only burn a source once," he said. "But, hypothetically, are they reliable?"

"I would say so."

"Have you tried to get someone else to confirm it?"

"Just you. I don't know how far to take this."

He understood her frustration. If true, breaking the story of Northcott's retirement would raise her profile at the paper and around town, but only if she beat the White House to its announcement. "Alright, so let's assume it's true. Why'd your source tell you?"

"What do you mean? It's news."

"Yes, but why is it news to your source? What's in it for them? We cultivate sources to report the news. That's our motive. But don't ever get it twisted; we're being cultivated right back. So what's your source's agenda? Because nine times out of ten, it's not patriotic loyalty to the First Amendment. Sometimes the answer to that question will lead you to the real story. Sometimes knowing *why* a source is telling you something is more important than *what* they're telling you."

"I don't think there was an agenda. He'd just drunk too much," she said, plucking a pen from the coffee mug on his desk and spinning it between her fingers, thinking.

Bernard had conducted enough interviews in his time to know when someone was about to unburden themselves. He sat quietly and let her get there in her own time.

"There's something else," she said finally. "They also claim the White House is being lobbied to add a name to their vetting list."

"That happens sometimes. Super PACs will try to influence the White House's decision."

She was shaking her head. "Not a PAC. An individual. Lobbying on their *own* behalf."

Bernard felt bad for her now. That wasn't how the process worked. Supreme Court nominations were coveted by administrations. The announcement was a carefully choreographed process that had been worked out over decades. First, the White House would announce Northcott's retirement. Then they would vet a slate of potential replacements for the vacancy, while simultaneously conducting soft, unofficial leaks to test public response before finally settling on a nominee. What an administration didn't do was entertain requests for the seat. It simply wasn't done. Whoever Isha's source was, they were full of shit. It happened. People liked to appear more important, more in the know, than they actually were. Especially guys, and especially after a few drinks with a woman.

"You're not buying it," Isha said, putting the pen back in his mug.

"Well, it would be highly unorthodox," Bernard said, as gently as he could. "Did they say who this mystery nominee is?"

"Yes, but it's so ridiculous I don't want to tell you."

"That's fine, keep it to yourself," he said, knowing she couldn't.

She rolled her eyes. "Paul Paxton."

Bernard stared at her down the bridge of his nose. A congressman with no judicial experience? It was beyond absurd. The funny thing was that if it had been anyone else, Bernard would have dismissed it out of hand. But Paul Paxton was such a specific name. The congressman and the president had a close relationship going back decades. Was that what had Bernard's hackles up? The appearance of cronyism? He felt a superstitious chill pass between his shoulder blades—a bad feeling, as if half remembering something terrible he'd said the night before after drinking too much.

"I know. I know," Isha was saying. "Maybe I just wanted it to be true."

Bernard smiled, hoping he looked reassuring. "We've all been there. The day you stop getting excited about a big story is probably the time to hang 'em up."

"Thanks, Bern. I just didn't want to look like a fool," she said gratefully and stood from his desk.

That decided it. He definitely liked her sitting there, talking things through, looking to him for advice. It made him feel relevant even if that wasn't how this should work. There'd been a time when new hires sought the approval of senior staff, not the other way around. Sign of the times, he reckoned.

"So that's it? You're going to let it go?"

She turned back. "Isn't that what you think I should do?"

"Doesn't matter what I think. What about you? What's your gut tell you?"

"That there's something here. Maybe not what I think, but something."

"So . . ."

"So I want to keep digging around?" she half asked with a grin.

"Then do it. But let's hold off mentioning this to Sidney for now." Sidney Lowenstein was their editor, and chief among his pet peeves was reporters bothering him with half-baked story ideas.

"Agreed. You're the best, you know?"

Bernard watched Isha walk briskly away to her cubicle. *The best.* He thought he liked the sound of that. It made him hope that there really was something to her Northcott story. Could he really be stepping down from the court? It didn't seem likely, or maybe it was that the implication stung. The Supreme Court was still Bernard's beat, and he hadn't heard so much as a whisper about Albert Northcott. But why would anyone make up a story like that? And if true, why would a source circumvent the *Post*'s Supreme Court reporter in favor of Isha, an unknown, untested rookie? His sensitive soul wanted to take it as another sign that his race was run, but what if there had been another reason for feeding it to Isha?

Bernard drummed his fingers on his desk and reached for the phone.

CHAPTER FIVE

Agatha was a light sleeper and an early riser, usually waking at sunrise. So did her house, which creaked and groaned as the sun warmed it like an old man standing up from a comfortable chair. After twenty-five years, she knew all its idiosyncratic sounds and could usually tell if Shelby was home. Especially if Agatha were listening for her, which she had been all weekend. She'd heard Shelby leave on Saturday afternoon after their conversation but hadn't heard her come home. It would've been hard to miss. The basement's front door stuck a little and usually needed a helpful shoulder barge to open.

Had Agatha been overly harsh? Enough to drive her tenant away? On the one hand, she had a legitimate point about the late rent, but on the other, she could have handled it better. A lot better. The only positive from the weekend was that she'd sorted through her dining room and thrown away or recycled nearly everything. If she'd had any friends, she could've thrown a dinner party.

Now that Monday had come, Agatha knew two things: that Shelby hadn't come home and that there would be no rent check under the door. She took pride in having a good radar for players, having been one herself in a former life, and it stung to think she'd been manipulated so easily.

But had she? Despite everything, she still wanted to believe Shelby. Not that it mattered . . . things had passed the point of innocent mis-understanding. She liked Shelby and felt for her, but a line had been crossed. Her tenant wasn't the only one on a tight budget. The rent covered the monthly shortfall in Agatha's makeshift finances with little to spare. Every penny was accounted for, and Shelby was putting her in a bad position.

Clearly it was time to admit this wasn't working out. But every time Agatha made up her mind to evict Shelby, she second-guessed herself. What if Shelby had a good excuse? What if she gave her the check the moment she got home from work? Maybe. If she was sincerely remorseful, maybe Agatha could let it slide. But even the thought of it made her feel like a sucker, and that made her angry all over again.

Still on the fence, Agatha went downstairs to make tea and power on her laptop. Waiting for the water to boil, she texted Shelby that they needed to talk this evening, then stood there frowning at her phone. This was going to bother her all day if she let it. Fortunately she had plenty of work to keep her busy. Unfortunately the four part-time jobs she worked remotely required only a fraction of her attention. So Shelby was never far from her thoughts, and every time Agatha took a break, she checked her messages. *Nada.* Frustrated, Agatha knocked off early and biked down to the gym and took two classes, back-to-back, hoping to work out some of her frustration. Nothing helped.

Shelby worked long hours and usually wasn't home before eight, but by ten Agatha still hadn't heard her come in. She sat up for a while in the front window with an Ian McEwan novel open on her lap but eventually gave up and went to bed. By Tuesday evening, Agatha's anger had largely given way to concern. She'd tried texting a few more times but heard nothing back. There was always Shelby's boyfriend, but she usually saw him only on the weekend. Monday to Friday, Shelby belonged to her job. And she never stayed at the boyfriend's place, because she hated his roommates with a white-hot passion. If she were hiding out there, it was not a good sign. Still, it was better than the alternatives, and Agatha wished she knew the boyfriend's number. At this point she just wanted to know Shelby was safe. How did people work up the courage to have children of their own?

She was in the bathroom washing her face before bed when she heard the basement door open and close. Her first reaction was relief, followed quickly by a spiky, resentful surge of anger that had been waiting for its moment. Was this how her parents had felt when Agatha sneaked in late after curfew? No wonder her mom had always been furious.

Drying her face, Agatha tiptoed back downstairs. She paused at the basement door, hand poised to knock. The muffled sound of voices trying and failing to talk softly drifted up from below. She couldn't make out what they were saying, but both voices belonged to men. Had Shelby sent someone over to pick up her things, trying to avoid paying? Well, that didn't work for Agatha at all. She unlocked the door and went down the carpeted steps. The voices stopped.

In Shelby's living room, two men stood staring up at her, frozen in place. Both were in their twenties, but they couldn't have been any more different. One was tall and outrageously fit, his clothes festooned with athletic logos as if he'd stepped off a billboard. His head of black hair was shaved at the sides and sculpted into a pompadour that leaned stylishly to the right. He'd been by the house a few times, and Agatha recognized him as the boyfriend, his name popping unbidden into her mind: Jackson. The second boy—and Agatha really couldn't help thinking of him as a boy—was short and doughy, like an uncooked oatmeal raisin cookie. He wore baggy khaki shorts in imminent danger of falling down around his ankles, and his mop of shaggy blond hair looked as if it had tumbled in off the high plains.

"What are you doing in my house?" she asked. Technically the basement wasn't part of her house so long as it was rented to Shelby, but since the rent was now ten days late, she was more than happy to reclaim it for the purposes of this conversation. Anyway, the boys appeared too flustered to argue the finer points of real-estate law. She pressed ahead before they gathered themselves. "You're the boyfriend. We've met."

"Yes." Jackson nodded, clearly relieved to be recognized.

"And you are?" she asked the second boy.

"Philip," he answered.

She knew the name, a friend of Shelby's from grad school. Dorky and shy, but according to Shelby, he was usually the smartest person in any room. The one who rarely got the girl and never the one who got a girl who looked like Shelby. A confidant, at least that was the sense Agatha got.

"So where is Shelby? Did she send you?"

Both boys shook their heads in unison.

"We haven't heard from her in a couple of days," Philip said.

"Has she been to work?" Agatha had tried calling but hadn't been able to reach anyone willing to answer her questions.

"No, and she didn't call out sick or anything either. We're just worried about her."

"I have her spare key," Jackson added, holding it up for inspection. "We were hoping we'd find something that would tell us where she was."

"When was the last time you talked to her?"

"Saturday," Jackson said.

"You had a date, right?"

Jackson's brow furrowed at the question. He had no idea what she was talking about. Shelby's date hadn't been with him. Philip, on the other hand, winced at the question, as if she'd brought up an awkward subject he'd been hoping to avoid. Agatha didn't know what to make of that and filed it away. Against all odds, had Philip somehow gotten the girl?

"No, she had a work thing," Jackson explained. "We were supposed to have brunch on Sunday. She didn't show."

"I've tried texting," Agatha said.

The two boys glanced at each other.

"What?"

Jackson held up Shelby's phone. "We found it."

"Where?"

He pointed to the floor by Shelby's front door. "On the mat. She must have dropped it."

The idea was laughable. Shelby practically lived on her phone. She would've noticed it was missing before she got to the sidewalk. It was obvious to Agatha that someone had dropped it back through the mail slot. The question was why, and also who, and also when, but mainly why. Smartphones were good for two things—unnecessary communication and keeping track of their owners' whereabouts. Agatha often thought about how much more difficult her job would have been back in the day had smartphones existed. Nowadays you couldn't do much without leaving a digital trail. Dropping Shelby's phone through the mail slot to prevent anyone from tracking her movements sounded exactly like something Agatha would do.

There was a chance it had been Shelby herself. After all, she'd told two different stories about where she was going on Saturday night, one to her landlord and another to her boyfriend. Agatha guessed neither was true but still wasn't buying that Shelby had left her phone at home. Not willingly anyway. If anything, Shelby would have left it charging on the kitchen counter. She didn't have the money to be so cavalier with her things and would never drop her phone through the mail slot and risk cracking the screen.

Agatha held her hand out for the phone, which Philip dutifully handed over. The screen was blank—no texts, missed calls, or alerts. She took out her own phone and texted Shelby's, which dutifully vibrated, but nothing appeared on the lock screen. Apparently Shelby kept her notifications turned off. Not a very convenient setting for a habitual texter unless discretion was a priority. And another data point that accentuated Agatha's unease. What did Shelby not want anyone accidentally seeing?

"Do either of you have her passcode?" She would have bet a fortune that they didn't, and the boys confirmed that suspicion. Her priority now was getting Philip alone so she could squeeze him like a pimple. There was something shifty about him, and she was curious why he would help look for Shelby while also holding back. There was a story there that she very much wanted to hear.

She sent Jackson off to search the bedroom while she and Philip scoured the kitchen and living room. Agatha dug through the stack of papers on the coffee table beside Shelby's laptop. Another thing she wouldn't leave home without for long. Philip puttered around, not doing much of anything useful.

"Where is she?"

"I wish I knew."

"Where is she, Philip?" she said, putting a little mustard on his name.

He twitched nervously and glanced toward the bedroom. Whatever he knew, he wasn't going to share with the boyfriend here.

Agatha leaned in close. "You have fifteen minutes from the time you leave here before I call the police and tell them that you are obstructing an official investigation into a missing person. Are we clear?"

The look on the boy's face told her that they were.

She'd barely finished boiling water for tea back upstairs when Philip knocked at her door. When she let him in, he looked even more disheveled, face mottled and pink, and forehead as shiny as the Reflecting Pool at night.

"Did you call the police yet?" he gasped, leaning against the doorframe.

Oh, bless your heart, Agatha thought. Whatever rights a landlord had in DC, conducting an official investigation wasn't one of them. How was it the well-read ones were always the most gullible?

She considered doubling down on the bad-cop routine and really putting the fear of God into Philip. But looking into his stricken eyes, she couldn't bring herself to do it. The boy was just this side of a heart attack as it was. Instead, she invited him back to the kitchen and offered him some tea. He accepted gratefully while she contemplated whether she'd gone soft.

"So . . . ," she led when he'd caught his breath.

"I don't know where she is. I swear."

She believed him. Whatever gifts he might possess, she didn't think he'd make his fortune at a poker table.

"So what *do* you know?" she asked, placing a mug in front of him.

A guilty look spread across his face. He put his hands around the mug and stared into the tea as if the answer were at the bottom. "She *was* on a date."

"But not with her boyfriend. So who was it?"

"You promise you won't tell him?"

"This has nothing to do with Jackson. I just want to know she's safe."

He said nothing for a long time, but she could see him debating whether to answer. Finally, he blew out his cheeks and said, "Cal Swinden."

Not a name she was expecting to hear. "The lobbyist?"

Philip nodded miserably.

That took her back to the old days. Swinden had been a DC institution, or tumor, depending on your view of lobbyists, for going on four decades. Agatha had crossed swords with him a time or two on Paul Paxton's behalf and could testify that his reputation as a hardball negotiator was well earned. A mercenary for hire who could either kill legislation or attach enough pork to open a BBQ joint.

Putting aside for a moment the fact Swinden was easily thirty years Shelby's senior, what was she doing with a man like *that*?

"Why?" Agatha asked.

"She's a sugar baby."

"A what?"

Philip turned an even deeper shade of red, and it wasn't from physical exertion. He repeated it, as if hoping that would clear things up.

"What's a sugar baby, Philip?" It was Agatha's turn to feel naive. "Is that another term for escort?"

Philip winced. He seemed to do that a lot. "Kind of. Yeah."

"What's 'kind of' an escort?"

"It's where an older guy has a financial relationship with someone younger."

"So exactly like an escort."

"Yeah."

Agatha swore at herself. Shelby had asked if she could pay the rent on Monday. That had been why she'd gone on this "date." Agatha had segued from landlord to accidental pimp. She suddenly felt ill.

"And why do you know all of this?"

"She needed someone to tell. I guess she thought she could trust me. Jackson doesn't know anything about it."

"And you didn't talk her out of it?"

"I've tried!" he exclaimed in obvious pain. "I tried so many times. But once I saw she was set on it, I just tried to support her. I didn't want her going through this all by herself, and she had no one else she could tell."

In a way, it was incredibly sweet. Philip was clearly in love with Shelby. Keeping her secrets and having her back were his love language. Agatha didn't think she'd ever had anyone who would do the same.

"How long has this been going on? With Swinden?" She could barely bring herself to say the name.

"Not long. She was seeing another guy, but he vacated his seat in October and moved back to Tennessee. She's only been seeing Swinden for about six months."

"Was there anything out of the ordinary about Saturday? Did she seem nervous to you?"

"No more than normal. She hates doing it, so she's always stressed out before."

So what had happened on her date with Cal Swinden? Whatever else might be true, Agatha doubted that Shelby had planned on being gone this long. Her toiletries were all still in the bathroom, her suitcase safely stowed under her bed. She hadn't called out sick at work, and if she meant to monitor her email and "work from home," she would have taken her laptop. The cell phone on the entry mat was simply the icing on a very disturbing cake.

"What are we going to do?" Philip asked.

"We? Nothing. You're going to write your number down for me. Then you're going home."

"What are you going to do?"

That was a good question.

CHAPTER SIX

The eager whirl of camera shutters announced the beginning of the press conference. Felix finished typing an email and slipped his work phone into the breast pocket of his suit. The president and Justice Northcott had just emerged from the Oval Office. The forecast threatened rain this morning, so there'd been discussion of making the announcement in the Roosevelt Room. Fortunately, and much to Felix's relief, after a few scattered showers, the clouds parted, and the sun shone down. It was better this way. The Rose Garden made for a more celebratory vibe, and it was a beautiful day to make history.

Justice Northcott had been in a dour mood when he'd arrived at the White House this morning with his wife. A terminal cancer diagnosis could do that to a person, and staff had been extraordinarily deferential, treating the justice with kid gloves. That only worsened the man's disposition, as Felix suspected it would. Retirement was hard enough without being treated like a porcelain teacup, especially when it was under these circumstances. Northcott reminded him of his grandfather, Sebastian Hector Gallardo, who'd fought lung cancer for years before passing when Felix was fourteen. Even when his grandfather smiled, Felix remembered the sadness lurking at the corners of his eyes. *I'm just tired,* his grandfather would say with a stoic wave of his hand. Felix had known that wasn't it. His grandfather had been such a vibrant, accomplished man before his illness. The cruelty of a slow death was that it gave you time to add up everything that would go undone and all that would be missed.

Fortunately President Clark saved the day, sweeping in and charming the judge. No consoling words, no trite platitudes, and inside of two minutes, the two men were chatting warmly like old friends. Despite having seen the Harrison Clark effect a thousand times, Felix still didn't know how the president made it seem so effortless. Spend enough time around a politician, and you could read the signs that they were only half paying attention to a conversation. With his former boss, Felix knew that a neck scratch signaled boredom and a shoulder touch meant that a conversation was about to wrap up, while a clenched fist meant the conversation had taken an unpleasant turn and that Felix would get an earful later. Felix could tell when autopilot had been engaged and that his boss was sailing along on a light breeze of stock phrases and well-rehearsed gestures. What else were politicians supposed to do? Sometimes it was the only way to survive the constant crush of human interaction that came with being an elected official.

At least that was what Felix had thought before meeting President Clark. The president possessed a seemingly bottomless reserve of energy and empathy for people and their lives. It didn't matter whether the cameras were rolling; Clark had no autopilot, so far as Felix could tell. No predictable patterns. When Clark spoke to someone, it was as if a powerful spotlight had been switched on. Everything else fell away, and it felt like you were the center of his universe. *That* was the Harrison Clark effect. And, remarkably, it seemed entirely genuine. It was what made him such an effective leader. And why Felix was willing to go to war for the man.

The president and justice stepped out from beneath the covered walkway and onto the platform that had been erected at the head of the Rose Garden. Reporters sat on folding chairs arranged on the grass immediately in front of the platform, ringed by more than a hundred photographers and videographers. Felix affectionately thought of this as the pit. Normally he loved the energy of a presidential press conference;

it charged him up. Not today, though. Today he was standing in the shadow of the West Colonnade so he could slip back into the West Wing once things were underway. His contributions to this morning's proceedings were already loaded into the teleprompter. He was here only briefly to see and be seen.

The president stepped up to the lectern and began his prepared remarks—a tribute to the life and career of Albert Lowenthal Northcott. Felix had written thirteen drafts and could've mouthed the words along with the president. The hard part had been nailing the tone—joyful, celebratory, but tinged with sadness at the reason for the premature retirement. It had been a challenging tightrope to walk, and he would have liked more time to rework the last section. But, as his father liked to say, paraphrasing Voltaire, "Don't let perfection be the enemy of the good, *mijo*."

To this day, Felix figured Voltaire for a quitter.

He lingered at the edge of the press conference long enough to make sure the first joke landed. When everyone laughed appreciatively, even the judge, Felix felt okay to step away. He went in the door by Lower Press and turned the corner at the press secretary's office to go down the hallway outside the Cabinet Room. Several new jumbos—the White House term for the enlarged photographs on poster board that hung in the hallway—had been displayed from the president's recent state visit to Great Britain. It was vain, and he knew it, but Felix always checked to see how many he was in. He couldn't help himself. The novelty of traveling with the president was still thrilling. The idea that he was a part of history now. He spotted himself in the background of three pictures and felt pretty good about his ratio. It also reminded him how thin he'd become and to try to eat, even if he wasn't hungry.

He ran into Linda Chen, the president's executive assistant, who was by every conceivable metric scarier than the marines guarding the West Wing. The trick, he'd found, was not to break stride and get caught in her kill zone.

"Shouldn't you be out there?" she asked.

"I have a call."

"It's always something with you."

"It *is* always something," he agreed and hurried past her to the safety of his own office. His plan was to barricade the door, put on music, and get work done until the luncheon.

No such luck. Affixed to his office door was a yellow sticky. On it, in a familiar hand, were two words: *my office*. No name, but none was necessary. Yellow stickies were a trademark of Steve Gilroy, the White House chief of staff, who believed that the invention of the computer was the greatest single misstep in human history. Gilroy was waging a one-man war against the National Archives to see how little he could put down in text or email. He preferred discussions be held face-to-face if possible, and yellow stickies were his preferred mode of intraoffice communication. That was all well and good in theory, but for those trying to get work done in the twenty-first century, it was incredibly frustrating. It was also possible that Felix had made his feelings on the subject a little too apparent.

The chief of staff's office was in the southwest corner of the West Wing. Felix rapped his knuckles on the door, which was always open except during meetings.

"You wanted to see me?"

Gilroy had his feet up on his desk and was scribbling notes on a legal pad. "How's it going out there?"

"Well, I think," Felix answered, glancing over at the television tuned to C-SPAN. The president was still giving his opening remarks.

"You did fine work on that speech."

"Appreciate it," Felix said, an internal alarm sounding. Steve Gilroy wasn't known for his compliments, especially not to the Romper Room—his nickname for the president's younger staff. In Gilroy's oft-shared opinion, anyone under forty should be seen and not heard, although he seemed to harbor a special disdain for Felix, whom he viewed as undisciplined and a liability. Whatever Gilroy wanted now, Felix was confident it wasn't to pat him on the back for a job well done.

"We've added a fourth name to be vetted for the Northcott vacancy," Gilroy said, pivoting to the topic at hand.

"Oh? Who?" Felix replied casually, the very picture of unflappable calm. At least he hoped so. Truth was, the news surprised the hell out of him. A short list of potential candidates had existed as far back as the campaign. Narrowing it to just three names had sparked intense, borderline messianic, debate within the president's inner circle for days. Felix glanced at the television again. Northcott's retirement was a matter of public record now. The vetting process of his potential replacements was well underway with an eye toward giving the Senate enough time to hold confirmation hearings before the August recess. A newly appointed justice would be an invaluable talking point ahead of the midterms in November. What possible reason could there be for adding a fourth judge this late in the game?

"Paul Paxton."

"You're joking," Felix said, his mouth getting out ahead of him, although in his head he followed the question with a string of ugly curses that he miraculously suppressed. It had been a week since his peculiar meeting with Tina Lu. He'd dutifully delivered her envelope to Gilroy. They'd shared a laugh over the story, and that had been that. It had been so absurd that he'd even told an old friend about it over drinks. *Why did I do that?*

"I am not. Paxton's approach might have been a touch unorthodox and perhaps even melodramatic, but the president sat with it over the weekend and now believes there is merit in the idea."

"Merit? What fucking merit?" Felix said, losing his cool. "The guy's a clown."

Gilroy took Felix's outburst in stride, as if he were a not-quite-house-broken puppy. "Paxton is an old friend of the president, so I would perhaps keep that sentiment to myself."

"Exactly. They're old friends. It looks bad. Not to mention the fact he's entirely unqualified. He's never practiced law, much less served as a judge. We'll get eaten alive."

"Well, nothing is set in stone. You know how the president is. He has a weakness for outside-the-box thinking. It's what makes him great. The man loves a good zag. In the end, I'm sure he'll settle on one of the more conventional candidates. But in the meantime, we're going to entertain this flight of fancy. Paxton will be vetted. Am I understood?"

Gilroy wasn't wrong about the president. Shaking things up by nominating a lawmaker, not a judge, to the Supreme Court was exactly the kind of move that Clark loved. Felix could even see himself being talked into the idea. Not Paxton, but in theory . . . he thought back to the strange, tense meeting with Tina Lu. The envelope. Nothing about this felt right.

"I understand."

"Good," Gilroy said and leaned forward to look at something more interesting on his computer screen. "I have something I need you to do. Are you still seeing that *Post* reporter? What's her name?"

"Isha Roy," he replied, instantly sure that Gilroy must know Felix had told her about Northcott and Paxton. This wasn't a meeting; it was an exit interview. Gilroy was toying with him until he got bored and fired him. "But no, I'm not *seeing* her." Why did his denial sound decidedly like a confession of guilt? "We went to school together. We're just friends." *Stop talking,* he told himself. *Stop now.*

"Mm-hmm," Gilroy agreed in a tone so patronizing a French waiter would have admired it. "And you're still school chums? Get together and sing 'The Princeton Cannon'?"

Gilroy had gone to Penn, and the fact that Felix didn't pay attention to the athletic rivalry between their two schools had been the first strike against him.

"Not much of a singer, but yes we do."

"Good then. We need to float Paxton's name in the press. A trial balloon."

This was standard. The names of the other three candidates were being passed to trusted contacts in the media immediately following the press conference. The White House would now sit back and factor in public reaction before making a final decision.

"I want you to give Paxton's name to Roy."

"Me?" Felix asked, relieved. Gilroy *didn't* know. He wasn't getting fired. Almost immediately, though, he felt his heart sink. This meant going back to Isha after telling her the Paul Paxton envelope story. It had been off the record, and he'd been a little drunk, but she would still be aware. And if he knew Isha, she wouldn't let it go. *What a mess.* He knew he should tell Gilroy now. Throw himself on the mercy of the president. It had been an innocent mistake.

"Yes, you. And today. Is that a problem?" Gilroy asked, his full attention now on his legal pad.

Instead of coming clean, Felix said, "No, no problem."

On the television, Justice Northcott had just been invited to the podium and was thanking the president for his kind words. What would Northcott think of Paul Paxton succeeding him on the bench? Felix imagined that would be a memorable conversation.

Gilroy nodded, satisfied. "Good. Come see me when it's done."

CHAPTER SEVEN

After Philip left, Agatha knew she wouldn't sleep. She made tea and got comfortable in the armchair by her front window to think. Her last conversation with Shelby kept replaying in her mind. Shelby asking to pay the rent on Monday, and it never occurring to Agatha to wonder how she would get the money over the weekend. Agatha tried arguing herself out of any responsibility, pleading her case to the grand jury hastily impaneled in her head.

She'd always had a knack for deflecting responsibility, and this should've been an open-and-shut case of *not her problem*. But the vivid image of Charlotte Haines's lifeless body curled around a hotel toilet kept appearing in her mind's eye as a rebuttal witness. *This has nothing to do with that,* Agatha told herself, trying and failing to corral the memory back into its well-padded compartment. Shelby Franklin was nothing like Charlotte Haines. Nothing.

For twenty-one years, staying out of trouble had been the first commandment of Agatha's state religion. Keep her head down; don't get involved; mind her own business. All she had to do now was call the police, tell them what she knew, and go to bed. She knew how that conversation would go, though—*My tenant hasn't come home in days from her date with one of the most powerful lobbyists in the city. Oh, and she may be an escort.*

Agatha sighed and rubbed her tired eyes. The police would get *right* on that. Missing sex workers were always a top priority. Either Shelby was alive or she was dead. If the worst had happened, the police would have plenty of time to investigate later.

So what was Agatha going to do? Well, if Shelby was still alive, then Agatha's priority was to give Cal Swinden a reason to keep her that way. Which meant moving fast. It might be a good idea to pay him a visit.

If she moved forward, would there be consequences? She'd made certain assurances many years ago. Would Paul consider this going back on her word? She didn't know. They'd had no direct contact in more than twenty years. What if she was the only one who still cared about the summer of 2001? What if she was another Hiroo Onoda, the Japanese soldier who'd dutifully manned his post on a remote island in the Philippines for nearly thirty years because no one told him the Second World War was over? How must he have felt knowing he'd wasted so much of his life for nothing?

They weren't the same, though, she and Onoda. Not at all. Hiroo Onoda had been assigned to his post by a country he loved. Agatha had banished herself. It would be a good idea to keep that in mind, because this thing? She *had* to do it. Shelby Franklin *would* come home. It startled Agatha how determined she felt. Mind made up, she spent the rest of the night thinking through tomorrow. By the time the sun rose, she knew what needed to be done. It felt good to have a plan, and she rose from the armchair to get to work as energized as if she'd slept twelve hours.

That was how she came to be standing in Penn Quarter at the corner of Twelfth and G Streets, trying to get her bearings. She'd just stepped off the Metro Center escalator, and nothing looked the way she remembered. It made her feel out of touch. She'd spent a lot of time in Penn Quarter as a kid. Police headquarters and the courts were on Indiana Avenue, and she'd loved visiting her dad at work. Back then the neighborhood had been blocks of run-down or boarded-up storefronts. Penn Quarter had never entirely recovered from the riots of '68, and Agatha remembered seeing fire damage on some of the buildings. She would get off the Metro at Gallery Place and wander through

Chinatown and say hello to the giant lobsters in the window of Tony Cheng's Mongolian.

Tony Cheng's was still there, but so much else had changed. It was hard to articulate the scale of the transformation since the sports arena had been finished in '97. Professional basketball and hockey had returned to the city from the hinterlands of Landover, Maryland, and with them an orgy of construction: new apartment buildings, offices, restaurants, and bars—you name it. Gentrification had brought in the law firms and power brokers. K Street might be the ancestral home of the lobbying class, but since its revival, Penn Quarter, which neighbored the White House to the east, had become a popular alternative. It was also where Cal Swinden practiced his dark arts.

She knew it wouldn't be easy to get a face-to-face, especially on short notice. It would be essential to look the part. Unfortunately, the only part she was fit to play these days was that of antisocial shut-in. She kept her hair long, only trimming it in the mirror as needed. Her nails were a disaster, and what passed for her wardrobe was mostly leggings and T-shirts.

The only solution had been an emergency makeover—haircut, manicure, Brunello Cucinelli business suit, Cuyana work tote, Stuart Weitzman pumps. It had taken all morning, but Agatha had to admit the effect was startling. She paused to check herself in a shop window and not for the first time. Call it vanity, but she just wanted to gape at her reflection like a downtown Narcissus. Her long and, let's be honest, stringy hair had been cut into a sharp power bob that accentuated her features and made her look ten years younger. She wished now there'd been time for color and highlights. The stylist assured her that silver was very trendy, but Agatha was curious how she'd look with black hair again. Not that she could afford to spend any more money. After her spending spree, she was already down $3,800. If she returned the suit tomorrow, that would help, but she couldn't afford to go any deeper in the hole.

Claremont East was a small, influential lobbying firm with three founding partners and a handful of associates. It kept offices on the fifth floor of a building on F Street three blocks from the White House. Agatha rode up in the elevator, getting her game face on. Everything depended on the first five minutes. She hadn't spent thousands of dollars on designer labels for Cal Swinden's benefit. Men didn't notice such things, but women did, and if she hoped to see Cal Swinden, she first had to get past his gatekeepers—his receptionist and assistant. If they didn't buy her act, then this was over before it began. And how could she be sure they'd be women? Well, anyone who paid for escorts but needed to call them *sugar babies* wouldn't have a man answering his phone.

The elevator opened onto a hallway where brass lettering directed guests of Claremont East to the glass doors at the far end. Inside was an enormous reception area with plush blue carpet and black-and-white photographs of Washington in the 1940s. A wall-mounted television replayed this morning's White House press conference announcing the surprise retirement of Justice Northcott. Exotic fish swam in an enormous tank, and inoffensive jazz played quietly over invisible speakers. Everything looked brand new. Pristine and untouched. Agatha doubted Claremont East saw much foot traffic; lobbyists didn't have advertising budgets and depended on recommendations and referrals for new business. But they also hosted fundraisers and special events for clients, which explained the excessive square footage.

The woman behind the reception desk looked up from her computer and greeted Agatha with practiced warmth. She was young and stylish, at least by Washington standards, which had never been a city that knew how to dress itself. Women's fashion in the DC political scene veered toward puritanical chic and was a vestige of which side of the Mason-Dixon Line the city lay.

"May I help you?"

Agatha swept off her new Tom Ford sunglasses and set them on the receptionist's desk. "Yes, I'm hoping for a quick word with Mr. Swinden. Is he available?"

The woman winced as if this were the most unfortunate news she'd ever heard. "I'm sorry. He's not currently in the office."

Agatha brushed this off. "I understand. He was recommended to my employer last night. I'm at the Willard and thought I'd stop in on the off chance he was free."

"He'll be sorry to have missed you, Miss . . . ?"

Agatha placed a business card on the desk between them. The receptionist leaned forward to inspect it without touching. In gold letters, the business card introduced Agatha as Olivia Furstenberg. Beneath her name read "Emirates Financial Group" followed by an address in Dubai and a phone number with a (971) (04) prefix. In blue ballpoint pen, Agatha had added a 202 number with "DC Cell." The receptionist's eyes widened slightly, exactly the reaction Agatha had hoped for. There wasn't a lobbyist in the city whose pulse wouldn't quicken at the prospect of petrodollars.

"It's a shame he's out of town, but I'm sure we can find an answer to our issue elsewhere."

"He's not out of town," the receptionist said, giving away more than Agatha would have tolerated if the woman worked for her. "His days are just very scheduled, but I'm sure Mr. Swinden would be available tomorrow if you're free then."

"We leave for Paris this evening," Agatha said and then, after a meaningful pause, added, "unfortunately."

"Will you excuse me for just one moment?" the receptionist asked, scooping up the business card and disappearing through a frosted-glass door behind her desk. To maintain the illusion of a busy representative of a Gulf investment firm, Agatha took out her phone and began a list of supplies she'd need to stop her downstairs toilet from running. It wasn't finished by the time the receptionist returned, accompanied by another young, attractive woman, who wore the expression of a surgeon come to update a worried family. It was quite a show.

"Ms. Furstenberg, I'm Tish Linklater, Mr. Swinden's executive assistant." The woman extended a hand, which Agatha shook perfunctorily. "I'm sorry for the inconvenience. I just spoke to Cal. Would you be able to meet him at Tosca in half an hour? He's just finishing a client lunch and has a little time before his next meeting."

"Thirty minutes?" Agatha said as if she'd been asked to make a quick trip to the moon. What she was actually doing was kicking herself for not checking there first, and in so doing saving herself several thousand dollars. Lunch was the preferred business setting for most of the lobbyist class. Tosca was one of their favorite boardrooms and only a block away from Swinden's office. Agatha unlocked her phone and swiped through to her calendar. She frowned, then said, "I can make that work."

"Again, I'm sorry for the inconvenience."

Agatha smiled graciously. "No problem at all. I have a long flight tonight; I could use the exercise. Thank you for your help, Ms. Linklater."

"Tish, please."

"Tish. Thank you. You've been most accommodating."

The two women shook hands again. Agatha was halfway to the door when the receptionist called after her. "Ms. Furstenberg?"

Agatha felt the hairs on her neck stand up. What had she missed? Had they found her out?

"Yes?" she said, turning back.

The receptionist was approaching, hand extended. "Your sunglasses."

"Ah, thank you so much," Agatha said, sliding them up onto her head. That was a lucky break. They hadn't been cheap either.

CHAPTER EIGHT

Ristorante Tosca had been an institution on F Street for decades, but Agatha never had the chance to eat there in her old life. It first opened in the spring of 2001, but by that summer, her world had been turned upside down—and then inside out for good measure. In August, she'd left the country—fled, if she were being honest. A monthlong trip to clear her head and think. That was all it was supposed to have been, but her return flight had been booked for September 12, and US airspace had been closed. The airline had offered to reschedule, but by then she'd met Denny Cross and begun, inexplicably, to fall in love with him. She hadn't come home for seven more years. By the time she did, restaurants like Tosca were the furthest thing from her mind.

If there was one thing insiders liked more than power, it was witnesses to their power. Choosing the right restaurant for a meeting was like picking the right theater for a new play. A well-staged lunch could send ripples of gossip and conjecture through the city before the check was paid. Tosca was the Carnegie Hall of DC restaurants.

The lunch rush was over, and the restaurant was officially closed until dinner. A few tables still lingered over dessert or coffee, but otherwise the staff was resetting for the evening. Agatha spotted Swinden alone at a table near the back but feigned ignorance and stopped at the host's stand. It was better if she didn't appear to know more than she should.

"Ms. Furstenberg?" the host asked before she could even clear her throat. Impressed despite herself, Agatha nodded. The host smiled and led her back through the sea of white-linen tablecloths and camel-colored upholstered chairs.

Cal Swinden sat as if posed for the jacket photo of an upcoming nonfiction history. His seat was turned forty-five degrees from the table so that he could cross his legs comfortably. He appeared deep in thought, one arm resting on the table near a cappuccino, while the other hung languidly over the back of his chair. Trim and healthy for a man in his sixties, he was meticulously handsome in a way that probably required constant maintenance. She thought the tweed suit and round, black-framed glasses a nice touch. He was one pipe away from cosplaying a kindly Ivy League professor from the 1940s. It was hard to imagine him as the ruthless bastard who'd built his kingdom on the ashes of the democratic process.

He felt her approaching and stood to offer his hand. "Ms. Furstenberg, good to meet you."

It was an impressive handshake, even if she wanted to break all his fingers. The host held a chair out for Agatha to sit.

"Thank you, Robert," Swinden said to the host, who had lingered by the table. "Can they bring you anything?"

"I was under the impression the kitchen was closed."

"Not to me," he said matter-of-factly. "Are you hungry? The agnolotti del plin is superb."

As it happened, she was starving. Her makeover had not come with a lunch break. "No, I'm fine. Thank you for taking the time to meet with me."

He nodded to the host that that would be all. "Well, I have a meeting on the Hill in forty-five minutes, so we will have to be brief, but I didn't want to miss the opportunity to put a face to the name."

Something about the way he said it didn't feel right, but she smiled through her apprehension. "The sheikh will no doubt appreciate it."

"Yes, the sheikh. May I ask who recommended me?"

"Aaron Burnett." Burnett was a former Clinton adviser who had done a stint as a lobbyist before landing a gig as a talking head on cable news. Agatha thought he was an idiot, but he looked good on television.

"Aaron? Really? Well, I owe him another one. So since we're pressed for time, why don't we cut to the chase? What is it I can do to help your employer?"

Swinden was staring intently at her face, but Agatha pressed on. "Congress is considering legislation to further limit foreign investment in certain American businesses."

"Senator Morton's bill."

"Precisely."

"He's evangelical on the subject, but I don't think it's going anywhere."

"We'd rather not leave that to chance," Agatha countered.

"I can understand that. What's the sheikh's desired outcome? A watered-down version of the legislation, or see it killed outright?"

"Killed outright, ideally, but we'd be open to the first option, depending on how much water it takes on."

"Well, I think that's . . ." Swinden paused, then smiled tiredly. "How far are we taking this?"

"Excuse me?"

"Sheikh Salman bin Abdul-Aziz Al-Qahtani is in London. His team is playing Chelsea this weekend. And Aaron, to my knowledge, is not a soccer fan."

"Well," Agatha said, realizing the jig was up, "shit."

Swinden's face brightened when she cursed, as if that were the missing piece of the puzzle. "Agatha Cardiff! I *knew* I knew you. Never forget a face, but it's been a few years. You were Paul Paxton's pit bull back in the day. A real pain in my ass, as I remember."

"I did my best."

"Agatha Cardiff. My, my, my, that's a blast from the Dark Ages. Looks like you've lost your fastball, though. This? This was weak. But

What is it you think you were doing here?"

"Honestly, I need your help arranging a meeting."

"Well, you haven't lost your nerve, I'll give you that," he said, signaling to the waiter for his check. "And, theoretically, to whom would I be introducing you?"

"Shelby Franklin. She's been missing since Saturday. You remember Saturday, don't you? Date night?"

The amount of blood that drained from Swinden's face could have transfused an open-heart surgery. She'd always loved these moments, watching someone realize they'd underestimated her and feeling the momentum swing in her direction. It was borderline erotic.

"Where is she, Cal?"

Swinden shook his head. "Take out your phone. Power it off and leave it on the table."

She did as he asked, holding up her phone so he could see. It felt like the scene in a movie where the hero had to surrender their weapon. She put the phone on the table in front of her, but that didn't seem to satisfy Swinden, who reached over and slid it out of her reach.

"Who are you really working for?" he asked, all the bass dropping out of his voice.

"What? You think you're the only rich old man Shelby is fucking for money?" she said, noting with disgust that he actually had the balls to look offended. Men and their egos. He'd paid a woman half his age for sex and still managed to feel hurt to hear it put in such unromantic terms. "Grow up. There are bigger fish in this town than even you, Cal. My employer is very fond of Shelby. And very, very protective. He wants her returned."

Swinden appeared to buy her bluff. "I'm working on it."

Agatha didn't know what that meant, only that a late lunch at Tosca didn't seem to be working all that hard. "So, she *is* alive?"

He nodded grimly.

Agatha felt her heart flutter in relief but kept her expression neutral. "That's a good start. Where is she?"

"It's complicated."

Agatha leaned forward. "Well, uncomplicate it. You want to destroy my reputation, Calvin? Take your shot. But I'll burn yours to the ground. We have Shelby's phone and laptop. Either you take me to her now, or my next stops are CNN, MSNBC, and Fox."

"I can't."

"Are you sure? 'DC Lobbyist Kidnaps Escort' is one hell of a headline."

He held up a pleading hand. "Keep your voice down, damn it. I can't take you to her. She's not even in the country."

"Where is she?"

"I don't know exactly," he admitted. "The Caribbean somewhere."

"The Caribbean? Somewhere?"

"She's on a yacht."

"What is she doing on a yacht in the Caribbean, Calvin?"

"Look," Swinden said, the tone of his voice changing to indicate he was leveling with her. "Her date on Saturday wasn't with me. It was with an associate of mine. Shelby met him a few weeks ago while out with me. He took a fancy to her and asked if she was available. I just set it up. She flew down Saturday afternoon to join him."

Agatha knew that had to be a heavily sanitized version of what had actually happened. Cal Swinden certainly wasn't the first person to use sex as a sweetener in a business deal.

"What happened?"

"I'm not entirely sure. Things . . . took a turn."

"A turn?" She wanted to shake him until all the euphemisms fell out.

"An unpleasant turn."

"Is she physically hurt?" Agatha demanded, punctuating each word to drive home the question.

"I've been assured that is not the case."

She didn't know that he believed that, but now wasn't the time. "So what's the problem?"

"They won't let her off the boat without certain assurances."

"She's being held against her will."

He grimaced. "On a yacht, where her every need is being met."

"It doesn't matter if she's in a suite at the Hay-Adams with a view of Lafayette Park, it's still against her will," Agatha said, avoiding the word *kidnapping*. For now. Swinden wasn't a stupid man. He'd thought the situation through. But thinking something through and hearing it spoken out loud were two different things entirely. He already looked visibly shaken, and intuition told her that throwing the *K*-word around would overwhelm him. She needed Swinden calm and took that as her cue to shift tactics. Time for them to be on the same side.

"Cal, look, I get it. You're trying to protect your client. I'd do the same thing in your position." God knew she had and more. "My employer doesn't want to make trouble for you. His strong preference is that this be resolved discreetly. He just wants the girl released unharmed."

"I just need twenty-four hours to straighten this out."

Somehow she doubted it. "I can buy you that, but I'm going to need proof of life."

"Right now?"

"Yes, right now. You want twenty-four hours? I want a photograph of Shelby Franklin having her every need met. In it she'll be holding her left thumb to her right ear."

He looked confused at the specificity of her demand but took out his phone and made a call. Whoever answered sounded none too happy and became even less so when Swinden explained what he needed and why. A terse back-and-forth ensued like two men playing tennis with a live grenade. The voice at the other end stubbornly resisted the idea, but gradually Swinden wore them down.

"Well?" she asked when he'd hung up.

"It'll be a minute."

A minute turned into five and then ten. They sat there in the world's most awkward silence. Agatha watched him, looking for any sign he was playing her. But unless the man could perspire on command, he was on the level. She was moments from lowering the boom on him when his phone buzzed to announce an incoming text message.

Swinden unlocked the phone and placed it on the table near Agatha. On the screen was a photograph of Shelby sitting in a cushioned armchair. It could easily be confused for an Instagram pic from a tropical vacation if it weren't for the dark-red mark on her face and that she was wearing an oversize sweatshirt instead of a bathing suit. Her left thumb was touching her right earlobe. The photo was current—Shelby Franklin was alive or had been minutes ago.

"You said they wanted assurances. What kind?"

"That she will not involve the authorities or the media. She says she won't, but they don't believe her."

"Why not?"

"Because her first move was explaining that in taking her into international waters against her will, they could be charged with kidnapping and human trafficking. She was extremely detailed about the statutory ramifications and sentencing guidelines. It put the fear of God in them." Swinden sighed. "She's very, very articulate. They were not prepared for that from a—"

"Prostitute?" Agatha suggested helpfully.

Swinden gave her a pained look. "She's not. She's actually brilliant. Her mind is—"

"Spare me." Agatha was in no mood for him to present his feminist credentials. "So they're in a standoff?"

"Essentially. She says now she won't go to the police, but they're too scared to let her go."

"So what's happening?"

"Nothing. They don't know what to do."

"And every day this gets worse."

"Don't I know it," Swinden said miserably.

"If they kill her, life as you know it is over. You understand that."

"It won't come to that," he said without conviction.

Agatha had seen this all before. These were men who'd made a mistake. Instead of cutting their losses, they doubled down. Tried to cover over the first hole they'd dug for themselves but succeeded only in making an even bigger one. At some point, a hole got so deep that the only way out was down, down into the darkness. From the look in his eyes, Agatha knew that they would keep digging now until they were caught, or by some miracle they got away with it. Throwing Shelby overboard and letting the sea dispose of the evidence would occur to them eventually, if it hadn't already. How long until they talked themselves into that being their only option?

"Can you get me on that boat?" she asked.

"Why?"

"Let me talk to her. Find a peaceful resolution. I can fix this, Cal. This is what I do."

"It's what I do too."

"Yeah, but you're involved. She needs a face she can trust."

"And she trusts you?"

"She will."

Swinden sat there a long time, thinking it over. Agatha didn't press him. She'd made her case and had always found repeating herself to be counterproductive. Finally, he reached for his phone.

"Let me make a call."

CHAPTER NINE

Isha arrived early, but Felix was already at the bar nursing a beer. In the entire time she'd known him, he'd never been early to anything. And the fact that he'd volunteered to trek out to Arlington made her uneasy. If she was being honest, she probably had it coming. She'd been a lousy friend. She knew that. Ever since Felix and Stephanie split up, things had been strained. She'd let their friendship drift. Before running into him last week, they hadn't spoken in months, only the odd text here and there. It had been a peculiar encounter, to say the least. He'd looked gaunt, worn out. And then there was the small matter of what he'd told her.

Since the campaign, there'd been an unspoken rule between them—Felix didn't talk about his job, and she never asked. There was no other way. She worked in the political press. He was the young star of the administration. It would be too easy to misinterpret even innocent questions as "working him for information," and she refused to tarnish their friendship that way. No matter how tempting it had been at times.

Their informal détente had held until that Sunday night. She'd seen a show at the Warner Theatre and stopped off for a drink at the Hamilton with friends. Felix had been at a corner of the bar, already a few high-thread-count sheets to the wind. In retrospect, she should have slipped away without saying anything, but guilt got the better of her. That had been a mistake. Felix had been *off* and not just because he was drunk. Unprompted, he'd launched into Albert Northcott's pending retirement and a crazy story about Paul Paxton pitching himself as Northcott's replacement.

After sitting on the Northcott story out of deference to their friendship, Isha had watched half of her scoop confirmed on national television this morning. It was painful but still felt like the right call. She'd owed it to Felix. Though that didn't mean she wasn't curious now whether there was also truth to Paul Paxton lobbying for the nomination.

Stephanie and Felix's divorce had sent a shock wave through their friend group. While Isha hadn't actively chosen a side, she'd found herself in Stephanie's camp almost by default. That had a lot to do with the starkly different approaches Stephanie and Felix had taken to the end of their marriage. Stephanie had been openly, heartbreakingly devastated. Isha had held her friend while Stephanie sobbed until she made herself physically sick. It had been easy to cast her as the wronged victim of the story. Felix, on the other hand, did what he always did: buried himself in work and soldiered stoically on. It didn't help that he appeared entirely unaffected by the divorce, and while Isha knew he must be grieving, it had been hard not to resent his unaffected calm on Stephanie's behalf. The easy villain, he'd chosen his career over a relationship that Isha had always placed on a pedestal.

Isha had been two years behind Stephanie and Felix in school and had met Stephanie working at the *Prince*, the university's newspaper. Stephanie and Felix had been an item even before Isha entered their social circle. She hadn't been alone in that. People gravitated to the pair, and much of their friend group had been scaffolded on the assumption that Felix and Stephanie were an unshakable pillar. Their separation marked the end of an era.

It wasn't overly busy for a Thursday night. Felix caught her reflection in the mirror above the bar and rose to greet her. They always hugged when they met up, so that was what they did, although it felt as awkward as a middle-school slow dance. It struck her how much she'd missed him, and she wished she knew how to get back to the way things had been. They sat and looked at the drink menu, filling the silence between them with questions about what the other would order. For a moment, it seemed that was all they had to say to each other.

"You really didn't have to drag ass out to Ballston. I work about a half mile from you," she said.

"Thought I should come see how you barbarians live out here."

"Well, we just discovered fire. Could be a game changer."

Their drinks arrived, and Felix proposed a toast to "fire." Another tradition begun as undergrads and carried into the real world. They always toasted to something ordinary, essential, and easy to take for granted. A reminder not to overlook the little things.

"And all it burns," she added.

They touched glasses. Isha braced for both barrels and the real possibility that Felix would then pause to reload. Instead, he downshifted into safe, familiar banter, perfected over countless late nights in college. She was grateful for the reprieve. As a rule, she loathed small talk, but with Felix talk never felt small, even when it was about nothing at all. She gave him a heavily redacted version of her life. No mention that she was struggling to find her footing at work and was worried that the paper might be running short of patience. She still had Bern in her corner, but the clock was definitely ticking to make her mark. A journalist was all she'd ever wanted to be, and it felt traumatic and a little embarrassing to admit that she might not cut it at this level. She wasn't accustomed to failure and didn't know what she was supposed to do with her life if not journalism. There'd been a time when she would have come to Felix for advice, but they didn't have that kind of relationship now. It made her heart ache.

"How is she?" Felix asked suddenly, signaling that their opening act had drawn to a close. "Have you talked to her lately?"

Isha texted with Stephanie every day. "She's okay. I saw her last week."

Felix hid his surprise well. "You were in Chicago?"

"No, she was here."

"Stephanie was in DC?" Hiding it a little less well.

"Beatrice's bachelorette party."

"Bea and Tommy are getting married?"

Isha stared at him in disbelief. "They've been engaged for two years."

"I know that. I just didn't know they'd picked a date."

Isha sighed.

"What?" he said defensively. "It's not like anyone tells me anything anymore."

"Well, whose fault is that? Jesus Christ, Felix. They're your friends too."

He stared glumly at the shelves of liquor behind the bar. "I just didn't want anyone to have to choose between us."

"That's a bunch of crap, and you know it. You wanted everyone to choose Stephanie, so that's what they did. Don't act like a martyr and then get hurt when people nail you up. You cut yourself off from all of us."

"Work's been so busy," he said, but he was nodding glumly that he knew she was right.

"I'm sure it is, but you do this kind of thing all the time—make a grand gesture and punish yourself in the process. We can be friends with both of you. It won't be like it used to be, but we all love you."

Without looking up from his glass, Felix put his hand on the bar between them. She put hers on top and squeezed. They sat there a long time, counting bottles behind the bar.

"Sorry about the other night. I was . . . not at my best."

No, you weren't, she thought. "It's okay."

"And I really appreciate you forgetting about Northcott. Gilroy would have roasted me over that."

She hadn't exactly let it go; finding anyone to corroborate the story had simply been impossible. "Between friends stays between friends."

"You're the best," he said. "So what did you think of the announcement?"

That caught her off guard. What was he doing opening *that* door after they'd just about closed it again? Maybe since Northcott was public knowledge now, he thought it was fair game. Still, the question irritated her. It felt like he was taunting her for her discretion.

"It's tough for Northcott. That's a sad way to go. But I like any of the three nominees Clark talked about during the campaign."

"There's a fourth," he said.

Now Isha's radar was pinging wildly. "Who?"

He arched an eyebrow but said nothing.

"Paul Paxton?" she guessed, wanting very badly to be wrong.

His nod was virtually imperceptible, like a seismometer registering a distant and faint tremor.

"So you were right?" she asked, then caught herself and back-tracked. "Wait. Are we on background or off the record here?"

Felix took his time answering. "Background."

She put her drink down and twisted in her seat to face him. "Alright, what is going on? Is giving me Paxton *your* idea?"

He shrugged. "They need to test the waters with Paxton like any other nominee. I suggested you. Got to admit, I owe you one."

Isha went cold all over and felt all the hairs on the back of her neck stand up. They weren't meeting as friends. Stephanie, the last six months, it had all been a pretext for him to whisper "Paul Paxton" in her ear. That was why he'd volunteered to come to Arlington instead of meeting in the city.

"And this was all Paxton's idea?" Isha put her phone on the bar between them and hit record. Felix made no objection.

"No, where'd you get that?"

"Sunday. You said Paxton had lobbied the president for the nomination."

"No, I misspoke. Too much to drink," Felix said, miming a glass in one hand. "Paxton definitely wants the nom, but it was the president's idea."

"But Paxton's not a judge."

"That's exactly why, though. The president is intrigued by the notion of having an experienced lawmaker on the bench. Adding a different perspective to decisions. He feels the court's makeup has become too narrow over the last fifty years. Earl Warren was the governor of California, and he was chief justice for sixteen years," Felix said and went on enumerating the case for Paul Paxton. When he was finished, he signaled the bartender for another round.

"There's no chance he's going to get it, though, is there?"

"I doubt it. You know how Clark is. He likes to shake things up, but in the end my guess is he'll go with a more traditional candidate."

The story sounded so plausible and even admirable in a way. But something about it didn't sit right with her, though she couldn't quite put her finger on why. Felix was too good a liar for that. It was part of his job, and she didn't enjoy having it turned on her. She started gathering her things to go as the bartender arrived with two more drinks.

"You're not going to stay?" Felix asked, toggling from work mode back to friends.

"Do you want this story run tomorrow?" she asked.

"Yeah."

"Then I gotta go." She put one arm around his shoulder and gave him a brief hug. He made no move to stand up. "I owe you for the drink. My treat next time."

"Definitely."

She looked back as she pushed through the door to the street—he was watching her from his barstool and gave a forlorn wave. As soon as she was out of sight, she dialed Bernard's cell.

"Bernard Goff," he answered as if she might not know who she'd called.

"The White House *is* vetting Paxton," she said.

"You got confirmation?" Bern sounded interested but skeptical.

"On background. Two minutes ago."

"Alright, we're in business. That's good work. Let's put our heads together in the morning and discuss next steps."

Isha felt a stab of disappointment. Tomorrow felt like a lifetime from now, and an internal timer had already begun counting down until the moment someone beat her to another big story.

Bernard must have read her mind, because he told her sternly to go home. Reluctantly, she agreed, although she didn't really see the point. It wasn't as if she'd be able to sleep tonight.

CHAPTER TEN

Agatha emerged into the bright Caribbean sunshine from the Cyril E. King Airport, glad for the sunglasses. Her early-morning flight had been out of Dulles, which meant leaving for the airport well before dawn. She'd watched the sunrise from her window seat, wondering how she'd pay for any of this. Her expenses had been piling up even before she'd sprung for a next-day ticket to the Caribbean. She dearly wished there'd been a way to stick Cal Swinden with the tab, but haggling over plane fare didn't exactly fit the image of high-priced political hatchet woman that she'd sold him. She still clung to the waning hope of returning the business suit, flying down in leggings and a sweatshirt to protect it from unnecessary wear and tear, and only changing once she'd landed. Call it irony or maybe just karma, but it wasn't lost on her that this had all started because she'd been a hard-ass with Shelby over the rent.

———————

Standing beside an idling car, a slight man held a sign that read simply "A.C." He looked young, no more than thirty despite his thinning hair and stooped shoulders. From his cheap suit and worn shoes, she pegged him for an assistant or aide. Judging by the hollow, jittery eyes behind black-framed glasses, Agatha suspected he'd begun to question the career decisions that had led him to this moment. He looked like a man desperate to be somewhere, anywhere but here. She stopped in front of him and looked at his sign.

"Ms. Cardiff?" he asked, his accent indistinctly southern.

She nodded.

"Welcome to Saint Thomas. How was your flight?"

He seemed eager to cling to a sense of normalcy, which Agatha found reassuring. These people hadn't come to grips with the seriousness of their situation. They'd kidnapped a woman but were trying to carry on like business as usual. That told her they wanted a way out of this situation. Agatha just had to give them one.

"And your name is?"

"Charles—" he began, his manners kicking in on autopilot; then he caught himself. "Sorry, I'm just here to help."

"Sure," she said, hoping the smile on her face communicated just how screwed she thought he was. "Shall we?"

"Do you have any other luggage?" he asked, indicating her shoulder bag.

"I'm not here on vacation."

In actuality, she'd be here until at least tomorrow. There was only one direct flight to Washington every day, and she'd already missed it. She'd packed only the essentials and had a reservation at a hotel near the airport.

"Is it far?"

As it turned out, they could have walked. The car had scarcely left the airport before pulling up at a small marina.

"Will you please power off your phone and leave it and your bag here. It will all be safe."

"This your idea of a good first date?" she said, doing as he asked.

"Sorry," was all he could muster. She wondered if it had been his first word as a baby.

They parked and went down the dock to a waiting tender. A broad-shouldered man in a painfully tight T-shirt and Bermuda shorts offered Agatha his hand to climb down into the boat. Under any other circumstances, she would have brushed it away, but there was no way she was making it in heels and this skirt. The aide, whom Agatha had christened Sorry Charlie, took a seat beside her at the back of the tender and handed her a black hood.

"This is going to ruin my hair," she said.

"Sorry," Charlie commiserated again, still sounding as if he meant it.

To be a good sport, she put on the hood without making a fuss. There was no sport in torturing someone already torturing himself. Anyway, she wasn't here for him.

The tender pulled away from the dock and gradually accelerated through the choppy surf. Even with the hood, the breeze and the sunshine felt good. She wished that she were here under better circumstances and realized immediately what a crock that was. Her mind felt sharper than it had in years. Tuned in. Alert. She could've described Charlie from head to foot, from the old scar on his chin to the unusually hairy knuckles to his pink, sunburned ears, where he'd forgotten sunscreen. It was exhilarating. How she'd missed this.

Time passed differently beneath a hood, but it didn't feel too long before the tender's motor cut out. They coasted until the bow bumped gently against the hull of a larger boat. Voices called back and forth as the tender was tied off. Strong hands took her by the arms and guided Agatha up a ladder, down a flight of stairs, and through a door. Air-conditioning prickled her skin, and she shivered at the abrupt change in temperature.

Before leaving, she'd squeezed Cal Swinden for information. The idea of going in without the full picture didn't thrill her, but he'd been resolutely stingy with details. He'd refused to give her any names and provided only the broadest possible overview of the situation. The gist of it was that Swinden had a client, a wealthy foreign national seeking political support from an American congressman. Because the client was not welcome in the United States, Swinden had brokered a sit-down with the congressman aboard the yacht of a second client who needed a favor of their own. To entice the congressman, the meeting had also doubled as a floating orgy complete with booze, drugs, and enough young women to start a travel soccer team. Shelby had been one of them, a last-minute demand by the congressman. Swinden had assured Shelby she'd be there only as eye candy. But the congressman had other ideas, and at some point things had taken an "unpleasant turn," to quote Swinden. He wouldn't elaborate, but Agatha knew what it meant when men started talking in euphemisms.

Apparently everything had gone wrong from the start. Even before the unnamed congressman assaulted Shelby, he'd made it clear that he had no interest in doing business and was only there for the "perks." Another direct quote.

Swinden's foreign client was holding Cal personally responsible for the entire mess. Not only had Swinden failed to deliver, but he'd created possible exposure at a time the client could least afford it. All Agatha had to do was make everyone happy and get Shelby safely off the yacht.

A hand yanked off the hood. Agatha blinked in the light, feeling like the rabbit at the end of a bad magic trick. It was disorienting—she knew she was on a boat, but it looked more like a palace. The walls were paneled in a dark wood, and oil paintings hung between crystal sconces. One she felt quite certain was a Degas and not a reproduction. A Persian rug covered much of the floor, and an enormous curved sofa was centered between a set of leather Chesterfield armchairs. It was telling that the three men facing her were as far apart as the room allowed. They were not on the same page, perhaps not even in the same book.

Agatha recognized only one of them, but seeing him here caused everything to come into focus. Of course it would be Congressman Dale Havitz over at the bar, using silver tongs to drop ice into a crystal rocks glass. Havitz had been in the House of Representatives only a short time, but he'd swiftly established himself as one of Washington's most mercurial and pugnacious congressmen. His immaculate blond pompadour was already a favorite feature of political cartoonists, as were his wide, tarsier eyes and pursed lips that gave the impression that no matter how much he ate, he'd never be satiated. It didn't surprise Agatha to find Havitz at the center of all this. His ethics complaints outnumbered the bills he'd sponsored, and he had an unsavory reputation as a handsy boss and a hard-partying man-child. An undergraduate at Georgetown University last fall had been the fourth woman to allege Havitz didn't take no for an answer. Charges hadn't been filed, yet, but there was enough smoke around the man to start another ice age.

The man on the couch looked about Havitz's age, but that was all the two had in common. The life experience etched into his pale granite features was a world away from Havitz's easy, privileged upbringing. It was a face accustomed to going without and one that knew complaining wouldn't change anything. His close-cropped hair belonged to a man who'd grown up in the military and didn't know any other way. But it was the eyes, predatory and still, that made Agatha uneasy. She felt him studying her, the way a wolf watched from the edge of a farm, waiting for the lights to go out in the big house. He wore a short-sleeved polo, and the tattoos on his arms were all in Cyrillic. Eastern European or Russian. Could *he* be Swinden's foreign client? She'd expected someone older, but that had been an assumption. The world turned out billionaires of all ages nowadays.

The third man stood away by the door, arms folded tiredly across his chest. He was older, with a halo of curly salt-and-pepper hair and a gregarious, sun-damaged face. Of the three, he was the only one Agatha thought she might enjoy spending more than five minutes with. He wore a crisp white uniform and looked to be the captain of the HMS *Clusterfuck. Am I expected to go down with this ship?* his face seemed to be asking. His expression told Agatha that the yacht's owner wasn't on board, and neither was Swinden's foreign client. The rich didn't hang around to clean up their own messes. That was left to bagmen like the captain and the wolf on the couch.

And, of course, Agatha herself. Because what else could she call herself? Twenty-one years had passed and not a damn thing had changed.

It appeared that, of the principals, only Dale Havitz remained. Sorry Charlie was probably his man, and Agatha didn't blame the congressman for not trusting him to handle this. She looked from face to face, meeting each of their eyes, and said nothing. She wanted to see which man was in charge here and which only thought he was.

"How's Cal?" Havitz asked. From his tone, Agatha could tell that he'd worked out in his head how this was all Swinden's fault.

"He sends his regards."

Havitz scowled. "He says you're some kind of miracle worker. That you can fix this."

Agatha appreciated the vote of confidence. "I'll need to know what's broken first. How is she?"

"Stubborn," Havitz said. "Talk some sense to her. You've got an hour."

"And then what?"

"Excuse me?"

"If I can't talk some sense to her in an hour, what happens then?" *Or are you just talking because that's all you know how to do?*

"We all have somewhere to be," Havitz said as if being late were his most pressing concern.

"I've been here five minutes. It will take as long as it takes, so put away your stopwatch."

"The girl is frightened," the Wolf said quietly, his Russian accent a silky purr. "She does not trust us. Nor should she."

"And you are . . . ?"

"My name is not important," he answered, "but you may call me Sergei. My employer sends his regards and is grateful for your assistance in this matter." He turned in his seat and nodded to the captain, who left the room without a word. That settled who was actually running things. "You believe the girl will trust you?"

"That depends on how far this has gone. To be honest, I wasn't given many details."

Sergei nodded. "Well, then, I will let the girl tell you herself. Our side of the story is not relevant at this stage."

It was the most sensible thing she'd heard since she got up this morning. "Agreed." Agatha felt the engines throb to life. "Are we going somewhere?"

"International waters," Sergei said. "We only came this close to Saint Thomas to collect you."

Agatha's maritime law was weak, but she believed that meant three miles offshore. Far from prying eyes, and the perfect place for a private meeting between a Russian oligarch and an American politician. It also meant they'd be outside US jurisdiction and subject to the laws of whatever flag the yacht sailed under. If Agatha couldn't negotiate a favorable outcome, what were the chances she or Shelby made their return flight?

CHAPTER ELEVEN

The same broad-shouldered man who'd piloted the tender led Agatha belowdecks and down a hallway lined with stateroom doors. It made her wonder how many people remained on board. The yacht would've been bouncing on Saturday night for Dale Havitz's party, but it was hard not to notice the ghost town it had become. The smart move after the assault would've been to isolate Shelby. Let the party continue and keep the champagne flowing, but quietly turn the boat around. That was how Agatha would've done it. Back in Saint Thomas, grant most of the crew some well-earned R & R and then deboard them along with the guests. The goal would be to create as much joyful confusion as possible. Shelby wouldn't have been missed. No one stops to count the escorts the morning after.

Agatha's hulking chaperone paused at the last door, produced a key ring, and unlocked it. His instructions had been in Russian, so she didn't know if he had any English. She suspected he did but that she was meant to think otherwise. That was a concern since there was a nonzero chance that the first word out of Shelby's mouth would be a confused "Agatha?" Not ideal, since supposedly Agatha worked for a mysterious and powerful client and wasn't, in actual fact, Shelby's recluse of a landlord.

Shelby sat huddled on the bed, knees tucked up against her chest inside an oversize sweatshirt. Her eyes were swollen and red, but Agatha didn't sense fear so much as burning resentment. Swinden's picture hadn't done justice to the livid purple-and-black bruise marking the left side of Shelby's face. Starting at the corner of her mouth, it ran along her jawline and terminated at the dark circle beneath her eye like a river reaching the open sea. Dale Havitz had a mean right.

Needing to be first in the door, Agatha squeezed past her chaperone and held an index finger to her lips. Shelby's eyes widened at the sight of her, face registering about six kinds of surprise, but to her credit she played her part and kept her mouth shut.

"Ms. Franklin. My name is Agatha Cardiff."

The silence that followed felt like an anvil falling from a great height. Finally, Shelby said, "Who are you?"

Agatha could have kissed her. "I work for a mutual friend. I've been sent to bring you home. Is it alright if we talk?"

"Yeah, that's okay."

Agatha looked back at her chaperone and gave her best you-may-go-now face. To her surprise, he went, key turning in the lock behind him.

When they were alone, Shelby stood up and threw her arms around Agatha's neck. "What are you doing here?"

"Never been to the Caribbean. Heard it's nice," Agatha said lightly, disentangling herself from Shelby's embrace. "How are they treating you?"

"Like this?" Shelby said, gesturing around the luxurious stateroom. It was a lot nicer than Agatha's basement, but a prison was still a prison, no matter how tastefully decorated. A tray of food sat untouched on a nearby table.

"Have you been out of this room?"

"Not since . . . ," Shelby began but trailed off. A spasm of emotion contorted her face like a squall with thoughts of becoming a storm, but she tamped it down and kept her composure. "I think I screwed up."

Agatha sat Shelby down on the edge of the bed. "Maybe. Maybe not. That's for you to decide. But worry about that when you're home. Deal?"

"Deal," Shelby agreed gratefully. "How did you find me?"

"Cal Swinden," Agatha said and told her about catching Jackson and Philip searching her apartment. How that had led her to Cal Swinden and their confrontation at Tosca. "I take it this was his idea?"

"He suggested it, but it was me that got on the plane. I'm so stupid."

"Reckless. Desperate, maybe, not stupid. I've done worse."

"Who *are* you?" Shelby asked for the second time, this time with an air of wonder.

"I wasn't always a landlord. Let's leave it at that. So tell me the situation here. They seem to think you're being unreasonable."

Shelby's eyes widened first in disbelief and then in scorn. "Me? I'm the unreasonable one? They're the ones who won't let me off this stupid boat."

"Well, you scared the shit out of them."

"Me? How did *I* scare *them*?"

"By not being what they assumed you'd be."

Shelby frowned. "It's not my fault they're idiots. They talked at me like I'm a child, so I explained human-trafficking laws and the consequences of taking me into international waters against my will."

"Which I'm sure was very satisfying, but now they're afraid to let you go."

"I just gave them the facts."

"Since when have facts meant anything to men like these?" Agatha barely kept the eye roll out of her voice. "Always keep in mind who you're talking to, not just what you're saying. These men? They like to move fast and break things. And people. They're not interested in getting bogged down in nuance. That means that everyone and everything that crosses their path gets sorted into broad binaries. This or that. Yes or no. Safe or dangerous."

"And now I'm dangerous?"

"You didn't fit into their worldview, so of course you're dangerous."

"They assumed I'd be a dumb whore, so that's how I should've acted to keep them happy? That's really your advice?"

"Be what you want to be. But next time? Know your audience and how they'll react. Always pick the right tool for the job."

"There won't be a next time."

"There's always a next time," Agatha countered. "But let's take this one step at a time. I'm going to ask you a question. It's going to sound pretty straightforward. It's not."

"Okay."

"What do you want, Shelby?"

Shelby answered like a slap; the heat and anger behind her words could've welded steel. "I want them in jail. I want them to be as scared as I am. I want to ruin them, and I want them to know it was me who did it."

"Okay, did that feel good? That looked like it felt good."

Shelby nodded and almost laughed in relief. "Yeah. It felt pretty good."

"I bet. You hear those engines?"

"Yeah?"

"We're heading back out to international waters, which is where we'll stay until this thing gets settled to their satisfaction," she explained. "Now, the simple solution? Dump us over the side and let us drown. If anyone comes asking questions, we got drunk and went for a midnight swim. Problem solved."

Shelby's relief vanished. "They'd do that?"

"They've considered it, but they won't if they can avoid it."

"How do you know?"

"They wouldn't have brought me on board otherwise. Havitz is a scumbag, but I don't think he's ready to graduate to murder. The other guy, though? The Russian? He's had his diploma for years, but my guess is he's done the math. Too many people know what went down on Saturday night and know his boss was on board. Otherwise you'd be dead already."

Shelby had already been through so much that scaring her felt cruel. But it was necessary cruelty. Hopefully Agatha would have the chance to second-guess herself later. For now she needed Shelby focused. Not on revenge but survival. The look on Shelby's face said that she understood.

"Will you do something for me?" Agatha asked and waited for Shelby to nod before continuing. "I want you to take a deep breath, close your eyes. Now tell me what you *really* want."

This time Shelby was slower to answer, as if weighing up the question. When she did, her voice never rose above a whisper. "I want to go home. Sleep in my own bed. I want to wake up and go to work."

"And do you want my help with that?"

"Yes. Please. But if they're terrified of me, what do I tell them? That I won't go to the police. Would they even buy that now?"

"If it were me? I'd blackmail them."

Shelby stared as if sure Agatha was kidding, as if she expected the real answer to follow. When Agatha didn't offer one, her eyes narrowed as if seeing her landlord for the first time.

"Are you being serious right now? Blackmail *them*? For what? Money? I don't want their money."

"Doesn't matter if you want it. You just have to take it. Once we're home, you can burn it, donate it to charity, drop it on the street from a helicopter. That's up to you. But if you want out of here, you have to take it. It's the only language they'll understand."

"Understand what? That I'll take a payday instead of justice?"

"These are blow-with-the-wind people. Everything to them is a political calculation. The only thing they believe is that any situation can and should be exploited for personal gain," Agatha explained patiently. "Right now, you have them over a barrel, and they know it. You could potentially destroy careers, end marriages. It's a trump card, but you aren't playing it. That makes them suspicious, because if the situation were reversed, they sure as hell would be looking to leverage the situation. That you won't doesn't compute. They don't know what it means, and that scares them."

"So you're saying I have to blackmail them to get them to trust me," Shelby said in disbelief.

"You have to speak a language they understand."

"And then we go home?"

"And then we go home," Agatha repeated.

Shelby thought it over. "So how much should I ask for?"

"Do you trust me?"

"Yeah, I do," Shelby replied, clearly surprised by it.

"Then leave that to me," Agatha said and went and knocked at the door.

"Who *are* you?" Shelby asked again.

CHAPTER TWELVE

Isha hadn't slept in twenty-four hours, and her eyes were beginning to feel like they'd been packed with lint. After seeing Felix, she hadn't gone home as ordered but had come into the office to work. She'd gone into research mode, acquainting herself with the tangled history of Congressman Paul Paxton and President Harrison Clark. The more she learned, the stranger it all seemed. She understood now why Felix had been so dismissive of it at the Hamilton. The nomination made no sense politically. So what was she missing?

By the time Bern arrived at seven thirty, a draft of her Paul Paxton piece was waiting in his inbox as well as a physical copy on his desk (she knew how he preferred paper). She'd tried to look busy but watched him out of the corner of her eye. He took his sweet time putting down his things and fussing around his desk. *Look at it!* she screamed silently. Instead, he'd wandered off to the kitchen with his Tupperware. It wasn't until he returned that she realized he'd been deliberately torturing her. He picked up her pages and read her article, standing at his desk, the faintest of smiles dawning on his face. When he was finished, he looked over and nodded.

If Isha lived to one hundred, she'd never be able to articulate how much that meant to her.

Her elation was short-lived.

She'd always considered herself a strong writer, but the redline that Bern dropped on her desk an hour later looked like a crime scene. She devoted the rest of the morning to drafting and redrafting. Each time she thought she'd nailed it, Bern would make a fresh round of changes and kick it back to her. The process was frustrating, but in the end, she had to admit the article was much stronger. In her enthusiasm, she'd taken what should have been a straightforward story—Paul Paxton added to vetting list for Supreme Court vacancy—and tried to connect dots that she couldn't. Bern knew his craft and helped her shape it, eventually trimming more than half of the original piece.

Shortly after noon, Bern rose from his chair and made the well-traveled pilgrimage to her desk. She braced herself for another round of edits, but he only patted her on the shoulder.

"This'll do," he said, holding up her pages. "Go get something to eat. Be back in an hour."

When she returned from grabbing a salad and her third venti of the day, there was a sticky on her desk that read simply CONFERENCE ROOM. Curious, she shoveled a few bites of her salad into her mouth, scooped up her laptop, and went to see what Bernard needed. What *she* needed was ten minutes to shut her eyes in the restroom. Not very dignified, but even caffeine had its limits.

Inside the glass walls of the conference room, Bern was locked in discussion with Roger Fitzgerald, the *Post*'s investigations editor. Fitzgerald had come over from the *Times* in '14, and his reputation was sterling. He was exactly the kind of editor Isha had hoped to work with when she'd taken the job. So how to explain the pit forming in her stomach? Was it the way the two men were huddled together at one end of the conference table, even though they were the only ones in the room?

"You wanted to see me?" she asked, after Fitzgerald waved her inside.

"Sit down, Isha," he said as though this weren't the first time they'd ever spoken. He tapped her article with two fingers. "This is good work. Very good work."

"Thank you," she said warily, glancing at Bernard, who sat there like a tweed sphinx, giving nothing away. There was either an *and* or a *but* coming; she couldn't decide which one Fitzgerald was teeing up.

"It will go up online this afternoon, and then we'll run it tomorrow. Above the fold."

The front page. Isha couldn't believe her ears, but from Bern's smile it must be true. Her first. A dream since she was a kid. It was embarrassing how many copies she would buy.

Would this be enough to save her job?

Fitzgerald continued. "I have a few questions about this, though." His hand moved from the finished article to a copy of her first draft. "There are some pretty startling assertions here. Specifically, you claim that Paxton directly approached the president about the nomination."

"I'm sorry. I know I got ahead of myself."

"That wasn't a criticism. I just need to understand where it's coming from," Fitzgerald told her.

Isha relayed her encounter with Felix at the Hamilton. That he'd been drunk and in a peculiar mood. How when she'd seen him last night, he'd tried to walk it back.

"But you don't believe him?" Fitzgerald prodded.

"I think he was honest at the Hamilton and covering his ass last night." She'd been arguing with herself all night about whether that was true or if she *wanted* it to be true for the story.

"I see. And you know Felix Gallardo how? From college? Princeton, isn't it?" Fitzgerald seemed to already know the answer and was only asking because he was too discreet to ask his real question: What was their relationship now? Was she sleeping with him? It was insulting even if she understood the need to ask.

"I've known Felix since sophomore year. I was a bridesmaid at his wedding. I'm friends with him and his wife. Ex-wife," she corrected.

"Mmm," Fitzgerald said with a neutrality that Isha found maddening—judgment without being judgmental. "And has he ever been a source before now?"

"No, never. We kind of had an unspoken pact not to cross that line."

Fitzgerald jotted something down on a legal pad. "Wise. Friendships don't always survive that sort of arrangement. And who broke the pact? You or him?"

"He did."

"So you didn't mention Paxton? Bring up the vacant seat, even tangentially?"

She thought about whether she'd unintentionally raised the subject. "No, it was totally unsolicited."

Fitzgerald and Bernard shared a look.

"What?" she asked, hating the feeling that she was missing something obvious.

"It's just curious that they chose you," Bernard said.

"They?"

"The White House. It wouldn't have been Gallardo's call. Someone would've directed him to give the name to you."

That wasn't how Felix had put it to her last night. "Why?"

"Well, that's the million-dollar question," Bernard said. "Administrations always leak nominee names to the press."

"They like us to do their job for them," Fitzgerald continued. "Dig up any dirt their people might've missed before a confirmation hearing. But normally those tips go to someone senior. Bernard, for example, whose beat this is."

Could that be what this was about? Was Bernard upset that she'd jumped the line? He'd always been supportive—curmudgeonly but fair. Had she misread him?

"So for them to bring it to someone at your level . . . it piques my curiosity. And something about this Paxton situation troubles me," Fitzgerald added.

"It's super weird, right?" she agreed and immediately wished she'd phrased it differently.

Fitzgerald and Bernard shared another of their looks.

"Tell us what you know about Paxton," Fitzgerald said.

Isha felt like she was auditioning for a part she thought she'd already won. She recited the bullet points that she'd committed to memory this morning. "Well, before running for governor of Illinois, President Clark served as a congressman for twelve terms from 1987 to 2010. Paxton was elected to the House in '98, and Clark took him under his wing. Basically acted as his patron saint, helping Paxton's career along. They were close allies."

"Which tells you what?" Fitzgerald asked.

"That even floating Paxton's name is a bad look."

"There's no law against the president nominating someone he knows," Bern countered, playing devil's advocate.

"No, but the optics are atrocious, and the other side will massacre him for it. Why take the political hit?" she asked.

"Which tells you what?" Fitzgerald repeated.

"That there's another reason Paxton is being vetted."

Fitzgerald nodded approvingly. "Good."

Isha glanced at Bernard, who was smiling like a proud papa. "What?"

Fitzgerald shuffled the papers in front of him. "Well, my first inclination is to hand this story off to Susan Radosta. Someone more experienced."

Isha's heart sank. "But?"

"But Bernard talked me out of it. He thinks it's your story and that you're ready to run with it."

How inappropriate would it be to hug Bern? Highly, she decided. "I am. I—"

Fitzgerald put up a finger to stop her. "Piece of advice. Don't keep arguing *after* you get what you want. The only thing that can happen is you'll talk your way out of it again."

Chastened, she nodded.

"You'll report to Bernard, who will keep me in the loop. Everything you're currently working on is still your responsibility. The first sign that you're in over your head, I bring in Radosta. Clear?"

"Clear. Where do you want me to start?"

Fitzgerald frowned at the question. "It's your story, Isha. Where would *you* start?"

"I'd dig into Paxton and Clark's history. Find out what else is there."

"Good. What else?"

Isha thought about it. "Figure out why Felix flip-flopped on Paxton. And why the White House picked me, not Bernard."

"You know who we ought to talk to?" Bernard said, half to himself. "Orson Maltese."

"Maltese?" Fitzgerald said. "He was before my time, but didn't he go off the deep end?"

Bernard sucked in his cheeks. "He had his struggles."

"That's a diplomatic way of putting it. Didn't he threaten to kill Thompson?"

"Just kick his ass."

"While holding a baseball bat," Fitzgerald added.

"It wasn't a good situation," Bernard admitted. "But Orson retired in '07, so he's probably had time to cool off."

"Probably?" Fitzgerald repeated.

"No one knows more about Paul Paxton than Orson. It kind of became his pet project after that staffer from Paxton's office died. What was her name?" Bernard rubbed his temple, trying to coax out the memory.

"Are you and he still on good terms?" Fitzgerald asked.

"Oh God no," Bernard said. "Me, he did threaten to kill. Thinks I betrayed him to management."

"Did you?"

"If warning them that he had a baseball bat and intended to use it is betrayal, then, yeah, I'm Judas Iscariot."

"What if I talk to him?" Isha said. "He has no reason to hit me with a bat."

The two men looked at her, then at each other.

"Do we know where he is now?" Fitzgerald asked.

"I think he had a place in West Virginia, but that was fifteen years ago," said Bernard.

"I'll find him," she said.

Fitzgerald stood and gathered up his things. "Sounds like I'm no longer needed. Bernard will take it from here."

"Thank you, sir," she said.

"Call me Fitz," he said, pausing at the door. "And keep me posted."

CHAPTER THIRTEEN

The aircraft lurched forward, engines powering up for takeoff. Agatha glanced over at Shelby, who'd trailed off midsentence. The girl was out cold, curled up into a ball, head resting against the window shade. As if her body, recognizing it was finally safe, had turned off the lights and quietly shut the bedroom door. It didn't look remotely comfortable to Agatha. That was the difference between being twenty-five and fifty-two—you could take more and bounce back faster. Or maybe it was just that you didn't recognize the damage your choices were doing, not until later, not until it was too late to do anything but live with it. An unfamiliar maternal urge caused Agatha to want a blanket to cover Shelby, but by the time the flight attendant returned, Agatha had shaken off the instinct. *Don't get it twisted,* she cautioned herself. *You're not anybody's mother.*

Still, it felt satisfying watching Shelby sleep. Things had turned out about as well as Agatha could've dared to hope—better, maybe. She'd played it down at the time, but walking off that yacht and not being thrown over the side was a small miracle. Shelby was safe, and they'd be home in a few hours. That was what mattered.

Shelby had impressed her too. In Agatha's experience, personal responsibility wasn't an abundant natural resource. Normally when someone got into a bad situation, there was an inclination to insist that something or someone else was to blame. But Shelby hadn't done any of that. There'd been no excuses, no pointing the finger. She hadn't apologized. She'd faced up to her predicament and done what needed doing.

People weren't usually so self-possessed and tough at her age. It made sense, though. The kind of poverty Shelby had escaped? No way she made it out otherwise. There would be those who would judge her harshly, but they hadn't grown up worrying about their next meal. It meant doing whatever it took, over and over. Most people were fortunate enough to never understand what that really required. Agatha counted herself among the lucky and accepted her part in backing Shelby into this corner.

Shelby slept the whole flight and woke only when the plane arrived at the gate. She hadn't traveled with any luggage, so there was only Agatha's small bag in the overhead. They deboarded and went down the concourse like any two tourists returning from vacation. Agatha didn't think anything of the cameramen waiting outside security. National Airport was just across the Potomac from DC, and politicians flew in and out every day. Judging by the size of the media scrum, someone had seriously put their foot in it.

Agatha was still pitying whoever was about to get ambushed when a cameraman caught sight of Shelby.

"There she is!"

It was like a starter's pistol. Every head pivoted toward Shelby, and then they were up and crowding around her like a pack of wolves taking down a kill. Shelby's eyes went wide, and her feet stuttered to a standstill. Rookie mistake. The first rule of the press was never, ever stop walking. If you stopped, they had you. Agatha took Shelby by the arm and wedged herself between two reporters and forced her way toward the exit. Microphones and phones were jammed in Shelby's face as reporters rained questions on her. The phrasing differed, but the shouts were variations on a theme: *Shelby Franklin, Dale Havitz, assault.*

They rode an escalator down to baggage claim, the media following with choreographed ease. Some trailing behind, some ahead walking backward, some even taking the stairs beside the escalator two at a time, all while firing off questions across the concrete barrier. It was chaos, the point now not to have their questions answered but to document Shelby Franklin's intransigence. These clips would be played on the news like a silent movie while pundits interpreted Shelby's downcast expression like the mind readers they weren't.

They went out the sliding doors to arrivals. Agatha glanced toward the cab line, grateful that she'd driven. She dug her keys out of her bag and held them in her hand like a talisman. With her other arm, she shielded Shelby and hustled her across six lanes of traffic to the parking garage. Many reporters gave up the chase there, but one in particular, a determined woman in a navy suit, dogged them all the way to the car, her questions pointed and startlingly personal.

Agatha threw her bag into the trunk and then guided Shelby to the driver's-side door.

"Climb across," she said, giving Shelby a helpful shove in the right direction.

Shelby finally seemed to snap out of her shock and scrambled over the center console. Agatha followed her.

Once in the car, Agatha backed out without bothering to put on her seat belt. She didn't want to give the press a chance to pin them in. No one was looking to get hit, and they danced out of the way like seabirds avoiding the surf. It was almost over now. Shifting into drive, Agatha reminded her passenger to buckle up. Then they were away.

Shelby hadn't spoken a word since the airplane. When traffic slowed inevitably to a crawl crossing the Fourteenth Street Bridge, Agatha asked if she was alright. Shelby just stared out her window at nothing. Agatha checked the rearview mirror for any indication they'd been followed. The good news was that it didn't look like they had. The bad news was waiting for them at home—the press was already camped out on the sidewalk in front of her house.

Agatha slowed, contemplating parking anyway and running the gauntlet. They'd be trapped and surrounded, but at least they'd be safe at home. Agatha really liked the idea. So what if reporters were outside?

That was what curtains were for, and after the last few days, she was really ready to be alone.

But then a sound exploded out of Shelby, a broken and sorrowful wail from behind the bars of her chest. She'd been calm and composed on the yacht, not a single tear. But sometimes a crisis was the easy part. No time to think about the trauma or the consequences of what was happening. That came later. If you survived. And for Shelby, the consequences had followed her home, literally. There would be no privacy for her. The world had no intention of giving her time to recover and heal in peace. It meant for her to relive her ordeal over and over for an audience to dissect and judge and tsk. Everyone would know. Forever. Her friends, her family, and especially her workmates. The career that meant everything to Shelby.

No, there'd be no hiding from this now.

A few blocks away, Agatha pulled over in the shade of an old church. Shelby was sobbing so hard the old car shook. Not knowing what else to do, Agatha unbuckled her seat belt and pulled Shelby into her arms. To her surprise, the girl sank into them and wept. They sat there like that while Shelby cried herself out. Agatha desperately tried to think where she could drop her. She didn't want to be responsible for this. She'd brought Shelby home safely. It was someone else's problem now, right? Shelby needed somewhere safe to decompress without facing the business end of a microphone. Maybe the boyfriend? But would he even take her? Her private life was a matter of public record now . . .

She did have her grad-school friend Philip. He'd take care of Shelby, no question, but how long before the press tracked her down to him?

And what *about* the press? It had been such chaos at the airport that Agatha hadn't had time to think, but how had they known to be there? So many different outlets. And the questions they'd asked had been so specific and personal. Only a handful of people knew what had happened to Shelby and what flight she'd be on. One of them had set her up. Agatha didn't know who or why, but she meant to find out.

"Is there anywhere you want me to take you?" Agatha asked.

Shelby sat back and shook her head miserably.

Agatha thought for a moment. "I know a place. Do you trust me?"

She shifted the car back in gear before Shelby finished saying she did. They took Pennsylvania Avenue across the Anacostia River and got on the Suitland Parkway toward the bay. Agatha had learned to drive on this road and had made the trip a thousand times. They were almost halfway along before Shelby thought to ask where they were going.

"Deale. My dad lives there."

"You have a dad?" Shelby asked, as if the idea contradicted her fundamental understanding of the universe.

"So he tells me."

Deale was a small waterfront community on the Chesapeake Bay, only forty minutes outside of DC. Agatha's parents had bought a small place on the water back in the seventies, when she was a kid. It wasn't fancy and hadn't been winterized for the first fifteen years, but it became their paradise. A refuge from the city. The plan had always been to grow old there, and her dad had spent years renovating the house for the day they could both retire. Cancer had other plans.

John Cardiff and Eleanor Manson met and fell in love as juniors at Montgomery Blair High School in Silver Spring, Maryland. That had been at the old Wayne Avenue campus, before the school moved to Four Corners. Eleanor's parents, academics at the University of Maryland, hadn't thought much of John Cardiff, a solid C student and the son of a police officer. They'd thought even less of him when he announced his intention to follow in his father's footsteps and join the Metropolitan Police Department. Parental feet had been put down, warnings and ultimatums delivered, but Agatha hadn't come by her willfulness by accident. Eleanor Manson made her daughter look like an amateur.

What both Eleanor's parents and the good teachers at Montgomery Blair failed to notice, but Eleanor knew, was that John Cardiff was usually the smartest person in any room. Some people just weren't meant for a classroom. But anything that interested him? John absorbed it as easily as taking a breath. He was a human sponge and read voraciously.

It took time for his colleagues to accept a partner bringing a book along on stakeouts. It helped that John Cardiff was one hell of a detective, but he was always viewed with suspicion by those who didn't know him well. Behind his back, they called him Professor Sherlock. It was not a compliment.

Over her parents' objections, Eleanor married John Cardiff in the summer of '67 after graduating from College Park. John, good to his word, joined the police while Eleanor went to work at Saint John's College High School. They bought a fixer-upper in Petworth and started a family. When Agatha was six, they bought the house in Deale. Life had been good for a lot of years, and Agatha's mother never once regretted her decision. Not even when doctors confirmed that the cold she couldn't quite shake wasn't a cold at all.

The cancer had done its work with brutal efficiency. One day her mom was a picture of health. Eight months later she closed her eyes forever. After the funeral, her dad retired quietly from the MPD. He'd already put in his twenty-five, and his love of the job had waned during the drug wars of the 1980s, when the District had been branded the "murder capital" of the country. The family home had sold quickly, and he'd moved out to Deale year-round.

It had always been her mom's favorite place in the world. When school let out in June, Eleanor would pack up and make her annual migration for the summer, rarely returning to DC until a few days before teacher meetings in August. Detectives didn't get summers off, but John made the drive every night to sleep beside his wife.

The same couldn't be said for their daughter, not after she turned fourteen. Deale was boring. There was nothing to do but stare at the bay, read, and watch one of the five fuzzy channels their little black-and-white television picked up. The city was where she belonged, especially on week- ends. Live music at d.c. space, the Bayou, and the 9:30; dancing at Tracks; trying her luck getting into bars on a fake ID. The drinking age had been only eighteen, and even then she'd been good at talking her way into places she didn't belong. It had been a running battle with her parents, who knew their teenage daughter couldn't be left unsupervised but also wearied quickly of her constant bad attitude. Maybe that was why, even now, Agatha didn't get out to Deale to see her dad as often as she should.

After Eleanor's death, John said it was where he felt his wife's presence the strongest. Never had two people been more in love or more perfectly matched. It made Agatha wonder how she could have grown up with them for role models yet turned out so cynical about relationships. Maybe the danger of being a gifted liar with a pragmatic, situational morality was it forced you to assume the worst of people. Agatha's greatest fear had always been letting her guard down and getting treated the way she treated the world. Now that she was older, she didn't know how to be any other way and would rather be lonely than change. It was probably why she watched so many Michael Mann movies.

When she pulled into the gravel driveway, her seventy-seven-year-old father was kneeling beside the back steps with a hammer. He was a well-preserved son of a bitch, she'd give him that. Still had the same wiry build from his police days, and under his Orioles cap grew a full head of hair that had never turned entirely gray.

He looked up at the car and went back to his task. The salt air took a toll on the property, and there were always repairs. It was a full-time job, and the house hadn't changed since the day his wife died. A fresh coat of paint, always exactly the same color. The flowers in the planters were always red and white impatiens. Nothing was ever updated. Everything the way Eleanor liked it. Agatha thought it was both the most romantic and most depressing thing she'd ever seen.

"Saw you two on the news," he said, putting one last nail into a loose stair. "Thought you didn't do this kind of work anymore."

"Special circumstances," Agatha said.

"Aren't they all."

"This is Shelby. Shelby, this is my dad, John Cardiff."

"Good to know you, Shelby," he said, wiping his hand on his jeans and extending it to her.

Shelby mumbled a faint hello and shook it.

"Can Shelby stay here for a few days?"

They didn't always see eye to eye, but to her dad's credit, he didn't hesitate. "Long as she needs. Come on inside."

He held the door for them and fussed over Shelby, who got the John Cardiff "nickel tour." By the end he'd even coaxed a laugh out of her, which Agatha would've considered impossible. He'd always had a way with young people. The detective who got called to the scene whenever a kid was involved. When Agatha had asked him his secret, he'd told her: "Don't talk down to them. They can smell condescension like a fart in a phone booth." Apart from needing an updated simile, it was pure John Cardiff.

He finished the tour in the guest bedroom and gave Shelby a set of towels so she could freshen up. When she didn't come back after twenty minutes, Agatha went to check on her. Shelby was on the bed, fast asleep, using the towels as a pillow. For a second time resisting the urge to cover her with a blanket, Agatha shut the bedroom door and tiptoed out to the kitchen.

"After a thing like that? She probably needs all the sleep she can get," her dad said, taking a couple of beers out of the fridge. They went out to the porch, where he opened the bottles and passed her one.

Touching the necks, Agatha sat back and stared out at the gray waters of the bay. They drank in silence. Without being asked, her dad went back inside for two more.

"Want to tell me what happened?" he asked on his return.

She tried giving him the redacted version but should have known better. After twenty-seven years eliciting confessions, her father didn't buy half-truths. He was like a genial cobra with those unblinking eyes of his. People were always telling John Cardiff things they shouldn't. In another life, he would have made one hell of a therapist. He of the patient questions and calm demeanor. It shouldn't have surprised her that she found herself inexplicably needing to talk about it. In the end, she told him everything.

"Who knew?" her dad said with a chuckle when she was done. They were on their third beer now.

"Who knew what?"

"Agatha Cardiff is a soft touch."

He didn't use her married name. Never had. Having not been invited to the wedding and never having met Agatha's husband, her dad had elected to paper over that entire time in her life.

"What are you talking about?" she said.

"You care about that girl."

"I just need my rent."

John Cardiff had never been much for sarcasm, but he rose to the occasion. "Sure."

"Oh, whatever, Dad."

He scratched his cheek idly. "Remind me, what's her rent again? And how much did you pay for these clothes, the round trip to Saint Thomas, the hotel?"

"I'm returning the suit."

He fixed her with a pitying look. "Good luck with that."

"What do you want from me? Someone needed to look out for her. They were going to dump her in the sea."

"I don't doubt it. You did the right thing. I'm proud of you."

"Just stop, okay?" She didn't know why it was so hard to accept praise from him. Maybe it was the way he always sounded a little bit surprised to be giving it.

"You never were any good with compliments," he told her.

"That's not a compliment."

"Oh, sweetheart. Maybe it should be."

"Can we drop it, please?"

He put up his hands in surrender. "It was funny, you know? Seeing you on TV the same day as the news about your old boss."

She looked at him blankly. "Paul Paxton?" It wasn't a name she liked hearing spoken aloud. "No, I don't know. What about him?"

"He's on the White House's short list for Northcott's seat on the court."

A cool, unwelcome tingle ran between her shoulder blades. "What are you talking about?"

He went into the house and came back with the front page of the paper. The lead article made her feel like she'd been in an underground bunker the last few days. It finished by saying that while the choice of a sitting congressman with no judicial experience wasn't entirely unprecedented, Paxton's nomination would break with a half century of tradition. The reporter noted that Paxton and the president had worked together closely in Congress in the late nineties. That was putting it mildly.

"Seems like an odd pick," her dad said. "If they really go that way."

"They won't. I'm sure it's just a stunt."

"You think?"

She did not, but what else was she going to say? Nominating Paul to the Supreme Court would put a gun to the president's head. The last thing he wanted was the media digging into their relationship. At best it would scream of cronyism. And at worst? At worst it would lead back to the summer of 2001. He would have to be a fool to risk it, and Harrison Clark was nobody's fool. The only reason he'd do something so stupid was if he'd been given no choice.

Agatha had a pretty good idea how that had played out.

"Are you okay?" her dad asked.

"Can I have another beer?"

"Want something stronger?"

"Yes, please."

When she was alone, she leaned forward and put her face in her hands.

What have you done, Paul? What on earth have you done?

CHAPTER FOURTEEN

Isha tracked Orson Maltese down to an address in Harpers Ferry, West Virginia. She assumed it must be the same person. How many Orson Caldwell Malteses could there be? A name that sounded straight out of one of the black-and-white movies her nani had made her watch growing up. Isha couldn't find an email or a cell number for him, and the listed landline just rang and rang. Still, she liked her odds well enough to borrow a friend's car and make the hour drive up 270. It was her first time behind the wheel in five years, so she white-knuckled it in the slow lane as cars whipped past going at least eighty.

The address belonged to a nondescript door beside a windowless dive called the Bulldog. There was no bell, so Isha knocked and then hammered after knocking got no response. Still no answer. Either Maltese was inside and not answering or else he was out and also not answering. Hell, he could be on vacation for all she knew. So how long was she going to wait? As long as it took, came the immediate answer. Anyway, did a guy who lived above a dive bar *go* on vacations? She didn't think so.

Hoping the Bulldog had Wi-Fi, she pushed through the heavy green door. A long bar with a lacquered top and a dull brass rail stretched the length of the narrow room. Small booths with dodgy tables and cracked leather upholstery dotted the opposite wall, which was decorated with a hodgepodge of framed pictures and newspaper clippings. In the back, a dimly lit hallway led to a solitary bathroom and maybe an office.

The only patrons were two old men in even older baseball caps sitting at a respectful distance from each other. Both nursed beers and cigarettes—smoking indoors was such a foreign concept that she had to remind herself that this was West Virginia. One of the men stared up at a television tuned to the news; the other dead-eyed his beer as if someone might make off with it if he wasn't vigilant. Both men gave Isha a disinterested once-over and went back to killing the afternoon. Either one of them could have been Maltese. Bernard had shown Isha a picture, but it was nearly two decades old.

She was going to need a minute before she felt ready to strike up a conversation with strangers. No one was tending bar, so she took the stool nearest the door to wait. She opened her laptop but couldn't find a public network. Her phone wasn't getting any reception, so her hot spot wouldn't work either.

An old man appeared from the back with a bar rag slung over one shoulder. Favoring one leg, he shambled his unhurried way down the bar, stopping along the way to check on the two men before finally getting to Isha.

"What'll you have?" Beneath a beard that looked to be more sloth than style, his white skin was a ruddy tapestry of broken capillaries.

"Coffee?" she asked. "You have anything to eat?"

"Chips. Regular or salt and vinegar?"

"Nothing else?"

"Hot Pockets, but the toaster oven broke."

"Salt and vinegar," she said, surprised at how disappointed she was about the toaster oven. She hadn't had a Hot Pocket since college. "Is there Wi-Fi, or is that broken too?"

"Nope."

He returned with her coffee and a bag of chips. Before he could wander off again, she decided to take a chance.

"I'm looking for someone."

"Aren't we all?"

Oh, he was one of those witty bartenders she'd read so much about. "Orson Maltese. He lives upstairs. I think."

The nearest barfly looked their way with mild curiosity.

"You think?" the bartender said.

"Do you know him?"

"Sure. What do you want with him?"

"Just a couple of questions."

He sized her up. "What are you? A reporter or something?"

"What makes you say that?"

"Because you're not a cop. Did you try his door?"

"There was no answer."

"Must be out, then."

"Does he ever come in?"

He considered the question. "Most days."

"Mind if I wait and just let me know if he does?"

"Long as you don't think I'll just refill your coffee for the next eight hours. Gotta keep ordering."

Seemed like a fair deal, so Isha sat at the bar, marking the passing of each hour with a cold bottle of beer. She hadn't come here to get drunk, so after the first two, she began passing them to her neighbors, who accepted the free drinks without questions or curiosity. It earned her goodwill and the right to be left in peace, which seemed to be the main draw of the Bulldog. A handful of people chatted and shot the shit, but most kept their thoughts resolutely to themselves. It was a pleasant change from bars in DC.

Whenever someone new arrived, Isha glanced at the bartender for a sign, but he never looked her way except when it was time to order another round. Music came on over the speakers. Old rock bands that she didn't recognize and categorized collectively as the Rolling Stones. The bar never got busy, but it gradually filled as day turned to night. By nine, every stool was occupied and several of the booths. By ten, the cigarette smoke was so thick it made her eyes water. Her dad told stories about bartending in New York City when he'd first arrived from

Pakistan, but she hadn't fully understood until now. The haze of smoke felt like a war crime, and she'd have to burn her clothes after tonight. It didn't seem to bother anyone else. Then again Isha was the youngest person in the Bulldog by at least five presidents. Maybe it just took time until you stopped noticing that something hurt.

With no Wi-Fi or cell reception, she found herself alone with her thoughts for the first time in, well, perhaps ever. Normally she did her thinking with a backing track: social media, a podcast, Netflix. Now her goal in life was to successfully peel the label off a beer bottle without a tear. The trick, she'd decided, was the amount of condensation on the bottle. Too little and the label would tear; too much and the label would come apart in her hand. To her right, Bill, of the gray Civil War mustache and Peterbilt cap, watched her progress with silent approval.

Between labels something unexpected occurred to her—she felt happy. Maybe the happiest she'd been since graduation. For the last six hours, she'd been killing time waiting for a man with serious anger issues to walk through the door. Or not. There was no way to know for sure. And yet she hadn't felt bored or frustrated. Not for a moment. If anything, she was exhilarated. Dialed in. She knew it was probably the wrong word, but it felt weirdly *romantic*. Following up a hunch with a mysterious source in a smoky dive bar in West Virginia? She'd been having this fantasy ever since joining her high school newspaper.

The journalism bug had struck her early. "Never show *All the President's Men* to a precocious ten-year-old" had been her parents' main takeaway. Not unless you wanted your kid going through the kitchen trash looking for "clues" or asking hard-hitting questions at the dinner table. The movie had filled Isha's head with daydreams of clandestine meetings in dimly lit parking lots, chasing down dangerous leads, listening to gut instincts, following the money, untangling far-reaching conspiracies. The challenge had been finding kids who wanted to play Dustin Hoffman to her Robert Redford (she was obviously Woodward). That had led to four years on her high school newspaper, four more at the *Daily Princetonian*, summer internships, and entry-level jobs, all of which had led, finally, to her dream job: young hotshot reporter in Washington, DC.

So not to be corny, but this was where she was meant to be, and this was what she was meant to do. Maybe it was the cigarette smoke, but she felt a little giddy. To celebrate, she ordered another beer and slid it silently down the bar to Peterbilt Bill.

By eleven Isha was contemplating packing it in. It was getting late and time to admit tonight was a bust. She'd stepped out a few times to knock on Maltese's door, to no answer. For all she knew, the bartender had warned him to steer clear. There was no reason to hang around any longer except out of pure stubbornness. She still had to drive back to the city and drop off her friend's car. She'd put a note through Maltese's mail slot. Hopefully he'd get in touch, but there must be other ways of learning what she needed to know about Paul Paxton and the president.

It would have been the sane thing to do, but stubbornness won out. She'd come this far. Would Linda Greenhouse have given up? Or Jane Mayer? Dorothy Thompson? She didn't know their names because they'd been easily deterred. She ordered another beer and offered it to Peterbilt Bill, who was a real artist at sculpting animals from bar straws.

The Bulldog began to empty out after midnight, and by one thirty only a handful of stalwarts remained, among them one of the pair who'd been at the bar when she first arrived. He hadn't moved in hours and was still nursing a beer and a fresh cigarette like an alcoholic statue. She wanted to catch his eye to acknowledge the kinship of seeing the night out together, but he never looked up from his glass. The bartender announced last call and started the slow process of ringing everyone out.

"You must be hungry," he said, dropping her tab on the bar.

She was starving. Three bags of salt-and-vinegar chips hadn't done the job. She'd been dreaming of cheeseburgers for hours. "I'll live."

"What did you want to ask Orson anyway?"

"Just have a couple questions about an old story of his."

"Paul Paxton?"

She looked up and studied the bartender's face. Orson Maltese had lost a ton of weight in the last fifteen years. She wouldn't have recognized him from his picture even if someone had pointed him out to her.

"You own the Bulldog?"

"Owner and proprietor. Honestly, I thought the name would give me away." He frowned at her blank stare. "Do you not even know what a 'bulldog' is?"

"Should I?"

"A bulldog was the early edition. Back when newspapers ran more than once a day." He swore to himself. "No wonder the profession has gone to hell. No one knows their history. You probably think Mark Zuckerberg invented the media."

"Is this your 'kids today' speech?"

He grinned at her. "It is at that, Isha Roy."

"You know my name?"

"I might not work at the paper anymore, but I still read it. You wrote the piece about Paul Paxton's vetting. Decent work for an Ivy League brat. Who put you on me?"

"Bernard Goff."

"Bernie Goff?" he repeated as if he'd just been told what kind of cancer had been found on his ass. "How is that wheezing hack?"

"Still wheezing. He speaks highly of you, though."

"Bullshit. What did he tell you about me?"

"That you were a good reporter but had a difference of opinion with management involving a baseball bat."

Orson chuckled, his eyes becoming unfocused as he recalled the moment. Judging by the way his expression fell, it wasn't a good memory.

"So what was this?" Isha asked. "Why'd you make me sit here all night?"

"Well, I'm not going to waste my breath on someone who gives up easily," he said. "No room for quitters in this racket."

He told her to sit tight and returned to closing up the bar. After the final glass had been washed and the last drunk shepherded out, Orson locked the front door and waved Isha over to one of the booths. He poured himself a whiskey and set a cup of coffee and a Hot Pocket in front of her.

She stared at it like a mirage appearing in the desert. "I thought the toaster oven was broken."

"I got it working," he said with a shrug and slid into the booth opposite. "You know, I was wondering when someone from the paper would show up. This is faster than I expected. What do you and Bernie know that has you spending Friday night in West Virginia?"

"The president is breaking a half century of precedent to vet a man for the Supreme Court with no judicial experience. On top of that, Clark has a long and cozy relationship with Paxton, which will raise every eyebrow inside the Beltway. It's a monumentally stupid political move from a president who didn't get where he is by shooting himself in the foot."

"So why is he?" Orson asked.

"That's the question."

"You know what that expression means, I assume. Shoot oneself in the foot."

"To make a situation unintentionally worse for yourself."

"Right, but do you know the origin? The etymology?"

She wasn't in the mood for an English lesson, but he seemed determined to give one. "No."

"It's from the Great War. Soldiers would give themselves nonfatal injuries to avoid going over the top and dying an almost certain death. Better to walk with a limp than lie in a pine box. But there was nothing unintentional about it. That meaning got tacked on later."

"So?"

"So, I think you're using the wrong expression. Everything this president does is calculated. If Clark shot himself in the foot, he had a reason. There was nothing unintentional about it."

"A small injury now to avoid certain death later. You think that's what's happening here?"

He spread his hands. "If he's willing to take the hit over Paxton, then there's a reason. Either he expects a bigger payoff, which I'm not seeing . . ."

"Or he's hoping to dodge a bullet to the head."

"Guess we'll know soon enough."

"How?"

"If he actually nominates the son of a bitch."

For some reason that possibility hadn't occurred to Isha. She slid her cup toward him. "Can I have a little whiskey?"

Orson smiled in commiseration and poured a shot into her coffee. "A lot to contemplate."

"Yeah," Isha said, overwhelmed at the prospect.

"How much do you know about Paxton's relationship to Clark?"

"Just that they were allies in Congress. Clark advanced Paxton's career, and in return Paxton was a good soldier. Voted with Clark and helped push his legislative interests."

Maltese scoffed. "Well, that doesn't begin to cover it. Paxton was Clark's hatchet man for ten years. They were a fearsome one-two until Clark left Congress to run for governor of Illinois. He liked to appear above the fray. Too dignified to get involved with petty politics. That's always been his brand. But it was an open secret that crossing Clark meant dealing with Paul Paxton, and no one wanted any part of that. Paxton didn't mind getting his hands dirty and could get biblical real fast."

"You think Paxton crossed the line?"

"That man couldn't draw a straight line with a ruler."

Isha's mind went back to Felix's story about Paxton asking for the nomination. Was that what had happened? "So where would you begin if you were me?"

"At the beginning—July 14, 2001."

"That's specific. What happened then?"

"The police found the body of Charlotte Haines in her car."

Isha had been about ten years old at the time, but the name rang a bell. "The staffer who died of the drug overdose?"

"Well, she had cocaine in her system, but that's not what killed her."

"Right," Isha said, the event coming back to her now. "What was it again?"

"Levamisole. Aminorex. Drugs that dealers used to cut their product. But it was mainly the rat poison."

"Rat poison? What the *hell*?"

"What can I tell you? Drug dealers aren't exactly regulated by the FDA."

"Sure, but why go out of your way to kill your customers?"

"Well, that's the thing about drugs. There are always more customers."

It was moments like these that made Isha feel incredibly sheltered. "So how does Charlotte Haines figure into any of this?"

"She was Paxton's intern. There were rumors at the time that she was having an affair with Clark."

"Was she?"

"I was never able to get anyone to go on the record, but that was my working assumption."

"And you think Clark had something to do with her death?"

"Again, I couldn't prove it, but I think so," Orson said, warming to his story. "Now, on the night in question, Clark had been in Middleburg at a fundraiser. He spent the night at an inn. A car service picked him up on Saturday morning."

"Did anyone see him with her that night?"

"No," Maltese admitted.

"Where was her car found?"

"In DC. On a side street in Cleveland Park. She lived in an apartment building on Connecticut Avenue near the zoo," Orson said. "But here's the thing, the police concluded that she didn't die in the car. She'd been moved and someone had re-dressed her."

"Re-dressed?"

"Someone put her clothes back on after she died. It's a common mistake and easy to spot. The car was arranged to look like she'd pulled over, done drugs, and OD'd. But she died somewhere else."

"And you think that somewhere else was Middleburg?"

"She'd been on a date and not with someone her age."

"And you know this how?"

"Because she was wearing lingerie. A little black dress. Heels. She'd had her hair blown out at a salon that afternoon. Now, I don't know how women in DC dress for dates now, but in 2001, twenty-three-year-olds didn't go to that kind of trouble for a date at Buffalo Billiards. This was a special occasion, but one which no one in her life knew anything about. So where was she Friday night?"

Isha furrowed her brow. This all sounded spectacularly thin. "So, *if* she was having an affair with Harrison Clark, which you can't prove, she might have done cocaine with him, although *he* didn't die of rat poison. He then moved her body back to DC without being seen and was back in Middleburg for his car pickup the next morning."

Orson nodded along as if everything she said were the most reasonable thing in the world. "Or someone did it for him."

"Who? Paul Paxton?" Isha would need to be fitted for a tinfoil hat at this rate. "Can you connect him?"

"No, not directly. But everything accelerated after that. Suddenly Clark was Paxton's champion. Paxton got a promotion within leadership that he wasn't in line for."

"And you think the Supreme Court nom is to pay Paxton back for covering up Charlotte Haines's death?"

"Not necessarily, but one thing I know for certain is that Paxton knows where the president's skeletons are buried. And don't lose sight of the fact that Charlotte was Paxton's staffer."

"How did this not get investigated at the time?"

"It did, but after the planes hit the Towers and the Pentagon, nothing else mattered. Not for a long time. I tried to keep the story alive, but the paper wasn't interested."

"So you took a baseball bat to the editor?"

"He was an asshole, but, yeah, maybe it wasn't the best career move." Orson sighed. "You ever been right about something but no one will listen? It just gets hard to take at a certain point."

"I'm sorry." She didn't know what else to say.

"So am I," he answered and poured them both another shot. "To being right," he said and held up his glass. They toasted and drank. He refilled their glasses, but she didn't dare touch it. She still had dreams of driving home tonight.

"Won't be easy to dig all this up now," she said, nibbling at the corner of the Hot Pocket to see if it was cool enough to eat yet.

He blew out his lips. "Shit. After all this time? Well, there was one person I never got to talk to. Paxton's chief of staff. She quit a few weeks after Charlotte Haines was found and left the country. Never could track her down. Might be easier now with technology."

"Any chance you remember her name?" Isha asked.

"Oh, fuck me," Orson said, staring up at the television above the bar. "Fuck me."

Isha followed his eyes. The news was playing a clip of two women, one young and very pretty, the other with silver hair and hard eyes. Both were surrounded by cameras and microphones. The chyron read: "Shelby Franklin Arriving Back in the United States Following Alleged Abduction by Congressman Dale Havitz. Accompanying her is long-time political operative Agatha Cross."

"Her," Orson said. "I'd start with her."

CHAPTER FIFTEEN

When it became clear that Shelby was down for the count, Agatha ordered pizza and sat up with her dad, watching the Orioles get swept by the Red Sox. When John Cardiff had turned fifteen, the Senators decamped to Minnesota, becoming the Twins. That was back in 1960, and for the next forty years, many DC baseball fans adopted Baltimore as their home-away-from-home team. Her dad, who prized loyalty above all else, had been one of them. From that day forward, he'd had two favorite teams—the Orioles and whoever was playing the Twins that day.

Some kids picked up religion from their parents; Agatha picked up baseball. Growing up, watching the O's was one of the few times there was peace between them. Sitting in the bleachers at the old Memorial Stadium for game two of the '83 World Series was one of her best memories as a child. Rick Dempsey hit a double in the fifth to drive in the winning run while they hugged and cheered their throats raw.

Then in '05, the Expos moved to Washington as the Nationals. A lot of DC folks, Agatha among them, had grown tired of Orioles owner Peter Angelos treating their city like his own personal fiefdom and were quick to trade orange ball caps for red. Not John Cardiff. The Orioles were his team and that was that. And although he'd never said a word, Agatha knew he frowned on her shifting loyalties. He'd always blamed himself for the way she'd turned out, and her becoming a Nats fan somehow exemplified his failures as a parent.

By the seventh inning, with the game well out of reach, Agatha disappeared down a rabbit hole on her phone, cataloging all the stories that mentioned Shelby Franklin. Clips of their arrival at National Airport were everywhere. Agatha chuckled at still being described as a political operative. The good news was that no one identified Shelby as a sex worker, only as a young woman who'd been assaulted on a boat in the Caribbean and held against her will. That was a relief, but as a narrative it wouldn't hold for long. If Agatha were handling messaging for Havitz, her first move would be to cast doubt on Shelby's character and motives. Sling mud and see what sticks. Discreetly, of course, through back channels, nothing that could be tied back to the congressman. It would work too. Sympathy for young professional women ran reasonably high. But if news broke about Shelby's side hustle, how quickly would the narrative shift to gold-digging opportunist? No, it was only a matter of time . . . unless something was done to stop it.

What had come to light since being ambushed at the airport was that the media had been incited by an audio recording of Dale Havitz arguing about what to do with Shelby. The recording had been carefully edited to play only one side of the conversation, but Agatha had a good idea of who was on the other end. The same bastard who'd likely leaked it—Cal Swinden. He had the best motivation, and she was kicking herself for not anticipating this move.

Havitz had embarrassed Swinden down in Saint Thomas in front of his client. Perhaps this was payback, or maybe there was more to it than that. It didn't much matter to Agatha. They'd had a deal, and Swinden had broken it. She'd gone to war for far less, though this was a lousy time to come out of retirement. With her old boss being bandied around as a possible Supreme Court nominee, she needed to keep the lowest of profiles. But Shelby wasn't some card for Cal to play. What choice did she have? That Agatha couldn't yet see a way to pin his ears back was only temporary.

It was a good thing the beer ran out, or she would have kept on drinking. After the game ended, she fought her dad for the right to sleep on the couch. Knowing he'd never won an argument with his daughter, he brought her a pillow and blanket before hugging her good night. She didn't quite know what to make of that but patted his back until he let loose of her. What had gotten into him?

She did her best to get comfortable and drifted off debating whom she wanted to slap sense into more: Cal Swinden, Dale Havitz, or Paul Paxton. It was a highly competitive field.

In the morning she woke to the smell of bacon frying. Shelby was already up and making breakfast, wearing Agatha's sweatpants and a Bad Brains T-shirt that she'd found in the guest bedroom. Agatha's dad was leaning against a counter, staring disapprovingly at Shelby over his coffee cup.

"What's going on?" Agatha asked warily.

"Tell her," he said to Shelby and, when she didn't immediately answer, turned to his daughter. "How dare you bring this heathen into my house?"

"What? What did she do?"

"She's never had crabs," he said. "Not once."

Agatha rolled her eyes. "Oh my God, Dad. You're going to give me a heart attack."

"She's lived here four years."

"I always meant to," Shelby said with an exaggerated grimace.

Agatha's dad shook his head in disgust. "'Meant to.' What kind of talk is that? Well, we're fixing that. Tonight. Beer, crabs, corn. A man can only tolerate so much."

Apparently they'd bonded while she was sleeping. Agatha didn't know how she felt about that. It was good to see Shelby smiling, but why was she smiling with her dad? He wasn't the one who'd flown down to Saint Thomas and pulled Shelby off that yacht.

Wait. Was Agatha being jealous? No, that was absurd. She shook it off and set the table. Maybe her dad was right, and she had turned into a marshmallow in the last twenty years. The important thing was that Shelby felt safe enough to let her guard down.

That settled, they tucked into breakfast around the small kitchen table. Shelby, who hadn't properly eaten in days, put away her weight in bacon and eggs and toast. Another good sign.

When they were finished, Agatha's dad announced he had some chores to do outside and excused himself. Agatha offered to help Shelby clean up, but she wouldn't hear of it.

"Do you think my work will find out about all this?" Shelby asked when they were alone, letting it out like a breath she'd been holding in.

Agatha's first instinct was to soften the blow, but what good would that do? It didn't feel kind, but the best thing Agatha could do was rip off the Band-Aid and let Shelby process the situation, so she'd be ready for the shitstorm to come.

"We were on the news," she answered simply.

Shelby paled and put the plate she was scrubbing back in the sink. "So they know."

"This is Washington. If they don't, they will soon."

"Will they know why I was really down there?"

"Secrets like this don't stay secrets. Not when careers are at stake."

"So everyone's going to know," Shelby said to herself, testing the awfulness of the idea. "Everyone."

"You should be prepared for things to get ugly."

"Uglier," Shelby clarified, her native determination returning.

"Uglier," Agatha agreed. "Can I ask a question? How did you meet Cal Swinden?"

"Online."

"How does that work?" Agatha knew nothing about any of this except what Philip had told her. It made her feel like a grandmother asking for help setting the VCR. The fact that a VCR was her go-to metaphor was itself a reminder that this was no longer her world.

"I have a profile on an app to connect older men with younger women." Shelby looked unhappily at her hands, maybe wishing they could fly her out of this conversation with her landlord.

Agatha was right there with her. The last thing she wanted was to pry into Shelby's business, but she had to know what she was facing. "And that's different than being an escort?"

"It's more of a relationship than an escort."

"But less of a relationship than a relationship?"

Shelby nodded. "Escorting is more one-off. With a sugar daddy, I get an allowance. Gifts. We go out to dinner. Travel sometimes. I usually saw Cal once or twice a month. It felt safer to just see someone regularly, you know?"

"He wasn't paying for sex?"

"No, he was. Just not explicitly. It's a way for a man to pay without feeling like he's paying for it." Shelby shrugged. "I guess that matters to them."

"Have you had any other . . . arrangements?" Agatha asked, making sure the version Philip had told her matched Shelby's.

"One, but it didn't last very long."

That was good. Made managing the situation simpler. "And your profile on this app, is it still up?"

"Yeah," she confirmed solemnly.

"You need to delete it. Everything connecting you to this. It all has to go."

"I need my phone for that."

That was a problem, since Shelby's phone was locked in the safe at the back of Agatha's bedroom closet. She'd put it there as an insurance policy in case things went bad in Saint Thomas, on the off chance it held something incriminating that Cal Swinden wouldn't want out in the world.

"I'm going to head back into town, then," Agatha said. "Pick it up."

"Should I come with?"

"That's up to you, but I don't hate the idea of you staying here a little longer."

"Your dad won't mind?"

"Long as you need. Like he said."

"I don't want to be a burden."

"Trust me, John Cardiff doesn't say things he doesn't mean. What do you need from the house?"

"Phone, laptop, some clothes . . ."

"Make me a list."

Shelby ran the hot water. "Can it wait until tomorrow?"

"Why tomorrow? Don't you want your things?"

"Would just be nice," Shelby said with a shrug that tried and failed to be nonchalant.

Agatha found it endearing, which was probably why Shelby wore her down even though it wasn't the best idea.

That afternoon, good to his word, John bought two dozen larges and a case of Coors. They spread newspapers out on the picnic table in the backyard and attacked the mound of crabs with hammers and knives. Agatha taught Shelby the ancient art of crab picking, and she took to it like a natural. It was early in the season, but it was a good batch. Agatha was fairly certain her dad could have eaten another dozen all by himself.

When Shelby discovered he'd been a detective, she pestered him into telling her about it. Agatha had heard his tales a thousand times, but her dad was a natural storyteller, and hearing them reminded her of her mother.

The beer was cold and light, but Agatha paced herself and reluctantly switched to water after a few. She meant to be on the road early the next morning and didn't want to be too rough around the edges. If the media were still staking out her home on a Sunday, though, they'd get what was coming to them.

It took a little cajoling, but her dad even got Shelby talking about herself while he polished off the last of the crabs. She told them about Stamps, population 1,200, the little town in Lafayette County, Arkansas, that her people called home. The way she danced around her mother and never mentioned her father at all made it sound like she was describing neighbors she hardly knew. It was only when she talked about her half sister that Shelby lit up. Lola Arthur was nine years younger, and clearly Shelby had served as the girl's second mother. At least until she left for college . . . the guilt in her voice was like a shot of strychnine.

"How's she doing without you?" John asked.

"My mom is hard to live with sometimes," Shelby said simply, but there was a lifetime of pain behind her words. "Lola's a sweet girl. Never could stand up to Mom on her own. I send money home, but I don't know that it always gets to her."

Agatha met her dad's eyes, which widened a hair. Shelby was paying student loans *and* supporting her little sister. No wonder she was always late with the rent and felt she had to find a second income. Agatha was beginning to feel like a monster out of a Dickens novel.

Her dad offered her a beer, and she took it.

Shelby leaned back in her chair. "It's not easy growing up there. I'm just praying she makes it to graduation without getting knocked up." She rapped her knuckles on the wood of the picnic table. "Lola's a smart girl, but she's seventeen and real pretty. Got boys on the brain, not books. Takes after our mom that way. Mom was only sixteen when she had me. I try to tell her there'll be time for all that later, but Lola's real stubborn."

"She get that from your mom too?" asked John.

"Yeah, guess we both did. Anyway, I'm gonna lose any credibility when Lola finds out about this." She looked down at her lap. "Mom's going to love that."

Crabs vanquished, they cleared the table by rolling everything up in the newspaper and dropped it all straight into a trash can. Shelby learned the hard way how difficult it was to scrub Old Bay off your hands and nails. Migrating up to the porch, they made themselves comfortable around the firepit. Her dad passed around beers from the cooler that had followed them from the picnic tables and stared out at the bay like it was his first time seeing the water. It was a beautiful night. The kind he'd planned to share with his wife for another few decades.

"Shelby," Agatha began. "You remember what I asked you back on the boat?"

"Yeah, I do."

"Well, things have obviously changed. The media at the airport? Someone set that up."

"Why?"

"I don't know yet, but you're not going to be able to slip back into your life on Monday. So I need to ask you the question again."

"What do I want?"

"That's right. What do you really want?"

CHAPTER SIXTEEN

The street was just waking up when Agatha pulled up to her house the next morning. It looked like the media had given up, or so she hoped, until a car door opened, and someone called out her name as she went up her front stairs. Not looking back, she fumbled the keys into the lock and disappeared inside. She stood with her back against the door, listening. Someone followed her up the stairs and rang the bell, waited, then rang it again. Eventually the footsteps retreated to the sidewalk, but Agatha wasn't green enough to believe they'd called it quits.

She went up to her bedroom and hung the suit on its original hanger. Pretending to be something she wasn't had served its purpose, but she was done playing dress-up. From here on, she would get by as Agatha Cross, landlord and card-carrying pain in the ass. She checked the suit for wear and tear. Steaming would help some, although nothing would erase the miles she'd put on it. Even with the tags still on, they'd laugh her out of the store if she tried to return it. Didn't mean she wouldn't try, though that humiliation would have to wait for another day. She had more pressing business.

First up was a long shower in her own bathroom with her own products. Afterward, she slipped on jeans and a straightforward top. She took Shelby's phone from her safe and went downstairs, where Riggins was waiting by his bowl. The little jerk appeared entirely unconcerned by her extended absence, except as it pertained to mealtime. *Good to see you too.* When the ingrate was fed and watered, she went down to the basement apartment and filled a bag with everything on Shelby's list. While she was hunting around for the laptop power cord, there was a knock at the door. The blinds were down, so Agatha froze in place and waited for them to go away again. They didn't. Instead, the knocking turned into pounding. When a man started calling Shelby's name, Agatha realized it wasn't a reporter. It was the boyfriend, Jackson.

She opened the door. Judging from the look on his face, she was happy that the metal security gate separated them. "Hello, Jackson."

He looked in no mood for pleasantries. "Where is she?"

"Ask her."

"She's not answering any of my texts or calls."

"Well, then, I can't help you."

He wrapped his fingers around the bars of the security gate. "Why was she on that yacht?"

"Go home, Jackson," Agatha said and went to close the door.

"Why was she on that boat?" he demanded and rattled the security gate.

"You understand that forcing your way into my home isn't going to win me over."

"I'm not forcing myself in," he said with a voice reserved for soothing cornered animals.

She looked at his hands still gripping the gate. "You're not leaving gracefully, though, are you?"

"Just tell her I need to talk to her," he said, giving the gate one final shake before letting go.

"If I see her."

"Bitch," he muttered when his back was turned.

Agatha watched him stalk off down the street. What was Shelby doing with this charmer? Then again, sometimes men didn't show themselves until things stopped going their way. Agatha went upstairs to reassure herself that her gun was in the drawer of the bedside table. Too many people knew where she lived and wanted something from her. It wasn't a comfortable feeling after so many years living anonymously. In the end, though, she left the gun in the drawer. Things weren't at that point yet, and the person she needed to see next would react poorly to firearms. Of course, she would have to find him first.

She reached for her phone and dialed a number she had never thought she'd use. The surprise in Kat Milbrandt's voice indicated she knew she'd been given the runaround when they'd bumped into each other at Eastern Market.

"How are things on the *West* Coast?" Kat asked, reminding Agatha of the lie she'd told.

"Brad Pitt says hello."

"Oh, well, remind him he owes me a phone call."

"I'm sorry," Agatha said, cutting short their banter. "You just caught me off guard at the market."

"It doesn't really matter, but thanks."

"I need a favor."

Kat scoffed into the phone. "And there it is. You have got to be kidding me."

"Come on, don't be like that. How many solids did I do you back in the day?"

"Those came with an expiration date."

"Fine, then. I'll owe you one. Or two. No expiration. Whatever you want. Please, I really need your help."

There was a long pause. Kat was either thinking it over or simply torturing her. Either was reasonable. "Does this have something to do with you and that girl on the news Friday?"

"It does. I just need to know where Dale Havitz is right now."

"Why?" Kat asked. "You know what . . . never mind. You're just lucky I hate that shifty prick. But this doesn't come back on me."

"You have my word."

"I feel so much better," Kat deadpanned. "Give me thirty minutes."

Agatha hung up and finished packing. While she waited for Kat to call back, she took Shelby's bag out to the car. Jim came out his front door, his old dog going down the stairs in little stiff-legged hops. They hadn't seen each other since the whole "flowers" incident—had it really been only last weekend?—and he tried to lead Regis up the street away from her. It wasn't Regis's usual route, though, and the dog planted his feet and held his ground. Jim stared pleadingly at his dog, who simply stared down the sidewalk in the only acceptable direction. It wasn't not adorable.

"Morning," Agatha said.

"Oh, hi," Jim said as though she'd jumped out from behind a tree.

"Listen, I'm sorry about the other day. I was kind of a jerk."

"I am too. It was presumptuous. I forget I'm not as charming as I think I am."

"Don't think your charm was the culprit," Agatha said. "Anyway, I'm sorry."

"Is she okay?" he asked, and from the weight he gave to the last word, she knew he meant Shelby. He'd seen the news and the media gaggle outside her house. No doubt the whole block was talking about her.

"She's tough. She'll be fine."

"It's a hell of a thing you did for her. She walks Regis for me sometimes. She's a good one."

"I think so too."

"Alright, well, I'm going to get the elder statesman on his way here. But if you need anything, let me know, okay? I'm only shouting distance away."

"Will do."

He let Regis lead him down the block to the first tree on their route. "And no flowers this time, promise."

Agatha watched man and dog make their halting way down the street. A woman passed him on the sidewalk coming toward her. Something about her body language told Agatha she was media. A certain head-down determination that looked out of place for a Sunday morning. Agatha went around to unlock the car door and get inside. The woman beat her to it.

"Ms. Cross?" the woman asked from the sidewalk.

"It's the weekend. Could we not?"

"My name is Isha Roy. I'm with the *Post*. I just have a few questions."

Agatha realized she'd lost her ability to judge the age of anyone under forty. Isha Roy might be twenty-six or thirty-six.

"I have nothing to say about Shelby Franklin."

"This isn't about Shelby Franklin."

Agatha put both hands on the roof of the car and stared across at the reporter. "What do you want?"

"You used to work for Paul Paxton?" It was framed as a question, but one to which Isha Roy already knew the answer.

"A long, long time ago," Agatha said, suddenly alarmed, her hand reaching for the keys still dangling from the lock. She needed to get gone.

"Well, surely you've heard the president is considering him as a candidate for the Supreme Court."

"I've been out of the country. Anyway, I don't know what help I could be. Like I said, it was a long time ago."

"We're just trying to get a better picture of Paxton and Clark's relationship during the president's congressional days. You were there at the start."

Agatha nodded as if she found the question entirely reasonable and appropriate while also wondering exactly what "at the start" meant. The trick was to not say anything while also not looking like she had anything to hide. It was a tough balancing act. Evasiveness was the blood in the water that told reporters there was a *there* there. Better to appear proactive.

She got into the car and rolled down the passenger window. "I'd be happy to help if I can, but I'm right in the middle of a situation. Do you have a number? I'll give you a call when I have a minute."

Disappointed but gracious, Isha Roy handed her a business card through the window. "Any insight you can give would be much appreciated."

Don't hold your breath. Agatha waved as she pulled away. She was at the end of the block when her phone rang.

Kat Milbrandt had come through.

CHAPTER SEVENTEEN

Isha watched the beat-up 2012 Chevy Equinox turn the corner and disappear from view. If she actually heard from Agatha Cross again, she would eat her phone on a bed of lettuce. The cordial, noncommittal brush-off was an art form in this town. It had taken her a while to recognize that "let's get lunch" was not an invitation but a goodbye. She knew the difference well enough now, and Agatha Cross had no intention of ever calling. But . . . that could change quickly. Sources were like diamonds. They took time and pressure to develop, and from what Isha could tell, Agatha Cross had too little of the first and too much of the second.

With a little luck, Isha would get another crack at her. Agatha Cross was a fascinating set of contradictions. Not at all what Isha had expected when she'd begun digging into the woman's history yesterday. Isha had lived in DC for six years and could count the number of people she knew who'd been born and raised here on one hand. It was a town of transients. Professional drifters who arrived in their twenties, put in their ten years in the political mill, and then either moved out to the suburbs or else left the area entirely. Agatha Cross was a unicorn—her childhood home less than six miles from Capitol Hill. As far as Isha could tell, she had spent her entire life in Washington. Except, of course, for one curious stretch in the early aughts when she'd fallen off the grid. That raised interesting questions, and Bernard was, at this moment, attempting to trace Cross's movements from 2001 to 2008.

On cue, Isha's phone rang. It was Bernard.

"How did it go?" he asked.

"She fled the scene."

"Super polite about it, though, I bet."

"Like we were best friends and she couldn't have felt worse."

Bernard chuckled. "They always think they're so smooth with that."

"She's hiding something, Bern."

"Is she, or do you just want her to be?"

The question slowed her down and forced her to be honest with herself. "Both? I don't know. You should have seen the way she changed when the topic of Paxton came up."

"How much light did Orson shed on her?"

Before leaving Harpers Ferry, Orson had bequeathed her his old files. She gave Bernard the highlights: "Agatha Cardiff, born in DC in 1970 and attended Saint John's College High School, where her mother taught English. Her dad was a cop, a detective with MPD. She graduates from the University of Maryland in '92 and goes to work on the Hill. Starts out as a staffer and climbs the ranks quickly for someone with no connections. Newly minted congressman Paul Paxton hires her as his chief of staff in '98. Appears to have been a marriage made in heaven. Paxton was apparently a merciless bastard in those days, and she was his right hand."

"His consigliere," Bernard suggested.

She didn't know why men Bernard's age insisted on describing the world in terms of *The Godfather*, but it was easier to just go along. "Right. She had a fearsome reputation, according to Orson. Played the game like it was art. Hell of a negotiator. And then out of the blue, she ups and quits in 2001."

"But was it?" Bern asked. "Out of the blue."

"Or was it related to Charlotte Haines's death? That's the big question that Orson was obsessed with. But by the time she resurfaced in '08, he'd already quit the paper and moved to Harpers Ferry. The world moved on from the Charlotte Haines story. Agatha Cardiff, now Agatha

Cross, returns home and lives quietly ever after. How about you? Were you able to turn up anything?"

"I was, but it wasn't easy. I see why Orson hit a dead end back then. Without the modern internet, this would have been impossible."

"So where was she?"

"Thailand," Bernard said. "Flew out of Los Angeles on August 30, 2001, for a two-week vacation. Her return flight was for September 12. It was canceled when the US suspended all air travel. The US began to reopen airports on the thirteenth, but she never rescheduled her flight."

"What'd she do instead?"

"Don't know exactly, but something changed her mind about coming home, because she rented out her house here. In '03, she married Denny Cross, a former Royal Australian Navy frogman."

"Frogman?" Isha asked.

"A navy diver. He ran a scuba shop on Koh Samui. That's where they lived until the accident in '07."

"What happened?"

"Cross was on a motor scooter. Went off the side of a mountain in the rain. Apparently it's not uncommon. She moved back to DC about six months later."

"It's weird. I talked to a couple of her neighbors. People who have lived here for twenty-plus years. None of them know anything about her. She's just the quiet, polite, gray-haired lady down the block," Isha said, flipping through her notes. "Any idea what she does to keep the lights on? She's not on LinkedIn or any social media I can find."

"Apart from renting her basement apartment to Shelby Franklin, it doesn't look like she's had a full-time job since Paxton. She cobbles together a living from a lot of freelance telework jobs. Sounds mind-numbing."

"I just wish we had more," Isha said.

"No, this is good."

"How is this good, Bern? The woman is a ghost."

"Exactly." He sounded almost triumphant. "She's a ghost. We don't know exactly why she quit working for Paxton, right? But here's the thing—she didn't just quit Paxton."

"She quit politics altogether."

"Bingo. Here's a woman who by all accounts was as ambitious and talented as they come. And she walked away. No," Bernard corrected himself. "*Ran* away from it and essentially hid in plain sight ever since."

"Until Friday, when she popped up on the news with Dale Havitz's accuser," Isha noted.

"Who also happens to be Agatha Cross's tenant."

"*That* happens the same week Paul Paxton gets added to the vetting list for the Supreme Court . . . Any way that's a coincidence?"

"If it is, it's an inconvenient one for her. Don't know I'd have found her if I'd gone hunting for 'Agatha Cardiff,'" Bernard said. "Agatha Cross, on the other hand? That woman has some explaining to do. Starting with what happened in the summer of 2001 that soured her on politics."

"It's got to be Charlotte Haines, right?"

"That would be my guess, but what happened, and does it have anything to do with Paul Paxton and Harrison Clark?"

"I don't know yet," Isha admitted, feeling a little discouraged. "And I'm not sure where to go from here."

"Never fear," Bernard said. "I've got you covered."

Her phone buzzed with his incoming text. "What's this?"

"That's the home address of Ben Roberts. Found it in one of Orson's files. Roberts is the detective who handled the Charlotte Haines investigation back in '01. He's retired and lives out in Largo. I spoke to him an hour ago, and he's happy to talk to you today."

"Happy?"

"Willing," Bernard amended.

"Don't you want to take it? It's your lead." But Isha had already started walking toward the Eastern Market metro.

"No, this is your story, so that makes it your lead. You're doing great."

To her surprise, Isha found herself on the edge of tears. "Thank you, Bern."

"You bet."

"Do you want to come with me? We could interview him together."

"What, and leave the comfort of my cubicle? Don't talk nonsense," he said. "No, I'll update Fitz and keep digging here. See if I can track down anyone who knew Agatha Cardiff back in '01. Keep your chin up and call me when you're done there."

Isha promised she would and rang off. She went down the broken escalator to the station just as a Silver Line train to Largo Town Center pulled in. Happy for the nice bit of luck, she found a seat on the mostly empty train and rode it to the end of the line. The whole way, she thought about Agatha Cross and the willpower, or desperation, it would take to walk away from her entire life. She wanted to ask if Agatha regretted it, if she woke up in the middle of the night wondering what might have been. Was there a secret to surviving it?

———

Ben Roberts's condo was a ten-minute walk from the Largo metro, and she liked him the moment he opened his front door. He had an infectious grin, like he'd just been told a good joke and was dying to share it with someone. Retirement had been good to him. Isha could still see the outline of the young, strapping man from his department photographs, but a substantial gut now overhung his belt and his once-black hair had been cut back into a neat gray fade.

"Let's take a walk," he said after she introduced herself, reaching for a jacket on a hook by the door. "Loretta doesn't have many rules, but she always hated when I brought work home with me."

His condo stood beside a small lake, and they walked down to the water's edge and sat on a bench.

"Mind if I smoke?" he asked. When she said no, he produced a pack of Newports like a magician. "Another thing Loretta don't tolerate in the house."

He offered her one, but she declined politely.

"I appreciate you talking to me," she said.

"Off the record. We clear?"

"Of course. I'm just trying to get a sense of what happened back then."

"How'd you get my name?"

"Orson Maltese."

"Oh, man, that guy." He chuckled. "What a piece of work. Why isn't he here, or did the little green men finally call him home?"

"He retired. Lives in West Virginia now."

"Retired, huh? Would've lost that bet."

"Well, it was sort of taken out of his hands," Isha said and told the baseball bat story.

The retired detective whistled. "Now that does sound like him. Guy was a pit bull. Wouldn't let go of nothing."

"Like Charlotte Haines."

"Drove me crazy with all that."

"What did he want?"

"What didn't he want? Guy was the Whac-A-Mole of conspiracy theories. Knock one down, three others popped up in its place. He was convinced Harrison Clark was sleeping with the Haines girl. Did Maltese have any proof? No, he did not. Still, he couldn't wrap his mind around why I wouldn't interview a congressman based on unsubstantiated rumors. Called me a coward to my face," Roberts said with a surprised look, as if he still couldn't quite believe he'd let it slide.

"Did Orson ever mention Paul Paxton?"

"Oh yeah. Paxton and his chief of staff. What was her name?"

"Agatha Cardiff, although she's Agatha Cross now."

"That's the one. He thought Paxton must be involved because Charlotte Haines worked in his office, and he and Clark became such good pals over the next few years. And because Cardiff—I mean Cross—quit her job and moved away. What was I supposed to do with that?"

"So you dropped the case."

"I didn't drop nothing. But I worked homicide in DC. Always another body. My job was to close cases, and there's only so long my sergeant was going to let one of his detectives chase a hunch," Roberts said and lit another cigarette. "If Charlotte Haines had been a Black girl from Southeast and didn't have a rich, well-connected father, I don't know it would've been investigated as a homicide at all."

"So you don't think there was anything to Orson's Clark theory?"

"Didn't say that. I didn't say that," Roberts said. "But juries and newspapers have very different standards of proof. Orson never could get that through his thick head. Just because I had nothing to go on doesn't mean something funky didn't go on that night. I just don't think it was murder."

"So why move the body if you didn't kill her? It doesn't make sense. Why commit a crime if you haven't committed a crime?"

"Lot of people in this town who couldn't afford to be explaining what they're doing with a dead girl in her underwear."

"Like a congressman."

"Wouldn't be the first time a politician risked jail to avoid a scandal."

"Do you think Clark and Paxton were involved together somehow?"

"Couldn't say. But I'm police. I see that much smoke, I assume there's a five-alarm fire somewhere. Conspiracy's tough to prove, though. Especially when there's power behind it."

"If I can confirm all of this, would you be willing to go on the record?"

"If you can *prove* it? Yeah. But you better have this locked up solid before then. I'm not about to get involved with accusing the president of the United States for anything less."

"I'm with you there."

Roberts finished his cigarette, and she walked him back to his condo. At the door, she shook his hand and thanked him again for his time.

"Anytime," he said. "You got my brain going again. Feels good. I think of anything, I'll give you a call."

"I'd appreciate it."

"And, hey, watch yourself out there."

She gave him a puzzled look.

"What happens if you do prove it?" he asked rhetorically.

Isha hadn't stopped working for long enough to think about that. "The president goes down."

He nodded in grave agreement. "You be real careful now, Isha Roy." She thought about that all the way back to town.

CHAPTER EIGHTEEN

It was a beautiful day for a round of golf. There were public courses in DC, but Agatha had never taken up the game. As someone whose competitive streak was known to get her into trouble, she'd witnessed people's obsession with the sport and foreseen catastrophe. But in her years on the Hill, she'd walked her share of courses while her boss networked over eighteen holes. One of the easiest—while also legal—ways for lobbyists to curry favor in Congress was an invitation to a round of golf at one of the dozen $200,000-per-year country clubs that formed a jeweled tiara around DC. There was a reason presidents took up the game and spent so much of their precious downtime on a golf course— the game was woven into the fabric of life inside the Beltway.

Congressional Country Club, straddling Bethesda and Potomac, was one of Paul Paxton's favorite courses. Back in the day, he'd called it his third office. Agatha found it disorienting being back here after so long. She'd gotten old while the club remained exactly the same, trapped in the amber of its own history. At least that was how she felt walking unchallenged through the stately clubhouse, which had long held the title as the largest in the United States. The strange thing about country clubs, even exclusive ones, was that they were easy to get into, providing you looked like you belonged. The staff didn't bother anyone until they attempted to use the facilities, and then they would descend in polite, soft-spoken phalanxes to escort interlopers away from the members.

Dale Havitz's foursome was waiting to tee off at the first hole. His companions were all in their fifties or sixties. One was the senior senator from Michigan. The other two would have been unknown to Agatha without Kat's help, but their easy confidence marked them as powerful insiders. Through Kat, she knew that only two of them had met before today, but you wouldn't have known it by the way the four men carried on like old pals. That was how the game was played. Handshakes, backslapping, and tall tales. A chance to get acquainted over a friendly round.

Havitz was looking for allies in the face of his newest scandal. In turn, his new friends wanted to know if he would be appropriately grateful for any cover they might provide. Given how Saint Thomas had gone down, Agatha would want similar assurances in their place. But the boys wouldn't be talking business, not yet. That would come after the turn, around the tenth hole. Until then, things would stay light and amiable. That way, if no deal could be struck, at least the golf wouldn't be entirely spoiled.

When Havitz saw Agatha coming down the slope, his pursed lips jutted out even farther. She'd seen that same expression countless times on C-SPAN during committee hearings. The other three men were either better at masking their emotions or else hadn't caught her command performance at the airport on the news.

Havitz excused himself and intercepted her. She felt a little of that old adrenaline rush that came before a negotiation.

"What are you doing here?" he demanded.

"Good to see you again," she replied, fixing a cheerful smile on her face for the benefit of their audience.

Like a mirror, Havitz matched her energy and demeanor. "Yeah, yeah. What are you doing here?"

"Believe it or not, the same thing as you, Congressman. I just need a minute."

"As much as I'd enjoy that, I'm about to tee off."

"Really? Because what it looks like is you covering your ass. Isn't that why Senator McCarty is introducing you to William Brewster and Jeremy Hobbes? Heavy hitters, and I don't mean off the tee."

Havitz frowned, unhappy at how much she knew about his business. "How did you find me?"

"I'm good at finding things. You should keep that in mind."

Havitz chuckled appreciatively and shook his head. "Do you want me to call security? Have them drag you out of here?"

"Well. That's always an option. Especially if you want to confirm your connection to Shelby Franklin for the media. But, what the hell, give security a call. I'm game. It's been a while since I made a real scene."

"Goddamn, you are a pistol," Havitz said, shifting gears. "Cal told me you used to work for Paul Paxton back in the day. When he was a freshman. You were his first chief of staff."

"That's right."

"Well before my time. What do you think of this Supreme Court business?"

"That's not what I'm here to talk about."

"Well, it's all anyone's talking about on the Hill, believe me. So come on, spill. What's going on between the president and Prince Paul?"

"I haven't spoken to the congressman in over twenty years, and I've never met the president." *At least not while he was president.* "So I don't have an opinion."

"This is America. Everyone has an opinion. And you definitely have one about Paul Paxton. I can see it in your eyes. C'mon, give your old pal Dale the unvarnished."

"I think the president has a good eye for talent."

Havitz shivered theatrically. "Now I know how the press feels talking to me. Can't say I care for this side of the microphone."

"Next question," Agatha said.

"Touché. So what is it you want?"

"Like I said, the same as you. To cover your ass."

"Cover *my* ass? Please. I'm paying that little tease three hundred and twenty-four thousand dollars, and she didn't even wait to get off the plane from Saint Thomas before running her mouth."

"Your campaign backers are paying," Agatha reminded him. She was proud of the deal she'd brokered on Shelby's behalf and didn't want him to forget it. One of Havitz's deep-pocket donors had agreed to "hire" Shelby as a consultant. No actual consulting would be done, of course, but they would pay her $9,000 monthly for the next three years. Shelby would have to report it as taxable income, but this way she didn't have to hide it. The money would be hers, free and clear, with no Form 8300 or Suspicious Activity Report to draw federal scrutiny. Most importantly, it had gotten them both off that yacht. "And even you are smart enough to know the last thing Shelby wants is publicity."

"Then who went to the press?"

"Well, you pissed off a lot of people on that yacht. I know for a fact it wasn't me or Shelby Franklin, so who does that leave? Could be Sergei's boss. You embarrassed him badly enough for him to want a little get-back, although leaking a story quietly to the press isn't really the Russian way. So who does that leave?"

Havitz weighed the logic of her simple arithmetic, lips pursed thoughtfully. "Cal is a friend."

"Is he?" she asked, looking over to the three men standing by. "I don't see him. If he's such a good friend, why isn't he here?"

The question appeared to momentarily knock Havitz off his gilt perch. She saw a glimmer of doubt in his eyes, but only for a moment.

"Who do you think set up this meeting?" he asked. "Cal came through for me."

"After you hung him out to dry in Saint Thomas?" She made no effort to keep the cynicism out of her voice.

"That was just business. Cal knows that."

She doubted that was how Swinden would characterize it. "So you're his client now?"

Havitz waved off the question. "Unofficially."

Agatha had only been mostly sure it had been Cal; now she knew for certain. In truth, she respected the play. He'd put Havitz in the crosshairs with one hand and offered to clean up the mess with the other. It was old-school.

Havitz sensed her indecision. "What makes you think it's Cal?"

"Nothing. Just speculating. I'm glad you two made up and are friends now," she said. "A man in your position can't have too many."

"And you're here to sell me on what a good friend you can be?"

"No," Agatha said. "To be honest, I've never been much of a friend. To anyone. And I wouldn't piss in your mouth if your tongue was on fire."

"Well, that's vivid," he said and grinned at her. "Then what's there to talk about?"

"I may not be much of a friend, but I make one hell of an enemy. And I know, I know, that sounds like an idle threat, but it's important that you take me seriously," Agatha said. "You were asking about Paul Paxton a minute ago. Well, I haven't lifted a finger for the man in two decades, and he just got nominated to the Supreme Court."

"Oh, and now you're taking the credit for that?" Havitz said but regarded her with newfound interest. "Last I checked, he's only on the vetting list."

"It's just a formality. The nomination's his," Agatha said, knowing that by the time she got back to her car she would regret saying any of this. But Havitz had rubbed her the wrong way, and she needed to make him a true believer. It was working too. She could see it in his face.

Senator McCarty called out that they were ready to get started. Havitz indicated that he'd be right there.

"Let me ride along," she proposed, looking over at the three golf carts standing by like noble steeds girded for battle. The senator had brought along one of his people, who texted in the driver seat waiting for his boss. Havitz's cart had an empty seat.

"Not a chance."

"Tell them I'm from your office and something's come up."

"I don't have staffers your age."

"Then a colleague's office," Agatha said through her teeth. "You're in Congress. Make something up."

Havitz weighed his options, then led her back to his foursome, where he introduced Agatha as an office director from Treasury. No one looked overjoyed by her inclusion, but they also accepted the interruption as part of life. Havitz was on the Foreign Affairs Committee, and things came up. He promised to keep it brief.

Agatha watched the men tee off from the cart. The senator had a beautiful, natural swing, and his ball bounced down the center of the fairway like it knew the way to the hole. Brewster and Hobbes followed after. Both were credible golfers. Havitz went last and sliced his tee shot into the trees that bordered the fairway. He came back to the cart and dropped his club disgustedly into his bag.

"Didn't you play in college?" Agatha asked.

"Captain of the Trinity golf team."

"Don't make the hustle so obvious, then."

He shook off her advice. "I'm distraught over my predicament. But I'm tough and a fighter, so I rally on the back nine when they pledge their support. In the end, I'll only lose by a stroke or two. It'll look good, trust me."

Agatha did. On this one thing, at least. She had no doubt Havitz was skilled at lying down when he needed a favor. If survival was an art form, then Havitz was a budding Picasso. In only his second term, he'd faced one potentially career-ending scandal after another. Through a combination of luck and timing, nothing had ever stuck to him. He also lacked whatever gene regulated shame and personal accountability. So it would serve Agatha well to remember that, to him, Shelby Franklin was simply one more nuisance to be stepped around, stepped over, or, worst case, stepped on.

They drove to find his ball, two sharks in search of an opening.

"So why are you really here?" he asked. "Because I'm not getting strong you-want-to-help-me vibes."

"I'm here because if this thing escalates any further, I know you'll feed Shelby Franklin to the wolves."

"What makes you say that?"

Spotting his ball, he stopped and selected an iron. He chipped his ball out between two trees and onto the fairway. It was an awfully nice shot under the circumstances.

"Because it's what I would do," she said when he returned to the cart. "Not that it's ideal admitting you were partying on a yacht in the Caribbean with prostitutes."

"I've survived worse."

"Absolutely. I just like to believe there's a third way that doesn't involved destroying Shelby Franklin's reputation."

"Make me understand how you fit into all this. Swinden said you work for unnamed deep pockets who are looking out for the girl. Or was that bullshit?"

"That was shit of the bull," Agatha acknowledged.

"So who is this girl to you?"

Agatha thought about a lie, but maybe the truth would put his mind at ease. "She rents my basement."

"You're joking," he said, peering at her closely for confirmation. "You're not joking."

"I am not," she admitted with a shrug.

He laughed hard at that. "Unbelievable. Well, one thing is for sure. You're setting a very high bar for landlords in this city." Still laughing, he got back out of the cart and went to take his next shot. He made it to the green in three but then three-putted for a six. True to his word, he finished the hole one stroke behind. "So what's she offering?"

"My client," Agatha began, aware that wasn't technically true and that it was a dangerous way to think about Shelby, "will stand by the terms of her NDA. You paid a not-inconsiderable sum for her silence, and she intends to honor that arrangement. If it comes to it, she will make a statement that nothing inappropriate happened aboard the yacht. She will back up your version of events."

"That's a good start," Havitz said and then didn't speak again while he played out the second hole, a tidy little par three that he holed out in four.

Agatha watched him pal around with his new friends, charming them effortlessly. She said nothing. Having made her offer, being the first to break the silence would only weaken her position and make her seem desperate.

After he crushed his tee shot on three, Havitz returned with a smile on his supremely irritating face—a mug that had been voted "most punchable" in Washington on more than one occasion. No small accomplishment in a crowded field.

"I will accept her offer," he said, and then after a deliberate pause, "but I need you to do something for me."

Agatha waited patiently for him to continue, in no mood to feed the little reptile his cues. He didn't until he took his second shot, which dropped neatly onto the green not far from the flag. He got back into the cart and drove them up near the green.

"Find out for sure if Cal was behind it."

"No, I'm not doing that."

"Excuse me?"

"There is no version of this where I get in the middle of your dick-measuring contest. I'm here to assure you that Shelby Franklin will back up your version of events. That's it."

"What if I insist?"

"Look, I wouldn't be any good to you anyway. I don't do this kind of work anymore. I don't have the resources to find out what you want to know," Agatha said. "But you want my advice? When you're done with your round, call him. Let him know I was here."

"Why would I do that?"

"Because he'll find out anyway. Hell, one of your golf buddies over there probably told him already. If he doesn't hear it from you, he'll wonder why."

"Smart," Havitz said. "What would you advise I tell him?"

"I accused you of leaking Shelby to the press. You denied it. Then I accused Cal. You got rid of me but want to know what he's going to do about me."

"You like to shake the tree, don't you?"

"Only way to get the nuts to fall out."

"Alright, lady landlord. Then we have a deal. For now," he said and exchanged numbers with her. With that, he pointed his putter in the general direction of the clubhouse. "Be an angel and find your way out. I have a date with a birdie."

Agatha watched him walk back to the green and coolly sink his putt. She'd learned a lot about him over three holes. Not much to like, but certainly much to fear. She would need to be careful with this one. He was a dangerous combination of arrogance and entitlement. And you never could tell what a sociopath would do when cornered.

CHAPTER NINETEEN

Felix woke to Steve Gilroy's hand on his knee. Disoriented, he thought he was back in his hotel bed, and that raised a laundry list of unpleasant questions. But then he felt the thrum of the engines and remembered he was on board Air Force One. The president's itinerary originally had them leaving Seattle early Monday morning. However, a developing crisis in the Strait of Hormuz had forced Clark to scrub Sunday at the last minute. They'd left for the airport the moment his Saturday-night event wrapped up.

Honestly, Felix was relieved to be heading home. The prevailing winds were always shifting around the White House, and these days it felt like he was sailing into them. He didn't know precisely why he'd been benched, but his number definitely wasn't getting called anymore. Meetings at which he'd once been a fixture no longer required his presence. The president was looking elsewhere for advice, and that meant Felix's seat at the table had a wobbly leg.

Felix had seen this happen to others—staffers whose loyalty had fallen into question or who'd given wrongheaded advice on one too many occasions. The president's confidence was hard-earned and dishearteningly easy to lose. And once lost, it was nearly impossible to find your way back in from the cold. Felix had foolishly believed the rules didn't apply to him. That his star had risen too high. The president relied on him, and that made him untouchable. He saw it now for arrogance but didn't know how to recover. Most of his friends in the administration had moved on, and in his hubris, he'd treated their replacements as second-class citizens. He had few allies left, and he could hear the knives sharpening behind his back. People were talking, avoiding him as if disfavor were contagious. His pride and a steep fall appeared to be making themselves better acquainted, and when he went down, no one wanted to be dragged off the ledge with him.

He'd hoped a West Coast junket might offer a change of fortune, a chance for some face time with the president. But it had been more of the same all weekend. As if to underline Felix's outsider status, the president had called a meeting shortly after takeoff. Felix had been the only senior staff omitted—the final, pointed humiliation of a demoralizing forty-eight hours. He wondered if that was why he'd been brought along.

Not for the first time, he wished he could call Stephanie, who always knew how to talk him through a crisis. She was far too classy to tell him she'd told him so, but he'd lost his phone-call privileges in the divorce. The thought left him miserable and lonely, so he'd faked falling asleep rather than endure the pitying glances of the support staff. At some point, pretend had become the real thing.

And now Steve Gilroy was patting him on the knee. Maybe there was one more humiliation yet to come.

"What's going on? Everything okay up front?" Felix asked, praying that it was.

They'd left Seattle a little after 2:00 a.m., which would put them into Andrews before ten. Once the president was safely away on Marine One, Felix planned on going home and crawling into bed to lick his wounds in peace. Maybe a sick day on Monday. He'd never taken one and didn't even know the procedure. Of course, then they'd know he'd been beaten.

"Yup. We're landing in ninety minutes."

Felix glanced at his watch. How long had he been asleep? "Do you need me to do something?"

"We need to talk. Come on."

Felix's heart sank as if the plane's engines had stalled and they were plummeting out of the sky. This was it. Gilroy was going to fire him at forty thousand feet, surrounded by colleagues, nowhere to hide. If nothing else, it would be a characteristically sadistic move from the chief of staff. Did everyone already know? Felix glanced around and saw how hard everyone was working not to look his way.

Crestfallen, he followed Gilroy up to the senior staff meeting room, where Collins, Frankel, and Zimmermann were hashing out the president's response to Iran's recent provocations. The sort of discussion that Felix was usually a part of.

"Folks, I need the room," Gilroy said.

They didn't ask any questions and cleared out like the chief of staff had called in an artillery strike on their position. Collins and Zimmermann kept their eyes down, but Eileen Frankel, who had been in the trenches with Felix since the beginning of the campaign, gave him the kind of wan, pitying smile usually reserved for death-row inmates and vice presidents. Well, Felix wasn't waiting while Steve slowly strapped him into the chair. If he was getting fried, he'd rather cut to the chase.

"Does he want my letter?" Many staffers kept a resignation letter on hand for the day when serving at the pleasure of the president became anything but.

"Don't be melodramatic. Sit down."

Warily, Felix took a seat at the conference table opposite Gilroy. "Then what's going on?"

"Felix, you have the full faith and confidence of the president. He told me so not fifteen minutes ago."

Felix shook his head as if he'd misheard him. "Then why have I been sidelined? And don't tell me I haven't. I haven't been in a room with him in over a week."

"It's been a rocky stretch. No one's denying that. But the president sees big things for you. The brightest of futures. We both do."

"Well, that means a lot to me," Felix said, relief washing through him like a narcotic. Stephanie teased that he had a praise kink. He denied it, but of course she was right. Sometimes he thought that the only things people wanted in life were what they'd lacked as children. He'd have liked to see anyone grow up under the terminally unimpressed watch of Hector and Felicia Gallardo and not crave a kind word. Even from a prick like Steve Gilroy. Felix wasn't proud, but there it was.

"Senator Childress is eighty-three."

Felix furrowed his brow, unsure where Gilroy was going with this. Lawrence Childress was a senator from Pennsylvania. An absolute legend who'd held his seat for more than forty years. As a young boy in Pittsburgh, interested in politics, Felix had obsessively followed Childress's career—much to his parents' chagrin. The summer internship in the senator's office after his freshman year in college had convinced Felix to major in politics. It was fair to say that Childress had been among his first political heroes.

Gilroy went on. "It's not public knowledge yet, but Larry is retiring in two years, at the end of his term."

Felix had heard rumblings to that effect but hadn't given them much credence. Reports of Childress's impending retirement had been making the rounds since as far back as 2006. If true, it would be a loss to the party, even if the old man had dropped a step. He'd always been a staunch ally of the president.

"I'm sorry to hear that."

"We all were. It's not a seat we can afford to lose, and an election will be much more competitive for us without Childress. Discussions have already begun among party leadership for possible replacements."

Felix was nodding. "It's good we've got this much lead time. Susan Altman would be an option if we can coax her back out of the private sector."

"Her name has been mentioned, but the president wants to go in another direction."

"Sure. Who does he like?"

"He likes you, Felix."

Time stopped cinematically, and a roaring white noise filled Felix's ears. "What?"

Gilroy smiled at Felix's confusion. "We think you should consider running for Childress's seat."

"What?" Felix said again.

"Hear me out. You're a perfect fit. Hometown hero. Rising star in the administration and the party. Youthful but with a decade's worth of experience on the Hill. You would shore up the Hispanic vote, and you poll well with women and voters under forty."

"You've done polling on me?"

"Last week. Quietly. Just preliminary stuff."

"The party will never go for it." Felix knew he was arguing against himself, but his job was to give the president good advice, and that was a hard habit to break.

"They'll go for it if the president says so. Childress has also indicated that he'll endorse you. My guess is that if you kiss the ring, he'll even campaign on your behalf. We think it's a no-brainer."

"I don't know what to say."

"Are you interested? Then say yes."

"Yes, God, yes," Felix said, still thrown by the notion. He'd always imagined a career for himself behind the scenes, advising the decision-makers. Now he wondered why. Why shouldn't he be the decider? In an instant he realized he'd been thinking too small all this time. *Senator Gallardo.* It had a nice ring to it. Even his parents would respect that.

"Good. The president will be delighted," Gilroy said, shaking Felix's hand.

"Thank you so much," Felix said. It all felt a little surreal to him. "What do I do?"

"Well, there's plenty of time for all that. Now that we know you're on board, the president will need to sell it to leadership. Strictly a formality, but it will require a delicate touch. And in the meantime, we still have work to do. We need you sharp. The old Felix. The killer we had during the campaign."

"Yes, sir." Felix could barely suppress a grin.

"If we're being honest here, Felix, you've slipped since the divorce. No one is blaming you. I've been divorced twice. I know. It's a hell of a gut punch. But we need you back and focused."

It stung to hear. Felix knew he'd been struggling but thought he'd kept a lid on it. There was no place for a personal life in the White House, and the idea that the president knew was mortally embarrassing.

"I am. I'm ready."

"Happy to hear that, because this administration is entering a new phase. The honeymoon is over, and the president is popular. Too popular for some with the midterms in November. You know how it works in Washington. Nothing that goes up can stay up. The media is looking to drag him back down to earth. It'll be open season, and they'll be looking for anything to smear him with. We can't allow that."

"I couldn't agree more."

"Good. Because it's likely to get ugly. The president's enemies fight dirty. We need someone in the trenches willing to roll up his sleeves and get his hands in the muck. A rapid-response team if you will. Snuff out fires before they have a chance to spread. Are you up for that?"

"Yes. Absolutely." Later Felix would think often about how quickly he answered, without even pausing to ask what it would entail. It was hard to think clearly with *Senator Gallardo* echoing prettily in his head.

"Good. That's good to hear," Gilroy said.

"So what do you need me to do?"

"Resign. Today. Effective immediately . . . so I'll be needing your letter after all," Gilroy said. "But don't worry. We've already put together an exit package that will speak glowingly of your service and accomplishments."

"Why? Is that really necessary?"

"Because you'll need a free hand. This will be off-the-books work, and we can't have you tethered to a desk in the White House. Do you understand?"

"I do, but . . ."

"It's okay, Felix. Speak your mind."

"Sir, it's just I can't afford to be unemployed. I wish I could."

"Don't worry. We've got that covered, too. Starting Monday, you are an employee at Fadden and Martin."

"F&M? The lobbying firm?"

"It's all arranged. You start at five hundred and twenty-five thousand."

"Dollars?" Felix asked in disbelief.

"Yup. You'll be attached to their public affairs arm, doing crisis communication. That will have better optics for you down the road." Gilroy slid a folder across the desk.

Felix flipped through the pages without absorbing a word. He needed a simple task, because his head was spinning. This was all happening so fast. He wondered how long it had been in the works. It occurred to him that Gilroy was still talking.

"You'll report directly to me. Never to the president. Understood?"

Felix nodded. "Understood."

"It goes without saying, but none of this goes into email or text. If we need to meet, it will be away from the White House. If anyone asks what you're doing now, you are a public affairs liaison at F&M. Your roles and responsibilities are outlined in the folder. You'll have an office and a secretary, but you can work out of your apartment. Whichever you prefer. You'll need to put in a little face time at client meetings, but there's no expectation that you'll do any substantial work. The firm has four-hundred-plus employees, so coming and going will be simple. Management will leave you be."

"Do I have a budget?"

"Whatever you need."

"Who else is on the team?"

Gilroy slid a business card across the table. "Call this number if anything comes up. He's a good man, a veteran of this kind of work. He'll get you anything you need. If you need more bodies, he has resources."

"Yes, sir," Felix said, picking it up and turning it over in his fingers. "So what's first?"

"First up, this absurd Paul Paxton story. The media is trying to make hay of the fact that the president had a cordial working relationship with a fellow congressman twenty years ago."

Felix nodded his agreement even if that was a fanciful way of putting it. "Won't that more or less take care of itself once our nominee is announced?"

"Paxton *is* our nominee," Gilroy said.

"Oh." It wasn't an eloquent reply, and Felix regretted giving voice to his first reaction.

"Is that going to be a problem?" Gilroy reached for the folder.

"No, sir," Felix said and pulled the folder closer, like a life preserver in frigid seas.

"We just need to be clear what is expected of you. You have a bright future. I would hate to think you weren't on the team. The president is counting on you."

"Whatever it takes," Felix said and then repeated it for good measure. "Whatever it takes."

"Alright, then," Gilroy said, standing and extending his hand across the table. "The president thanks you for your service, Felix."

CHAPTER TWENTY

Agatha stood in the dark of her father's kitchen, wondering what she was doing. After talking to Dale Havitz, her plan had been to deliver Shelby's things and then drive straight home. Sleep in her own bed, wake up in her own house. Since this all began, she hadn't had a moment to herself. She missed her solitude. After fifteen years spent more or less on her own, she felt worn down and over-peopled. All she wanted was to lock her front door and bask in the quiet. But then an unexpected thing had happened—her home began to feel suffocating. A lonely prison. No . . . *prison* wasn't the right word. *Prison* implied someone else had put her there. But that wasn't what had happened, was it?

Restless, she'd stalked circles around her house like an animal that couldn't find a comfortable place to lie down. In the kitchen, she poured herself a glass of water and stared at her reflection in the window above the sink. You know who else lived in the dark by themselves? Trolls. Was that what she'd become? Was that the sum total of her life goals at fifty-two? To shut herself off from the world and wait for billy goats Gruff to ring her doorbell?

Without knowing why, she'd packed a bag for herself and herded Riggins into his carrier before driving back to Deale. That this was where she wanted to be confused her, but opening the back door to the kitchen and hearing the sound of the television in the next room, she felt immediately calmer. The sense of relief that accompanied touching down on a runway after a turbulent flight. It was hard for her to trust it, though. A familiar feeling of not belonging crept over her. Had anyone heard her come in? Maybe she could slip away without anyone being the wiser. It had been a mistake coming here.

At the door to the living room, her dad flipped on the lights. "Thought I heard a raccoon."

Raccoon was an old family joke. A nickname he'd used for her in high school—a nocturnal animal that got into places it didn't belong. She'd hated it even if it was funny in a dad-joke kind of way. It had begun the night he'd caught her sneaking back into the house after missing curfew to see Minor Threat and Trouble Funk at the Lansburgh Cultural Center. She'd been thirteen at the time and was grounded for a month. It would be a stretch to say she'd learned her lesson. The show had been incredible, so to teenage Agatha, the punishment had been totally worth it. Her defiant battle of wills with her parents, and especially her father, had raged throughout her high school years. John laughed about it now, at least to a point. She loved her father but didn't understand him. The feeling was mutual.

"No such luck," she replied. Committed now to staying at least one night, she put her bag down on the counter. She'd been clutching it like the flight risk she was. Riggins mewled plaintively from inside his carrier on the floor, sounding like a lifer with no chance of parole.

"How did it go?"

"Good question," she admitted. "I think we're in the clear. For now. Havitz was receptive to our offer, but the man is half-weasel."

In truth, she was more concerned about Cal Swinden. He'd leaked the story to the press for a reason and wouldn't let Havitz off the hook simply because she'd struck a side deal.

"So what now?" her dad asked.

Another good question. There was an argument to be made that she should reach out to Swinden. Make the peace. But she was inclined to sit back until he made his next move. It would tell her more about his intentions than anything he might say. He hadn't exactly proved himself to be a man of his word.

"Now? Now, we wait," she said.

"I was hoping it would be more definitive."

"That's not how this works."

"Just would have been nice for the kid to have some peace of mind."

"I know that, Dad. I'm trying."

There must have been more heat in her voice than she'd intended, because he put up his hands. "Hey, I'm sorry. I know you did your best."

"It's fine. How is she doing?"

"Watching TV in the other room."

"Orioles?"

"Yeah, no." He smiled ruefully. "Got myself talked into a *Harry Potter* movie. She'd make a real good lawyer."

Agatha looked at him quizzically. Who was this man and what had he done with her father? He didn't watch movies and shows, or even read novels. He said the real world was all the fiction he could handle.

"Which one?"

"There's magic. That narrow it down any?"

She laughed at that. It wasn't as if she'd seen any of them herself. "But she's alright?"

"She will be," he said, looking at the wall as though he could see Shelby through it. "Just not ready to think about the mess she's in. I saw it all the time on the job. The mind has a way of protecting itself. It'll pass, but today she needed to just watch movies from when she was a kid and pretend tomorrow isn't Monday."

"Tomorrow is Monday. She's going to have to rally up."

"And she will. You know where most people end up in life? Exactly where they started. Born rich, die rich. Middle class, middle class. Born poor, go out the same damn way and usually within a few miles of where they were born. Pull yourself up by your bootstraps? That's a fairy tale. We don't sell bootstraps in this country anymore. But Shelby? That girl made her own. The kind of poor she was raised? People don't escape that often unless they can throw a ball a long, long way. Then she moved across the country to a city where she knew nobody. Put herself through college and graduate school. Figured it all out on her own, every step of the way. So, my bet? She'll wake up on Monday and do what needs doing."

Agatha thought the same, and she trusted his read on people. "Thanks for keeping an eye on her, Dad."

"It's been nice having her here. I've missed the company."

There was no indication he'd meant it as a dig, but that was how she took it anyway. Her pride began to unfurl like a stubborn flag over an outpost in an undecided war. That was the thing about family—all it took was one offhand remark to drag decades-old tensions back to the surface. She took a deep breath and told herself to let it go. Her thin skin was not his responsibility. Instead, she asked if they'd eaten.

"We did, yeah, but I can make you something real quick."

"I'm okay for now."

"Got a call from Ben Roberts," he said in the neutral tone he reserved for bad news.

Agatha searched her father's expression for some hint as to who Ben Roberts might be. The name rang a bell, although it was faint and far away. She had a feeling she'd wish it had stayed there. "How do I know him?"

"He was MPD. Younger guy. Came up in the First District, so we knew each other a little. A good detective. Transferred to the Second after I retired. He was lead on the Charlotte Haines investigation."

That was how Agatha knew him. She could still picture the man— tall, handsome, impeccably dressed, and with a tone of voice that suggested he didn't believe a word coming out of your mouth. Long-suffering-cop voice—she'd instantly recognized it after years of being grilled by her dad.

Ben Roberts had done the initial interviews about Charlotte's death. Routine background questions, trying to get a picture of Charlotte's life in the days leading up to her death. Charlotte had been a pain in everyone's ass, but the office had grieved for her and offered to help in any way they could. Agatha remembered Paxton appearing especially affected by the news. It had been one hell of a performance, and the exact moment she realized what it was that she had become.

After the toxicology report came back on Charlotte, Roberts had reached out to do a follow-up interview, but by then Agatha had quit her job. She left the country without returning any of his calls. When she moved home from Thailand after Denny's death, she'd spent the first few years expecting Roberts to knock at her front door. There was a time when she probably would have told him the truth if he'd asked. But the knock never came. The world had moved on from Charlotte Haines, even if Agatha never had.

She tried to keep her feelings hidden, but her dad read her better than anyone, which was probably why they avoided talking about anything real: she didn't want to be seen that clearly, and he didn't want to know her *that* well. Their relationship was built on sports, the weather, and nostalgia for old DC before gentrification. He'd never asked why she'd quit working for Paul Paxton and moved to Asia for seven years. No questions about why she hadn't invited him to her wedding. And when she finally came home, he hadn't asked about that either. And her dad sure as hell had never mentioned Charlotte Haines's name to her before today.

"What did he want?" she asked casually and went through her bag, looking for nothing as an excuse to turn her back to him.

"Just giving me a heads-up. He had a visit from a reporter. Some cub from the *Post*. She was asking about Paxton and Charlotte Haines. Your name came up."

"Yeah, I think I ran into that same reporter this morning." At least Agatha hoped it was the same one. She didn't need the whole press corps looking into her life story. "She stopped by the house when I was there."

"Why is she asking questions about that now?"

"You know how these things go, Dad. Paul's name is getting floated for the Supreme Court, so the media's going to dig up every old story from his past, no matter how minor. That's what they do."

"So there's nothing to worry about?" he asked, and right away she heard his tone of voice shift from Dad to cop.

"There's always something to worry about. Right now, that something is Shelby."

Thankfully, her dad took her invitation to change the subject. "She's in a tough spot."

"She told you everything, didn't she?" Agatha could hear it in his tone.

"I wasn't prying. Think she felt guilty about staying here if I didn't know. Wanted to give me the chance to kick her out, would be my guess. Told her I'll go before she does," he said with a smile.

"Thanks, Dad."

He shrugged it off. "It's a good thing you're doing for her."

"Like you said, she's got no one."

"Apparently she's got you," he said. "Can't think of anyone I'd rather have in my corner for a fight."

Agatha looked to see if he meant what he'd said. Compliments weren't exactly her dad's love language. But he'd already turned his back to rummage through the refrigerator.

"Does this reporter asking questions about Paul Paxton and Charlotte Haines have anything to do with Shelby?" He stood up with two beers, cracked both, and handed her one.

She'd hoped they'd left Paxton and Charlotte behind, but no such luck. "Not directly. It's bad timing mostly. My name popping up in the news because of Shelby just as this Supreme Court thing happens."

"So just a coincidence?"

"What? You don't believe in coincidences?"

"'Course I do. I was a cop for almost thirty years. Ever tell you the story of Nico Hawkins? Career bank robber, did a long fall at Lorton in the seventies. Had only been out about six months when he finds himself in a bank during a robbery gone wrong. Young crew who didn't know what they were doing and tripped all the alarms. MPD responds, and Hawkins winds up among the hostages. Afterward, the lead detective arrests him on general principle. What are the chances Hawkins isn't in on it? But it becomes clear pretty quickly, though, that the perps had never heard of Nico Hawkins or vice versa. Turned out Hawkins had found Islam inside and was just at the bank to open an account. Detective wouldn't let it go, though, and harassed him for two years, dead certain Hawkins was the crew's inside man. Got pretty ugly. A lot of people just aren't wired to accept randomness."

"Well, this *is* random."

"Good. It's good they're unconnected. But don't forget the legend of Nico Hawkins. Lot of times people will overreact to a coincidence because it undermines their faith in how the world works. You can't afford to be anyone's crusade."

"I'll be careful."

"Will you?"

"I could always move back to Thailand," she snapped. "I'm doing my best here."

He put his hands up a second time. "I know that, sweetheart. But they're gunning for Paul Paxton now. You know who gets caught in the cross fire of these things."

Of course she did—bosses never saw the inside of a prison cell. Nixon received a pardon and flew off into the sunset aboard a marine helicopter while forty members of his administration went down. That had been the blueprint for political scandals for fifty years. The two parties flung mud at each other by day and broke bread at night. Rocking the boat was permissible, but at the end of the day, everyone knew they were all making the crossing in the same leaky ferry. There was too much invested in the status quo to ever capsize it entirely. Washington would string her up before a scandal like this would be permitted to touch Paul Paxton or the president of the United States.

"I just want you to be sure," her dad said. "Don't just do this because of what happened twenty years ago."

She knew he'd always had his suspicions, but this was as close as he'd ever come to directly addressing the night Charlotte Haines died.

That he was willingly tiptoeing into this minefield only underscored the seriousness of the decision before her. She'd been circling the question ever since Shelby went missing, but it had taken her father to articulate the dilemma clearly. This was fork-in-the-road time. Do, or do not: there would be consequences no matter what she decided. Funny thing was, as soon as he framed the question for her, she realized she'd already made up her mind.

"Look, hopefully I tied things off with Havitz, Swinden lets it go, and Shelby can get back to her life in a few days."

"And if not?" he asked.

"She's got no one else," she said for what felt like the hundredth time. At this rate, it might be her epitaph.

"Alright, then," he said approvingly and held out the neck of his beer bottle for her to clink. "Been thinking. We haven't spent Christmas together in a couple of years."

That felt out of left field but also not. He wasn't just talking about the holidays.

"I just haven't been in the holiday spirit for a long time."

"Well, maybe we should change that. We could spend Christmas Eve here, open presents, and make your mom's family's breakfast in the morning. Drive up to Towson in the afternoon and see your uncle Pat. Family would love to see you. They ask about you all the time."

"Sure," she said, surprised at how good that sounded. Christmas Day at Uncle Pat's had been a Cardiff family tradition growing up, but Agatha hadn't attended in years. Families were often held together by big personalities. Her mom had been that personality, and after she'd passed, there'd been no one to take her place. The family had slowly drifted apart, but Agatha had warm memories of big gatherings when everyone was together under one roof. It brought back her mother and a feeling that she'd missed. "Let's do that."

"It's a plan," he said, taking a sip of his beer. "No matter what."

"No matter what," she echoed, feeling something significant pass between them.

They went out and joined Shelby, who was sprawled on the couch with a huge bowl of popcorn. Shelby scooched over. Agatha sat beside her and helped herself to a fistful of popcorn while Shelby explained the plot of the movie. The gist was that Harry Potter was in danger and that it had something to do with Gary Oldman. Beyond that, Agatha didn't much care. She was content to put her feet up, eat popcorn, and let the movie wash over her. She didn't remember falling asleep, but she woke to her father tucking a blanket around her.

"What happened?" she asked.

"You fell asleep."

"I was just resting my eyes." She didn't know why she always felt the need to deny the obvious.

"Sure," he said with a kind smile. "Rest them a little more."

In the morning she remembered another reason she'd planned on staying in town. Three nights on her dad's couch had done a number on her back. It felt like she'd been used as the floor of a mosh pit. The fact that she hadn't been to the gym or yoga in a week didn't help.

Out on the back porch, she stretched while the sun rose above the bay. When she was finished, she made tea and sat at the kitchen counter, scrolling through her phone. So far the coast looked fairly clear. No calls, texts, or emails that were out of the ordinary. There were follow-up articles in the press about Dale Havitz, but none of them mentioned Shelby Franklin by name. She knew better than to hope they'd been forgotten, but, deprived of oxygen, the press had nothing new to report. That could all change quickly, of course. It was frustrating, but there was nothing to do but wait and hope for the best.

When Shelby emerged from her bedroom, she looked like a new woman. She'd showered, and there was a focus in her eyes that had been missing since Saint Thomas. They acknowledged each other with nods, neither willing to break the morning peace just yet. Agatha watched her move around the kitchen like she'd lived there for years. When she'd put on a pot of coffee, Shelby sat across from Agatha and told her that she'd talked to her boss. He'd sounded sympathetic and agreed that it made sense for her to work remotely for a few days.

"He said to take as much time as I needed."

"Sounds like a good boss," Agatha said.

Shelby seemed surprised by it too. "Nicest he's ever been to me."

"Never too late to rise to the occasion," Agatha said, although she suspected that there might be pragmatism behind the World Justice Initiative's support. The public reaction to coming down hard on a traumatized employee wouldn't play well.

"I'm really sorry."

This felt like a change of subject. "For what?"

"You've done so much for me, and I kind of checked out there. It was wrong."

"I'm not sure you had a choice."

"Still. I just want you to know how much I appreciate it. No one's ever done anything like that for me before."

Shelby stood and threw her arms around Agatha, who wasn't by nature a hugger and felt surprised by how much she liked it.

"You're welcome," Agatha said, putting an arm around Shelby's shoulders and squeezing affectionately. "Now get yourself some coffee, and I'll bring you up to speed."

They sat there at the kitchen counter for more than an hour while Agatha described her meeting with Dale Havitz. Shelby listened intently and asked a thousand questions, all of them smart and insightful. She had a gift for taking the world as it was and not as she wished it to be.

"You been asking me what I want," Shelby said. "Can I ask you one back? Would you keep the money, you were me?"

"Are you thinking about going to the police?"

"Was, but I talked it through with your dad. The yacht was in international waters flying under Brazilian colors. The US doesn't have jurisdiction."

Agatha nodded.

"You answered my question with a question," Shelby said and smiled ruefully. "You're real good at that."

"Sorry, force of habit," Agatha admitted. "So would I keep the money in your place? Yes, I would."

"Why?"

"Because it would change your life. Let you do the work you want to do, which is important but—let's face it—doesn't pay the big bucks. And you could take care of your sister. End of the day, it'll do more good in your hands than theirs."

"It makes me feel disgusting."

"I know, which is why you shouldn't ask someone like me."

"You think I'm being foolish."

"I think you're being a human being. That's not really my strong suit."

Outside, a vehicle pulled off the road and crunched to a halt in the gravel. John Cardiff appeared in the doorway, holding a box of dough-nuts, a bag of groceries, and the newspaper.

"Morning, sleepyheads. Finished solving the problems of the world?"

"Just about," Agatha said.

"Peace in our time," Shelby agreed but was still staring at Agatha with troubled eyes.

He grinned at them. "Alright, I like a productive morning. Now who's hungry?"

The answer was everyone. He put on a Van Morrison record he'd been playing since Agatha was a kid and got to work at the stove.

CHAPTER TWENTY-ONE

Over the past few years, Agatha had become more and more a creature of habit. She did the same things at the same time, day in, week out, and had come to depend on her routine. It kept her busy, her mind on autopilot. Was that a function of getting older? She'd wondered. It wasn't that she feared change; it just bothered her. So it came as a surprise how quickly she adapted to life in Deale. She was coming to see how fine a line there was between a routine and a rut, and how hard it was to know which you were in until you stepped out of it. Yes, Agatha was seeing things more clearly than she had in years.

Mornings in Deale started early. Shelby appeared briefly for coffee and to review the day's doughnut selection before setting up in the guest bedroom to log in to work. Agatha didn't know why her dad was crawling around under the house, but it seemed to make him happy, so who was she to argue? Her plan had been to sit on the porch and get some billable hours under her belt. One look at her mother's garden put a pin in that. As handy as her dad might be around the house, he wasn't much of a gardener. The flower beds were a disaster. It would have made her mother sad, Agatha knew that much. Borrowing her dad's truck, she drove to a nursery in West River and returned with compost, topsoil, mulch, and pallets of impatiens—the kind and colors her mom had always favored. When her dad emerged from beneath the house around noon, he toured her progress with a delighted smile.

Because everyone was filthy apart from Shelby, lunch fell to her. She made sandwiches and served them out on the porch with cold beer and Utz potato chips. Shelby ate quickly so she could get back to work. Although she didn't say anything, it was plain that she feared for her job and was determined to remind her bosses that, despite recent events, she was indispensable. Agatha and her dad lingered over their lunch. They talked some, but mostly just enjoyed sitting together in silence, each lost in their thoughts.

In the evening, after everyone had washed up, they made dinner together and ate out on the porch. Afterward, her dad adjourned to the living room to watch the Orioles. Toward bedtime, Agatha announced that she'd head back into town in the morning. She meant it too. But what was the hurry? She hadn't heard a word from Cal Swinden or Dale Havitz since the golf course, and at least for now the media had moved on to other stories. So when morning came, she found herself back on her knees in the dirt, pulling weeds. And, dare she say it, happy? That was where she was on Thursday morning when her dad called her inside. He was standing in front of the television. The news was on. A White House press conference was in full swing. They'd settled on a nominee for the Supreme Court. Agatha felt her heart sink. Paul Paxton stood beside the president looking humble and reserved.

"That was fast," her dad said.

That was putting it mildly. Usually it took at least a month to vet candidates and come to a consensus. The president had the final say, but everyone had their personal favorite and would be given the chance to make a case. Paxton had gone from dark horse to the winner's circle in a little more than a week. That was some serious fast-tracking. The press would howl, but the White House knew that and had done it anyway.

Her phone vibrated in her back pocket. Then again and again—text messages coming in rapid fire. She checked her lock screen. It was Cal Swinden. The timing couldn't have been more suspect. She read his texts:

We need to talk.

Today.

3pm, National Cathedral, Bishop's Garden.

She frowned and put the phone back in her pocket without answering. As if he were psychic, her phone vibrated again.

I'm serious.

This time she replied that she wasn't interested. That wasn't precisely true, but she needed him to play all his cards.

His reply shot back: Well, get interested.

A moment later a series of photographs arrived—screenshots of Shelby's now-deleted profile on the sugar-baby app. How long had he been keeping those in his back pocket?

4pm, she replied. Not that it made a difference, but it felt important to negotiate.

4pm. My boy has a game at 3:30, so don't keep me waiting.

"Trouble?" her dad asked.

"This thing might not be as buttoned up as I hoped."

"Is this a coincidence?" he asked, pointing to the press conference.

No, she didn't think it was. Not this time.

Washington, DC, was divided into four unequal quadrants: Southeast, Southwest, Northeast, and Northwest. Of the four, Northwest was the largest and wealthiest. The White House, the National Mall, and the monuments were all in downtown Northwest. As you drove north up Massachusetts Avenue, through Dupont Circle, along Embassy Row, past the Naval Observatory and the vice president's residence, the National Cathedral would rise up on the right. In a way, it was a gateway to Upper Northwest DC, land of multimillion-dollar homes and the city's most exclusive enclaves: Cleveland Park, Spring Valley, Foxhall, Georgetown. Even now, all these years later, Agatha felt a little of the old animosity stir back up.

Growing up in Northeast, Upper Northwest had seemed like another world. In the late eighties and early nineties, as crack corroded the city, annual homicides had approached five hundred souls. Agatha remembered maps of the city with dots to represent each death. What stuck with her was that the dots had been clustered in the south and east as if an invisible wall shielded Upper Northwest from the crisis engulfing the rest of the city. And that was how her Black friends had talked about it—a wall. It wasn't on any map, but they all knew where the line was. They didn't "cross the park," especially after dark—the park being Rock Creek Park, which bisected the city and created a natural boundary between Northeast and Northwest.

Agatha made a point not to cross the line herself. There was nothing there she wanted. Upper Northwest wasn't the real Washington, not to her, not at fifteen. Years later, working on the Hill for Paul Paxton, she'd come to understand that Northwest was the only Washington that mattered in the wider world. Politics followed money and power like a stalker, and Northwest was home to both. She'd sold more than a little of her soul that way, licking bootheels all over Upper Northwest. That was okay, she'd consoled herself at the time, because that was how things got done in the real world.

She parked and walked up Garfield Street. In some ways, the National Cathedral was also the epicenter of Upper Northwest because of the two private high schools that sat in its shadow: Saint Albans for boys and the National Cathedral School for girls. The scions of the city's elite matriculated here. Annual tuition was north of forty thousand and competition for admittance fierce. Over on the athletic field, the Saint

Albans lacrosse team was hosting rival Georgetown Prep. She didn't know which boy was Cal Swinden's son, but it made perfect sense that he'd be enrolled here.

The entrance to the secluded Bishop's Garden was through a limestone arch. Such a serene, contemplative space felt like a perverse spot to meet, but she doubted Swinden thought about his life in those terms. Self-awareness could be an occupational hazard in his line of work. She followed the stone path until she spotted Swinden alone on a bench, scrolling through his phone, the natural beauty of his surroundings wasted on him.

"Agatha Cross, in the flesh," he said with a sugar-frosted smile, slipping his phone into the breast pocket of his sports coat. "No suit this time? Bit of a letdown."

It irritated her how good he looked sitting there like an avatar for the silver-fox brigade. She reminded herself that he'd been paying someone half his age for sex, which was precisely the cold shower she needed. "Your boy's team is losing."

"What's the score?"

"Seven–three, Prep."

"Well, they're a second-half team. They'll rally. That's what good teams do," he said and patted the seat on the bench beside him. "You, on the other hand, have not been a team player."

She remained standing. Once you started sitting on command, it was a short distance to rolling over and playing dead. "You have to be on the same side to be teammates."

"We had an understanding."

"Which you broke by leaking Shelby's name to the press."

"That wasn't me," he said, pure as the driven snow, but with the faintest of smiles, as if even he couldn't quite believe his own bullshit.

"Of course it was. You couldn't get what you needed out of Havitz by feeding him carrots, so now it's the stick. Straight out of the Jack Abramoff playbook. Manufacture a crisis that only you can solve and then swoop in as the guardian angel."

"Jack was the maestro," Swinden said, as if admiring a painting from the High Renaissance.

"Until he went to jail," she reminded him. Abramoff was a legendary lobbyist whose 2006 conviction had rocked the Washington establishment. "What I don't understand is why send me down there to put out the fire if you were just going to throw Havitz right back in?"

"Saved myself a trip. That was a headache I didn't need," Swinden quipped, then turned serious. "It was always the plan, Agatha. My client—"

"You mean the Russians," she interrupted.

"*Russian*, singular," he corrected. "My client was not impressed or pleased. He's a man who expects results."

"Terrible for you."

"Yes, it was," he said, ignoring her sarcasm. "I put in a lot of effort setting up that meet. I cashed in favors to get it done. Too many. Havitz got treated like a damned prince on that boat and then didn't come through."

"He never intended to," she said.

"That's my impression as well. He played me, so he was always going to get his, but not until he was safely off the boat."

It had been bothering Agatha why the Russians hadn't simply thrown Shelby overboard and been done with her. Now she saw it. "That was you. You convinced the Russians not to kill Shelby."

Swinden nodded in false modesty. "I needed a scandal to hold over Havitz, not a crime scene."

"It was already a crime scene," she reminded him.

"Yes, it was," he conceded, "but it could've gotten a lot worse without you."

"You're welcome," she deadpanned.

"And I appreciated it, until you showed up on that golf course and pointed the finger at me. Have to admit, I did not see that coming."

"All I did was convince him it wasn't Shelby. That left a short list of other candidates. Not my fault you're at the top of it."

"You made my life considerably more difficult."

"Shelby hasn't been home or to work in a week. Because of you. 'Difficult' is relative."

"That it is," he said philosophically. "But the only difficulty that concerns me is my own."

Those might be the most honest words the man would ever speak.

"Whatever is going on between you and Havitz, I just need Shelby left out of it. She doesn't deserve this, Cal."

"No. No, she doesn't. She's a good girl, but my client requires Dale Havitz's cooperation. As fond as I am of Shelby, she is my only leverage."

"Leave her out of it."

"Make me a better offer."

"Like what?" Agatha asked, although she suspected she knew what he had in mind.

"I start most days on the exercise bike. Answer emails, get in the zone. I keep the news on in the background. Guess what I saw this morning? The president of these United States nominating Paul Paxton to the Supreme Court." He paused for dramatic effect. "Now, I thought the whole Paxton thing had to be a stunt. Everyone in town did. Everyone but you, that is. Because you told Dale Havitz on Sunday that the nomination was a done deal. 'Just a formality' were your exact words. Now here it is Thursday, and the deal *is* actually done."

"That was just me blowing smoke," she said, trying to deflect. "I needed to make an impression."

"Well, that you did, which is why we're talking. And we both know you weren't blowing smoke. You have a unique insight into this situation."

"I have zero insight. I swear."

"Well, then let me offer you some. People only do things for one reason in this town, personal gain. Whenever someone does anything unexpected, my first question is always, What's their angle? How will they benefit? And here's the thing—nominating Paul Paxton doesn't benefit the president. He's going to take a hit and a big one. Now I've known the president a long time, and he is a man obsessed with legacy. So why would he risk tarnishing his with such a boneheaded appointment? There's only one answer to that question."

Agatha arched her eyebrows. "You sound like an internet conspiracy theorist. Need more tinfoil, though."

"I'd appreciate you skipping the denial stage. I need to get back for the end of my son's game."

"Then get to the point, if you have one."

"The only reasonable explanation is that Paxton has something on Clark. Something from the old days. *Your* days. And I want it," Swinden said. "If it's big enough to command a seat on the Supreme Court, then I won't need Dale Havitz anymore. Shelby will be free to get on with her life."

"*If* Paul has something on Clark—listen to me closely, Cal—I have no idea what it is." Agatha could tell from his expression that she wouldn't be winning any Oscars.

"Not only do you know, you took credit for it."

"That was all for show."

Swinden carried on as though she hadn't spoken. "Let's keep it simple. Paul Paxton for Dale Havitz. Shelby's skeletons go back in the closet."

"I can't give you what I don't have," Agatha said.

"Then let me sweeten the pot. Call the past week an audition. With no budget and no backup, you've made yourself a real thorn. Consider me suitably impressed. Come and work for me. I'll put you on the payroll starting tomorrow. How does 450K sound? To start. That's more than the president makes. You're good, and I could use you. If you take the job, your first assignment is to deliver whatever Paxton is holding over the president."

"I haven't spoken to the man in twenty years."

"Come on, Agatha," Swinden said like a man trying to sell her a used car. "Get back in the game. I don't know you, and even I can see how much you missed it. We could run this town. Aren't you tired of playing hausfrau in that run-down shack of yours? Wouldn't it be nice to be able to afford a fresh coat of paint and a change of clothes?"

"You should get back to your kid," she said and took a step away.

Swinden stood and took her by the arm.

"Don't," she warned, shaking free of him.

"Okay, okay, okay," he repeated, circling around to get between her and the way out. He had his hands up, palms out, the way people did around animals known to bite. If he put his hands on her again, he'd wish she'd only bitten him. "I don't know why you benched yourself twenty years ago, but, sweetheart, this is where you belong."

"Even if what you want was real, and I'm not saying it is, I couldn't get it for you. There's no world where he'd let me anywhere near it."

"So it *is* physical," Cal said. "It's a thing."

"I didn't say that." She was pretty sure she had, though.

"New deal. Just give me confirmation that I'm right. Paxton has something on the president. Just nod. I'll take it from there."

She stood as still as she had in her life. "And Shelby?"

"Protected as if from on high. You have my word."

Later, Agatha would have no sense of how long they stood there, two fighters waiting for the bell. What she did remember was that in the end her chin did drop—no more than an inch, but it was enough—and the way Cal Swinden smiled at her, so wide she could see his canines.

CHAPTER TWENTY-TWO

When Felix arrived at Fadden and Martin early Monday morning, his name and title were already affixed to his office door. He ran a finger over the embossed letters, wondering how they'd made him a nameplate this quickly. He'd accepted the job only yesterday morning. Well, if this was life in the private sector, he could get used to it. He loved working in government, but speed wasn't exactly its hallmark. Then again, there was another explanation, both simpler and much more complicated. They'd known he'd take the job. How long had this been in the works? None of the answers to that question were wholly reassuring—they left him feeling like a trained rat that had run its maze exactly as predicted.

The new office was massive compared to his White House cubbyhole and might even be bigger than his apartment. He dropped his bag on the broad walnut desk and made a lap touching each piece of furniture in turn, as if confirming it was all real. There was a private conference table, a sitting area with a leather couch and armchairs, a stocked refrigerator, and not one but two wall-mounted televisions. Out the floor-to-ceiling windows, the morning commute was beginning to back up down K Street.

He'd been to plenty of meetings in offices like this but never pictured himself as the one behind the desk. He still couldn't. Less than twenty-four hours ago, he'd been on Air Force One worrying that his star had fallen. Now a glittering future beckoned, one that he'd never dared imagine. It was giving him a serious case of career whiplash.

Felix wasn't naive. He knew accepting this assignment would mean getting his hands dirty. Any fool could see that there was more going on between Paul Paxton and the president than a "cordial working relationship," as Steve Gilroy claimed. The White House wouldn't be dangling a Senate seat in front of Felix if that was all there was to it. He'd spent a restless night thinking things through and realized that he simply didn't care. The details of the president's deal with Paul Paxton didn't concern him. Harrison Clark was a decent man with a vision for the country that Felix shared. Maybe the fact he'd already sacrificed his marriage for the president helped make this feel like a reasonable next step. Bottom line—if the president won a second term, just think of the good Felix could do from inside the Senate. He fished a bottle of antacid out of his bag. Chewing them like candy, he set up his desk the way he liked.

One minute before nine, a woman in her forties knocked at the door. She introduced herself as Sheryl Davis and said that she'd be right outside if he needed anything. Something in her tone told Felix that she'd been briefed and knew the drill. Her job was to guard his door, discourage lookie-loos, and make Felix appear essential to Fadden and Martin. After that a visitor from IT set him up with a computer that he had no intention of touching except to maintain the illusion that he was a busy partner. He would use his own laptop and would rely on a personal hot spot and VPN rather than leave a digital trail on the F&M servers.

The televisions were each tuned to different cable news networks. Around eleven, he glanced up and saw both channels running stories about his departure from the White House. "Ongoing Shake-up in the West Wing," one chyron read. Felix stopped what he was doing and turned up the volume. The gist of both stories was that Felix Gallardo was the latest and highest-profile administration departure. Officially, the administration was speaking glowingly of Felix, but there was also speculation attributed to "sources inside the White House" that he'd left under a cloud. After all, the departure had been announced only on Sunday after the president returned from Seattle, and reportedly

Gallardo had cleaned out his desk that same night. The news went on to sketch an outline of Felix's accomplishments before segueing to the latest speculations about Paul Paxton's nomination. That felt dangerous juxtaposed with Felix's departure.

Uneasy, he muted the televisions and then turned them off entirely. Even after all this time, he wasn't comfortable hearing himself discussed on the news. The details the media got right, the aspects they mangled but reported with appalling confidence—it felt like being conscious for his own dissection. He didn't entirely recognize the media's version of Felix Gallardo but worried sometimes that they knew him better than he knew himself. From experience, though, he could say with certainty that nothing good came from thinking about it.

What he needed was to put his head down and get some work done, keep himself busy. The only problem was there wasn't any work to do. Not yet, anyway. After spending the last few years working eighty-hour weeks, he didn't know what to do with himself now that he was in sentry mode. That was what Steve Gilroy had called it—*sentry mode*. Wait and watch.

Well, that wasn't in Felix's nature. He was supposed to be the new prestige hire at Fadden and Martin. The least he could do was act the part. That resolved, he spent the next few days settling in. He made the rounds, shook hands, met the partners, and put in face time around the office to build the impression that he was a legitimate employee. It all felt very clandestine, and he found himself enjoying the idea that he was some kind of spy. By Thursday, he was starting to feel at home. He had a lunch scheduled with two partners who wanted to pick his brain about a client issue that touched on the administration. That wasn't until noon, though, so he hunkered down and continued his deep dive into all things Paul Paxton. Around ten, the phone on his desk rang.

It was Mrs. Davis announcing that he had a visitor.

Felix frowned at the receiver. Wasn't her job to fend off visitors?

"Who is it?" he asked.

"Isha Roy."

Shit, he thought.

"Send her in."

"You work at Fadden and Martin now?" Isha repeated. It was the third time she'd asked the question, and he'd given up answering. She would wear herself out eventually. At least he hoped she would. They were sitting on the leather couch, which she was studying like she'd been beamed up to an alien spaceship. "I don't understand. When I saw you last week, this move was already in place?"

"Ninety-five percent. I'm sorry I couldn't say anything. Just had a few last details to work out." Felix thought lying to her would be harder, but it came easily. Then again, he wasn't lying to Isha Roy, his friend, but Isha Roy, the reporter. Until this was over, she was the enemy, and this would be the first of many lies. He didn't have the luxury of a guilty conscience.

"And this was your decision?"

"Yes, it was," he said, hoping to sound definitive. He couldn't afford to have her thinking otherwise. "F&M came to me with an offer, and I realized I was ready to move on."

"But six months ago, when Stephanie needed you to step back? You weren't ready then?" Isha said, her voice hard and accusatory.

Everything had been such a blur that Felix hadn't stopped to think about how his new job would look to his friends. His face reddened. What *would* Stephanie think? Choosing his career over their marriage had been a betrayal, but taking this job at Fadden and Martin—especially so soon after the divorce—would be a knife in her back. He wished he could call her and explain what was really going on but knew that would be selfish and inadvisable.

"Does she know?"

Isha looked at him like he was stupid. "Of course she knows. Everyone knows. It's been on the news."

Felix winced; he hadn't even thought to tell his parents. Taking this job had been like stepping into a parallel dimension where friends or family no longer existed. "How is she?"

"That stopped being any of your business the moment you decided she wasn't a part of your happy ending."

"You're right. You're right. I'm sorry," he said, bracing for her to continue tearing him a new one.

Instead, she sat back and stared up at the television blankly, like a boxer who'd fought the first round of a fight that had no end in sight. "Just tell me you're okay and I don't need to worry about you."

"I'm okay," he replied, unsure whether that was the truth or another lie.

Both of their phones buzzed simultaneously. Isha checked hers and then looked up at the news, which was just returning from commercial. The volume was off, but the chyron read, "White House Announcement." Beside the anchor appeared a photograph of Congressman Paul Paxton.

"Turn it up," she said.

Felix went to the desk for the remote and to check his own phone. He had a text message from an unknown number that was only one word: Gametime. Unmuting the television, he sat calmly on the edge of the desk and listened to the anchor report that the White House would nominate Paul Paxton to the Supreme Court. It sent a jolt of anticipation through him. Not at the news itself—he already knew all this—but because he would finally have work to do. Real work.

"This is insane. Did you know about this?" Isha asked. She'd twisted around on the couch to face him.

"No."

"Really?" She was looking at him intently.

"I mean, I knew he was among the finalists, but that's it. Nominations are the White House counsel's purview, and they're very tight-lipped about all that."

"Yeah, I know." She didn't sound convinced. Gathering her things, she rose to her feet. "I have to go."

He followed her to his office door, where she hugged him briefly and gave him a conciliatory pat on the back. The kind you gave relatives you loved but didn't really like much anymore.

"Honestly, I'm glad you're not there now," she said.

"How come?"

"There's something weird going on with this Paul Paxton nomination. I mean . . . you know what a lizard Paxton is. What the hell is the president thinking?"

"I am no longer paid to care," Felix said, meaning for it to sound airy but feeling it land with a thud. "Are you still working the Paxton story?"

Isha fixed him with a curious look. "Does the name Agatha Cross mean anything to you?"

"Who?" he said, although the name sounded vaguely familiar. It was a reminder that even though he was right in the middle of this situation, there was still so much he didn't know.

"One of Paxton's former chiefs of staff."

That was how he knew the name. He'd been reading about her yesterday, although she'd been Agatha Cardiff then. "What about her?"

"Talked to her on Sunday. She's mixed up with Dale Havitz's latest troubles; otherwise I would have missed her entirely. Wondered if her name came up before you left."

"No, not that I remember," he said evenly, aware she'd been testing to see if the name got a reaction.

"Forget it, not important," she said. "Drinks soon?"

"Absolutely." Now that was a lie, and they both knew it.

As soon as he shut his office door behind her, Felix went to his desk and found the business card that Steve Gilroy had given him. Beneath a phone number was written, "Call Sam for the best tuna fish in the city." Whatever that meant.

Felix dialed the number from his cell phone and went and stood by the window. The phone rang three, four, five times before someone picked up.

"Hello?" a man's voice said.

Felix wasn't sure how this was supposed to work. "Is this Sam? I was given your number."

"Password?"

Felix furrowed his brow: Gilroy hadn't said anything about a password. He looked at the card again. *That couldn't be it, could it?*

"Tuna fish?"

"Good, thanks. Where are you right now?"

Felix gave him the address.

"Okay, sit tight. I'm going to courier something over to you."

The line went dead. Forty-five minutes later, Sheryl knocked at the door and handed him a padded envelope with his name scrawled on it in Sharpie. Felix hadn't given his name.

"This just got dropped off," Sheryl said.

Felix thanked her and waited until the door was closed before reaching for the scissors. A cheap old-fashioned phone slid out into his hand. The kind that hadn't been popular since before the first smartphone. He looked in the envelope for instructions, but it was empty. At a loss, he flipped open the phone. There was one missed call from a half hour ago. It wasn't the number from the business card, but not knowing what else to do, Felix hit redial.

"Hello," the man said when he answered as if their first conversation had never happened.

"Sam?"

"Sure," the man answered with an attitude that sounded like pure New York City.

"Do you need the password again?"

The man whose real name definitely wasn't Sam chuckled. "No, we're good."

"So how does this work?"

"You tell me what you need. I take care of it."

"That's it?"

"You want I should make it harder?"

"So we don't need to meet?" Felix asked, feeling very much like the new guy.

"If we meet, something's gone bad."

Felix couldn't decide if there was an implicit threat there, or if that was how he was hearing everything today.

"So," the man said, "what do you need?"

"Surveillance."

"What level?"

"Round the clock? Is that a level?"

"Yeah, that's a level. Who's the subject?"

Felix stood there with the phone to his ear, staring at his shoe. His laces had come untied. When had that happened?

"Felix," the man prodded. "I need a name."

He swallowed, though there was nothing in his mouth but his tongue. "Isha Roy. She works for the *Post*."

"No problem. It'll take a few hours, but I'll be up on her by this afternoon."

With nothing left to say, Felix hung up. He had one more call to make. It would be unpleasant, but he couldn't afford to put it off. And he couldn't text either—someday, someone might subpoena his phone records. The phone rang, five, six times. He thought it would go to voicemail when she answered.

"Felix Gallardo. To what do I owe the pleasure?" Tina Lu said in the tone of voice of a woman taking a well-earned victory lap. In the background was the noise of what sounded like a very busy office.

"Congratulations, Tina. Your boy really did it."

"I told you everything would work out."

"That you did."

"Listen, I appreciate the call, but as you can imagine, we're pretty busy over here this morning."

"That's actually why I'm calling."

"Sorry, we don't have any openings right now. But if you want to send me your résumé, I'll keep it on file."

Tina Lu, hilarious as ever. "No, this is just a courtesy call. We have a problem."

"Oh, what's that?"

"Agatha Cross."

Tina Lu's condescension evaporated. "We're keeping an eye on her."

"Well, so is Isha Roy at the *Post*. I'll manage Roy, but you need to put a muzzle on your girl."

"I'll do it today," Tina said and hung up.

CHAPTER TWENTY-THREE

Agatha drove home nursing a hollowed-out feeling in her chest and couldn't put her finger on why. What she should have been was happy. She'd done what she'd set out to do—Shelby was safe and the loose ends tied up as tight as possible. This was all good news, right? Then why did she feel so uneasy?

For one thing, she'd given away too much at the cathedral— confirming the existence of Paul Paxton's blackmail to Cal Swinden was a mistake. She'd known that even as she did it. So why had she? To protect Shelby? Yes, of course. That was incredibly important to Agatha. But there'd been more to it than that. The old, primal need to win at any and all cost had returned. She'd made a rash calculation that it made no difference if Cal knew about the blackmail. He couldn't prove anything, and no matter how slick he thought he was, Paxton would eat his lunch if he interfered. She'd won. It was over.

And maybe that was the problem. Back at the cathedral, she'd laughed off Cal Swinden's job offer, but everything he'd said had been right on the mark. She did miss the work. Desperately. She felt like she'd come out of a coma and was slowly returning to consciousness. The thought of going back to her old life, disappearing from view again, filled her with a bitter, existential dread. Better to have remained in darkness than to catch a glimpse of the sun. Melodramatic, perhaps, but that was how it felt. Maybe that was why she couldn't entirely shut the door on Swinden or his offer. Why she was tempted even though she knew how bad it would be for her.

Agatha thought back to the night Charlotte Haines died. It would be self-serving, revisionist history to say she'd suffered a crisis of conscience and given Paul Paxton her notice the next day. Far from it. She'd stayed on for another six weeks and loved every moment of it. They'd taken the photos of then-congressman Harrison Clark moving Charlotte's body in the event that he developed amnesia, but it never came to that. Clark had shown his gratitude without any arm-twisting, so the photos went into Paul's safe, and Agatha buried herself in work. There'd been so much to do before the August recess—plans to formalize, relationships to iron out, new responsibilities to delegate. The MPD's investigation into Charlotte Haines's death was a nuisance that required finessing, but in truth it wasn't a serious concern. Agatha had never been happier. It was everything she'd ever wanted.

Ironically, it had been the police that caused her to quit. Not because she was worried about getting caught but because of how easy it had been to get away with. And how proud she was of that fact. She'd been sitting in on Paxton's interview with the police, admiring Paul's deft handling of the detective. He'd seemed so compassionate, empathetic, genuinely devastated to lose such a bright young woman to the scourge of drugs. Even Agatha felt herself buying his performance. Never mind that fifteen minutes earlier, he'd thrown a tantrum over the inconvenience. There'd been no kind words for Charlotte Haines then, only contempt and irritation.

Agatha remembered having an out-of-body experience, stepping back to watch herself watch Paul lie to the police. The fawning way she hung on his every word, looking forward to the moment the detective left so they could laugh at his gullibility. It made her cringe. The woman sitting in that office was nothing but a sycophant. A cheap lackey. She wasn't an employee; she was an addict. And Paxton was less her boss than her dealer. She also recognized in that moment that it wasn't Paul's fault. He might have been looking for someone like her, but she'd certainly been looking for him too. Someone who would let her off the leash and reward her for embracing the worst version of herself. This was what she'd wanted. And to what end? She'd caught a momentary glimpse of herself ten years down the road. Would there be anything left of her other than what Paul needed her to be? The thought appalled her, but she also knew how addiction worked—moments of clarity never lasted. It would get shoved back down into an unexamined recess of her mind so she could keep chasing the high that only working for Paul gave her. Because she loved the game that much, and all she valued was the win. She'd quit that night and bought a ticket to Thailand because a friend had vacationed there once and said how beautiful it was.

On a whim, she'd signed up to learn to scuba dive; the thought of drifting silently underwater among the fish sounded peaceful. Her instructor had been an Australian named Denny Cross, a granite slab of a man who spoke so softly she had to lean in to hear him. He'd done multiple tours in Afghanistan with the Australian Defense Force and was haunted by the person he'd become there. Maybe that was why they'd fallen in love—two people broken in similar places. Normally that was a recipe for disaster, but against all odds, it had worked. Denny had come to Koh Samui to open a dive shop and live a quiet life. Directionless, she'd been content to drift in the slipstream of his ambition. They'd been happy and even healed a little. Together. It had been a good life and better than she deserved.

After Denny's accident, Agatha tried to keep the business going, but it had been his dream, not hers. Within a year she closed the dive shop and flew home, determined not to forget the person she'd become with him. That had meant staying away from her old life. Agatha knew she was weak, weaker than most. She'd moved to the far side of the world to put temptation out of reach. Push came to shove, she wasn't a good person, but if she avoided pushing and shoving, then maybe she could be . . . if not good, at least harmless. Net zero. She dedicated herself to leaving no footprint in the world, no trace that she'd been there at all.

Her self-imposed purgatory had worked for a long time. But now along came Cal Swinden, whispering silkily in her ear and offering her a way back in. The worst part was she had the perfect excuse to take him up on his offer. She wouldn't be going back for herself. No, no, it would be for a good cause—Shelby Franklin's honor. People would call her Saint Agatha for doing something so selfless. She let out a cynical laugh. This was how the devil got you in those old folktales.

She parked outside her house and sat arguing back and forth with herself. There was only one possible right answer, but she held out hope that if she added it up enough times, then eventually two plus two would equal five.

She reached for her phone and made a call she should have back at the cathedral.

"How did it go?" Shelby asked after she picked up.

"I think you can come home this weekend."

"Really?" Shelby's voice filled with relief. "What did he say?"

Agatha recapped her conversation with Cal Swinden, leaving out any mention of Paul Paxton or the Supreme Court. There was no reason to involve Shelby in any of that. The ends were what mattered here, not the means. From Shelby's questions, it was clear she sensed she wasn't getting the whole story. They both knew Cal wouldn't just let it go this easily, but she was too grateful to say so out loud. While Agatha gently parried Shelby's questions, a Suburban pulled over to the curb with other-shoe-dropping energy.

Black SUVs were a common enough accessory on the Hill, but somehow Agatha knew it was here for her. There was an air of inevitability when the rear window opened and a woman's face leaned into view. They'd never met, but Agatha recognized the stern, humorless expression from C-SPAN. Tina Lu. It was petty, but Agatha kept track of her successors, of whom there'd been more than a few. The congressman seemed to chew through another chief of staff every few years like a spoiled child who was too hard on his toys. Tina Lu had lasted longer than most and was, based on everything Agatha had seen, very good at her job.

"I have to run," Agatha told Shelby.

"Will you be here for dinner?"

"Wouldn't miss it."

As Agatha lowered the phone from her ear, Tina Lu beckoned her with two presumptuous fingers. It should have rubbed Agatha the wrong way. Well, it did, but she also felt strangely grateful to her. She'd been sitting in her car feeling at loose ends, but now she had a fight, and a fight had always given her a sense of purpose. It also confirmed her suspicions. From the start, she'd guessed that Paul was blackmailing the president for the nomination. That he'd sent Tina Lu to read Agatha the riot act was all the proof she needed.

She was surprised only that it had taken this long.

It would probably be in Agatha's best interests to take her kicking, to appear chastened and penitent. She knew it. Intellectually, she knew it. But taking it on the chin wasn't in her nature. Her father would testify to that. She'd be damned if she was going to let this sentient doorstop with her stubby fingers interrupt her day unscathed. Call it professional courtesy, but Agatha needed Tina Lu to know the congressman could do better, and had.

Buoyed by the thought, she got out and crossed the street. A driver emerged and held open the back door. Agatha acknowledged him with a nod and got in. The door closed with a muffled thump, leaving the two chiefs of staff, past and present, alone. Tina Lu didn't look up from her phone, continuing to pound out a text or email with one veteran thumb. In her other hand, she balanced a coffee on her knee, which bounced in a way that made Agatha think that more caffeine was not in her best interests. But the deeply etched worry lines and dark bags beneath Tina's eyes also suggested that she probably wouldn't get through the day any other way.

Agatha remembered the drill. She'd never had children, but there wasn't much difference between a congressman and a newborn. Both required constant attention, praise, and supervision, so regular exercise and a balanced diet were rarely in the cards. She knew firsthand what working on the Hill could do to your health. Agatha might be twenty years older, but she was in far better shape than she'd ever been working for Paul Paxton.

The texting continued. It was a tedious, childish power play and did little to improve Agatha's opinion of her replacement. Tired of being made to wait, she reached over and took the phone out of Tina's hand.

"Excuse me?" Tina said. "Give me my phone back."

"Tina, I need you to focus. Can you do that for me?"

"Oh, so it's Tina? Have we met?"

"I have other things I can call you."

The corner of Lu's mouth twitched as she caught Agatha's meaning. "No, you can save that for when I'm gone."

Agatha handed the phone back. "I'll just be thinking it in the meantime, then."

Tina chuckled despite herself and took a sip of coffee. "He warned you'd be a lot."

"It's been a day."

"Well, yes, that's why I'm here. You don't seem surprised to see me, so I think you know why."

"Honestly, I was expecting him."

"I'm sure you were," Tina said, "but his schedule is a little tight today."

"The Supreme Court. Very exciting."

"Yes, exactly. The Supreme Court. And you're drawing too much attention. It's a bad time for your name to be back in the spotlight."

Tina said it with a knowingness that told Agatha her successor was aware of the photographs and the blackmail. Paxton must really trust her. She couldn't contain herself any longer. "You're actually blackmailing the president of the United States for a Supreme Court appointment? Are you two out of your damn minds?"

Tina seemed momentarily thrown by Agatha's directness but recovered her poise admirably. "We're just calling in a favor. The president understands that. We need you to understand it too."

"Why? What's Paul's angle?"

"There's no angle. The congressman just wants to serve his country."

Agatha couldn't contain her laughter. "No, seriously, what's his angle?"

"I am being serious."

"Fine, whatever. Don't tell me."

"All I'm here to do is to understand why you've chosen this precise moment to go back on your word to the congressman."

"I agreed to stay out of his business and to retire from politics."

"Is that what you call showing up at Congressional Country Club and harassing Dale Havitz?"

There it was. "'Harassing' is a little strong. It was a private conversation between two concerned parties. Nothing more."

"And you honestly think that doesn't qualify as politics?"

"I honestly don't think you've ever looked up the definition of 'politics.'"

"Don't get semantic with me."

"Calm down, I'm not registering as a lobbyist. I just needed a word with the congressman."

"About your tenant, the whore."

"Aren't we all, Tina?" Agatha shot back while imagining punching her in the throat.

"Agatha, I'm just trying to do my job," Tina said, downshifting to a more amenable tone.

Agatha was well versed in that maneuver. Any minute now, Tina would be making common cause with her. How they were just two cogs in the machine, but if they worked together, then they could sort this mess out.

"I've nothing to do with that anymore."

"You gave him your word," Tina reminded her.

"Yes, I did. My word. Didn't ask for anything. Didn't take anything. And I could have, believe me. I left of my own free will, and I've always kept my end."

"Until now," Tina said like a conductor announcing a key change. "So what do you want? What game are you playing?"

Agatha realized what was really going on here. It wasn't just that her old boss was pissed that she'd reneged on their deal; he thought she was making a move. That Shelby Franklin was some sort of gambit intended to hurt him. The ego on that man was breathtaking.

"Hasn't gotten any less paranoid, has he?"

"He didn't get where he is by trusting people's better angels."

"Well, then let me be clear. This has nothing to do with His Highness and whatever deal he made with the president. I didn't even know what he was planning. Maybe if he'd thought to give me a heads-up, I could've handled things differently."

"So this is all just bad timing? Is that what you want us to believe?"

Agatha sighed, remembering her dad's story about Nico Hawkins. Tina wasn't ever going to be persuaded this was a coincidence. "Let me talk to him."

"Impossible. He can't be seen with you."

"Then I think we're at an impasse."

"This girl's *that* important to you? That's the story you're sticking with?"

"She has no one else."

"Then you're really leaving me no choice," Tina said and held out a folder that had been sitting on the seat between them.

"What's that?"

"Consider it insurance."

Reluctantly, Agatha took the folder and opened it on her lap. Inside were a series of photographs that brought back a flood of memories, none good. In the first, Agatha held Charlotte Haines by the ankles while the then-congressman Harrison Clark struggled with her shoulders. Flipping through them, the pictures became a short film reel that told a damning story. Agatha remembered how messy Charlotte's little BMW had been and how they'd had to wedge her body into the trunk. The light wasn't the best, but she had to give Darius credit. He'd really captured the moment. What would Cal Swinden give to get his hands on these?

She'd always known there were photographs from that night. That was why she'd brought Darius along. But she hadn't known until now that she was *in* any of them. How was that possible? She'd specifically told Darius to leave her out and checked his negatives afterward to make sure he hadn't accidentally caught her. Well, not all of them, clearly. Agatha shut the folder delicately and handed it back to Tina. In a perfect world, she would have kept her composure and given nothing away. But this world was far from perfect. She didn't know where her blood had gone, but it wasn't in her face. Tina was watching her like a vulture who'd happened upon a dying animal and was waiting for it to give up and lie down.

"I want nothing to do with any of this," Agatha said.

"But you have *everything* to do with this. And you need to remember that. Because if your crusade to save Shelby Franklin costs the congressman this opportunity . . . if the press puts two and two together . . . you need to know you will be tarred with the same brush. So I strongly recommend that you sit this one out. Shelby Franklin got herself into this mess. She can get herself out."

Agatha tried the door. It was locked. "Let me out."

"Don't forget, Charlotte Haines wasn't the first time you crossed the line. You try me, and I will bury you. Do you understand?"

"Let me out."

"Do. You. Understand?"

"Yes," Agatha said through clenched teeth. "I understand."

Tina nodded to the driver, and with an audible thunk, the doors unlocked.

"I'd like to say it was a pleasure to meet you," Tina said as Agatha opened the door and climbed out into the sunshine. "I'd heard so much about you. But if I'm being really honest? You're a bit of a letdown."

Agatha turned back, searching for a clever reply, but for the first time in her life, she found herself at a complete loss for words.

CHAPTER TWENTY-FOUR

Agatha rang the doorbell and stepped back. Years had passed since she'd last been here, and she didn't know what to expect, only that it would be different. Still, she wasn't ready for the man who answered. It wasn't that Darius had changed—time had marched on for both of them—it was how. A Thursday evening, but he came to the door wearing a charcoal, pinstriped suit, sky-blue shirt, and peach tie with matching pocket square. Agatha wasn't religious—neither was Darius, far as she knew—but she recognized church clothes when she saw them. Back in high school, Mrs. McDaniel had taken her son to church every Sunday. He'd gone, not because of his close personal relationship with Jesus, but because back-talking Mrs. McDaniel might lead to meeting the Lord ahead of schedule. Apparently her determination had paid off in the end.

His head was bald now, and it didn't look like it was entirely by choice. He'd also grown a beard, more gray than black, and put on a little weight. Honestly, it worked for him. Agatha thought so, anyway—it filled out his face and softened his features. Darius always had a smile that could charm paint off a wall, but there was a warmth behind it now that hadn't always been there. Agatha guessed the little girl in the orange bubble ponytail holders and barrettes, perched on his hip, might have something to do with it; the gold band on his left ring finger too. Whatever the source, his smile wasn't meant for Agatha, because it vanished at the sight of her.

"What's up, A?" he said as though it had been twenty minutes, not twenty years. He looked her up and down, the eyes of a free safety who saw the whole field and diagnosed the play before the center snapped the ball. She could tell he knew exactly why she was there.

"Darius," she replied, much more civilly than she'd intended on the drive over. Credit her unplanned restraint to his adorable daughter. Cursing him out in front of a child felt wrong, and an irrational part of her suspected he'd brought the girl to the door as a shield. But another part of her was just glad to see him. Her unexpected arrival notwithstanding, he looked happy, and to her surprise, that made her happy as well.

"Who's that, Daddy?" the little girl asked.

He lowered the girl to the floor and shooed her back into the house. "Go find your mama."

The girl pouted but did as she was told, scampering off in her floral-print dress.

"Beautiful kid," Agatha said. "What's her name?"

"Let's leave her out of this. What do you want?" Darius stepped out onto the stoop, closing the door behind him.

"Not going to invite me in?"

"Can't be bringing this into my house. You understand."

"Thought this was your mom's house."

"Moms passed, left it to me."

"Sorry to hear that." Mrs. McDaniel had never liked Agatha and hadn't worked too hard pretending otherwise. Unvarnished honesty was hard to come by in this city, and Agatha had always admired the purity of her disdain. Mrs. McDaniel couldn't decide what kind of trouble Agatha represented, only that it had no business around her son.

"What about you? Where you at these days?"

"Still on the Hill. Same house too. Guess neither of us went far."

He nodded but not in agreement. "Depends how you mean 'far.'"

"Maybe just me then," she acknowledged.

"Maybe."

"So you know why I'm here."

"Been twenty years, A. Reckon you're not here to reminisce," he said, leading her down his steps to the sidewalk.

"Tina Lu was at my house this afternoon."

"She came by my work," he replied.

"Forgot what a good photographer you are."

Darius crossed his arms over his chest and looked past her down the street, his expression a blank.

"You have nothing to say?" Agatha pressed.

"What? You here for an apology? This is Trinidad. There's no sorrys here."

Trinidad was Darius's neighborhood, bounded on the south by Florida Avenue, Gallaudet University to the west, Ivy City to the north, and Bladensburg Road to the east. Gentrification had swept steadily south and east through Washington since the late nineties, but back in high school, when Rayful Edmond III had brought crack to DC, Trinidad had been at the heart of the city's drug wars.

"We were friends."

"Oh, come on, A. Just because we schooled together didn't make us friends," Darius said scornfully. "Only time I ever heard from you was when you needed something done. That's not a friend; that's an employer."

"So now I'm the bad guy for getting you work when you needed it?"

"That's true, you did. But why? There's the question, isn't it? You're saying it was because we were friends? That's a feel-good story, but sell that shit uptown. Truth is, I was broke and needed the money. You knew I'd do just about anything." He paused and appraised her. "But that was always your gift, wasn't it? Spotting weakness, exploiting it."

"That's not fair."

"The night we did that business in Middleburg. You even think to tell me what we were going out there to do?"

"A job's a job."

"Moving a body in the middle of the night? That's not just another job."

"*I* moved the body."

"Yeah, because Virginia police are all about those technicalities."

"Honestly, I didn't think you'd care."

"Well, I always appreciate when a white lady does my thinking for me. You know how thinking tires me out."

Agatha wasn't quite buying all this. He certainly hadn't tried to opt out. "Where's all this coming from? I don't remember any complaints out of you at the time."

"That's true. Just saying, though. A friend would have told me why we were going out there. Given *me* the choice," Darius said. "And then afterward, when the police started asking questions? Were you a friend to me then? Or did you leave the damn country without telling me? Face it, A. You used me like you used everyone. But I get it. I do. That's just how the world is, but you're on one with this we-were-friends bullshit."

"Is that why you took those pictures with me in them? You were pissed?"

"Oh, you think the pictures were *my* idea?" Darius said, realization spreading across his face. "You still haven't figured it out."

The truth dawned on her then, so obvious it embarrassed her. "That's why you didn't ask any questions when I called. You already knew why we were going to Middleburg."

Darius shrugged. "Paxton called me fifteen minutes before you did."

She put her hands on her hips and stared at the ground as the history she'd been telling herself for twenty years began rewriting itself. "Paul told you to put me in the frame."

He nodded. "Click, click."

"And you didn't think to give me a heads-up?"

"Like I said, you and me? We weren't in the heads-up business. Taking pictures was a job, not a favor to a friend, and Paxton was paying, not you. You were just what we call middle management. So if your head's in the lion's mouth now, well, I feel for you. I've been there, and it's a bitch. But I'm not sorry, and we're not friends. So say what you got to say so I can get back to my family."

"I'm sorry." The words were so unfamiliar in her mouth that she wondered if she'd ever said them before and meant it. A car passed, not even going that fast, but it startled her. She felt lightheaded. Darius had put it in harsher terms than she would've, but he wasn't wrong. She was no one's friend.

Something in his expression softened. "What?"

"You're right. I don't know what I was thinking coming here." She felt her face redden. Blushing? She was blushing now? What was happening to her?

Darius seemed to have similar questions. "You alright?"

"I should go," she said but instead felt him take her by the arm to ease her down onto his bottom step. Time passed while she blew the dust off her memories of that night in Middleburg, altered in important places now that she knew Paul had set her up.

An unwanted thought entered her mind like a bullet fired a long, long time ago—what if instead of torturing Charlotte to force her to quit, Agatha had taken her seriously?

The only reason Charlotte Haines had gotten a job in the congressman's office was because her daddy had been a major donor to the campaign. Agatha had resented Charlotte and her connections, mostly because, as the daughter of a cop and a schoolteacher, she hadn't been born with any. It hadn't helped that Charlotte lived down to Agatha's expectations. What a piece of work she'd been. Bad Charlotte had been a liability from the day she arrived.

With the benefit of hindsight, Agatha now saw Charlotte for who she'd really been—a spoiled, lonely young woman who'd never been taken seriously. How different things might have been if she'd taken Charlotte under her wing. But what had Agatha done instead? What she always did, according to Darius—spotted weakness and exploited it. She'd spun Charlotte around like a pretty top and pointed her at Harrison Clark in the hope that chaos would beget chaos.

Look how that bet had paid off.

"What do you think Charlotte Haines would be doing today if she were alive?" she asked.

"You didn't kill that girl, A," Darius said, sitting down beside her.

"No, but I sure didn't try to talk her out of it either."

"No one talks anybody out of bad habits."

"But that's my gift, right? Exploiting weakness."

"Didn't mean it like that."

"Yeah you did. And it's true," she said. "I'm really sorry I got you involved in any of it. I mean that."

"Alright, then," he said and tapped his fist on her knee twice like a judge gaveling his courtroom out of session.

"That's it?"

"Far as you and me are concerned."

They sat there for a spell, watching cars pass.

"So, Tina Lu," he said quietly, as if speaking her name too loudly might conjure her.

"Yeah," Agatha agreed.

"Don't care where she works, that lady's a gangster."

"What'd she tell you?"

"Said you might show up, warned me to stay out of it." He turned somber. "Paxton's blackmailing the president with my pictures, isn't he?"

"Looks that way."

"That why you stuck your nose in?"

"Funny thing is, no. Didn't know anything about it. I just have my own situation that put me back in the spotlight, and now Paxton can't believe it isn't secretly all about him."

"That girl I saw you on television with. What's her story?"

Agatha gave him a rundown of the past week.

Darius chuckled at her. "You haven't changed a bit. Probably why Paxton wanted you in those pictures. You never were one for minding your own business."

"I suppose not."

"So what are you going to do?"

It was a question she'd been avoiding since getting out of Tina Lu's SUV. She'd used her anger at Darius as a distraction to put off thinking about it, but now that it had passed, she couldn't avoid an answer she wasn't proud of.

"Nothing," she said. "I'm doing nothing. If Paul wants to blackmail his way onto the Supreme Court, more power to him. I'm not getting involved. I don't have much of a life, but what little I do have, he could easily snatch away."

Darius was nodding grimly.

"What's he got on you?" she asked.

"What?" Her question had caught him off guard, and she heard his voice flinch warily.

"Come on, Darius. Tina Lu didn't show up and ask you nicely. She's a gangster, right? They have the pictures on me. What are they holding over you?"

He was shaking his head, but not at any one thing. "Can't mix up in this again either, A. Just can't. You feel me? I have something to lose now." He glanced back at his house.

"That sounds nice. What's it like?"

"Keeps me straight, I promise you that."

"I'll let you get back to your day," she said and stood up. "Sorry for showing up unannounced."

Darius rose too. "You want to come inside? We're cooking and looks like you could stand to eat. Could fix you a plate."

"Thought we weren't friends."

"Wasn't friends with Agatha Cardiff. Might could be friends with Agatha Cross, though. Come on in and meet my wife."

It surprised her how tempting she found the offer, but not how undeserving she felt. There was no place for her inside a happy home.

"Rain check?"

"Cool," he said and put out his hand. When she took it, he drew her into a half embrace and patted her back affectionately. They exchanged phone numbers, and Agatha promised to keep him in the loop.

"Candice," he said out of nowhere.

She gave him a questioning look.

"My daughter. That's her name. Candice."

CHAPTER TWENTY-FIVE

Agatha drove Shelby back into town on Saturday morning. It was a win, so why did she feel so melancholy? They arrived home in silence and parted awkwardly in her small patch of front yard. She waited until Shelby disappeared into her downstairs apartment like it was the international terminal at Dulles and Shelby was catching a flight to the far side of the world.

For an hour Agatha puttered aimlessly around the house, wondering what happened next. Did life simply go back to the way it had been before? Drifting through the days in her anonymous cocoon, the Shelbys of the world safely back in their respective boxes. Just landlord and tenant again, speaking only at the first of the month, when the rent was due. She was so lost in thought that at first she didn't register the knock at the basement door. No one but Riggins would ever know she rushed to answer it.

"Everything okay? What's going on?" Was it too much to ask for a minor catastrophe to give Agatha purpose again?

Shelby held out a check. "Last time it's ever late. I promise."

"Oh, thank you," she replied, chagrined at how disappointed she felt.

"Hey," Shelby said as Agatha went to shut the door. "What do you think about inviting your dad over tomorrow? We could eat out back. Crabs, maybe?"

There was an unfamiliar pressure behind Agatha's eyes. She realized that, if she'd been a crier, things would have taken an awkward turn. Instead, she blew out her cheeks. "Sure, that sounds good. Dad's probably lonely without you."

With a grin, Shelby followed her into the kitchen, where they made a shopping list and called John to see if he'd bring the crabs.

"For how many?" was his way of saying yes.

Shelby asked if she could invite Philip, whom she hadn't seen since before Saint Thomas. No mention of Jackson, the boyfriend, who'd clearly been shown the door after Agatha told Shelby about their run-in. Whatever else could be said of Shelby, she wasn't indecisive, and she didn't second-guess herself.

Including friends sounded like a nice idea and made Agatha wish she had someone to invite. She didn't have any friends like that, though. That was a reality check and a half: not a single living soul she could ask to a simple dinner in her backyard. A month ago, she would have considered that a triumph . . . and didn't that just tell the whole story of her life? In desperation, she even considered Kat Milbrandt, but a fistful of lies and favors weren't the basis of a friendship. Kat would probably be more suspicious than anything, and Agatha wouldn't blame her. In the end, Agatha texted Darius, who said he had plans with his family but would try to stop by if he could. That actually seemed like a minor victory—being politely brushed off at least felt like something that happened to a normal person.

With that settled, Agatha's mood improved dramatically, and she spent the day working in the backyard. It had been a perfect spring with plenty of rain, and everything was a tangled, overgrown mess. She played Elvis Costello out the kitchen door and pulled all the weeds from between the badly overgrown brickwork. After that, she did her best to tame the small beds along the fence. Was gardening going to be her new thing like it had been her mother's? It had always looked boring as hell growing up, but she was starting to see the appeal.

After sweeping up, she took the car to Schneider's to pick up beer and wine. Shelby walked down to Eastern Market to buy sides. All in all, it was a good day. Having something to look forward to really helped.

It was raining when Agatha woke up Sunday morning, and her heart sank a little—crab feasts were definitely an outdoor sport. Fortunately the forecast held, and the sky cleared before noon. By the time her dad arrived, the sun was out and looked to stay that way. Shelby emerged from the basement with potato salad, mac 'n' cheese, and corn on the cob ready for the grill. She set everything down and then went around to let Philip in the side gate. They returned with bags of ice for the cooler and Jaya, a friend of Shelby's from grad school, whom Philip had surprised her with. *The more the merrier,* Agatha thought. Shelby looked happy, and anyway they had enough food for an army.

They settled in around the table and tucked in to the crabs. Her dad, with a familiar twinkle in his eye, was the life of the party. Philip and Jaya were immediately smitten, and Agatha reckoned that at this rate, John Cardiff would be the city's honorary grandpa by Labor Day. She watched him and wondered what it felt like to be a genuine version of yourself, and not just what circumstance called for? She cracked another beer and filed that question away for further consideration. This wasn't the time. For once, she was just going to sit in the sunshine and enjoy herself.

Halfway through, they had to pause to clean up and reset the table, clearing away the mountain of crab shells and empties. Agatha carried the garbage out to the bins on the side of the house. On the street, Jim was patiently guiding Regis on the dog's shuffling tour of the block's trees. Her neighbor saw her, started to wave, and then seemed to think better of it.

That was no good. She'd been a jerk and needed to sort this out now before it became permanently awkward between them. Following him up onto the street, she called his name. Jim stopped, much to Regis's displeasure, who was just getting on a roll, and said hi.

"Having some people over," she said, and on cue, Shelby shrieked with laughter from the back of the house.

"I can hear. Try and keep it down," he said with a wink that she found unexpectedly charming. Men could either wink or they decidedly could not. Jim Talbot could.

"We're having crabs," she said. "If you're not busy . . ."

"Crabs? Yeah, I'd like that. Just let me get his lordship settled, and I'll be over."

"Good," she said with a wink of her own. "I've got some landscaping work I'd like you to look at."

Jim chuckled resignedly. "That's going to be a thing, isn't it?"

"Well, at least until you do something better."

"Challenge accepted," he warned and let Regis lead him away.

A car door opened. Darius got out and crossed the street to her.

"You wear anything but suits?" she asked.

He grinned. "Just coming from church. Been thinking over what we talked about."

"Yeah, me too." She'd been definitive about not getting involved, but it had been gnawing at her.

"Imagine the damage that fool could do on the Supreme Court."

"Imagine being the ones who put him there."

"Yeah," he said and looked away.

"What's on your mind?" she asked as gently as she could.

"You asked me what they're holding over me. Figured you deserved to know, but you gotta give me your word you'll keep my name out of it."

She gave it, charmed that he thought her word was worth anything. It would be in this case, though.

He paused as if weighing the value of her promise on an invisible scale. Then, satisfied but wary nonetheless, he asked a seemingly rhetorical question: "What killed Charlotte Haines?"

"Drugs. Well, not the drugs themselves; they were laced with poison."

"Right. So who was her dealer? Who sold them to her?"

"They never figured that out."

"Well, let's say, hypothetically, that she never *had* a dealer. What if she was a beautiful, rich white girl and men just gave her whatever she wanted?"

"Sure." That was Charlotte to a tee, but Agatha was still unsure where this was going.

"Now let's say, again hypothetically, that she's got a habit now, but she's dating Congressman Harrison Clark, who doesn't touch the stuff. Where's she going to cop from, then?"

"Well, then she really would need a dealer."

"Right," Darius agreed. "Except she's too scared to make a buy on the street."

"So she'd do what she always does, get someone to do it for her."

"Right again. She found herself a sucker. Some fool she twists around her finger to keep her in powder," Darius said. "So the day she's supposed to go out to Middleburg to meet Clark, Charlotte's stash is on empty. She calls her fool, but by now he's wise to her and tells her to forget that. Now she's desperate and calls Paxton, says she's going to cancel on Clark unless she gets a little touch to cool her out."

"You're telling me that Paxton knew about her coke habit?"

Darius looked at Agatha in wonder. "Who do you think got her hooked in the first place?"

"Bullshit."

"You never saw what he was all about, did you? Not really."

"Wise me up then. What happened?"

"What happened was Paxton showed up at my door and gave me a thousand dollars and a package for Charlotte."

"Paxton personally handed *you* the cocaine that killed Charlotte Haines." It wasn't a question; she just needed to say it out loud to see if it sounded plausible. Did it also sound plausible that Paxton knew the drugs would kill Charlotte? It did, and that changed everything.

For twenty years Agatha had been tortured by the memory of that night. At how easy it had been for her to treat Charlotte Haines's death as an opportunity. To capitalize on tragedy. But if what Darius said was true—and she knew in her bones that it was—then Charlotte's death hadn't been an accident at all.

"Like I said, you didn't kill that girl," Darius said. "I did."

She didn't bother contradicting him, even if that wasn't quite true. Guilt couldn't be argued away with facts any more than love or hate. Paul Paxton had killed Charlotte Haines, but they were his accomplices. They were all responsible in their own way.

"I gotta get home," Darius said. "You watch your back, A. You imagine sitting on those pictures all this time? Waiting twenty years to make your move? That's some trigger discipline."

"Paul always did play the long game," she agreed.

Agatha went back to the party, thinking through what Darius had said. When Jim appeared twenty minutes later, bottle of wine in hand, she'd almost forgotten what he was doing here. Fortunately Shelby jumped in and made introductions. Everyone shifted around and made room for Jim next to Agatha. She didn't think that was at all necessary. Across the table, Shelby kept looking from Agatha to Jim and back again, a gentle grin spreading across her face. Even worse, Jim and her dad hit it off immediately. This had been a terrible, terrible idea, but she was in it now.

And then, despite her best efforts and much to her surprise, Agatha had a wonderful time. The best she could remember. Three generations at one table, but it all just worked better than she would have dared hope. Maybe it was the miracle of a Sunday afternoon in late spring, but the conversation tripped lightly from topic to topic. Everyone laughing and happily overserved with nowhere special to be.

When it came time to clean up and cut the watermelon, she was already calculating how long she should wait before throwing another party. *Seriously, slow down.* This was a one-off and best not to get ahead of herself.

At the far end of the table, Shelby wiped her hands on a paper towel and looked at her phone, a concerned frown crossing her face. She excused herself and walked away toward the house, holding the phone to her ear. Even with her back turned away, Agatha could tell from the way Shelby's shoulders slumped that it wasn't good news. Shelby stopped at the kitchen door, locked in discussion while everyone fell awkwardly silent. Not to eavesdrop but because it was difficult to carry on. Shelby was obviously upset, and they watched her from the table as the Isley Brothers sang about summer breezes.

Agatha got it in her head that it was Cal Swinden. Had to be. The idea that he'd have the nerve to call her now, after everything he'd done, made her furious. Some might even call it irrationally angry, but Agatha would have countered that there was nothing irrational about it. As it turned out, Cal Swinden wasn't on the other end of the call.

Shelby hung up and came back to the table with the poker face that Agatha had come to recognize as her tell for bad news.

"I need a beer. Anyone have a beer?" she asked with a forced smile.

Agatha's dad reached behind him into the cooler, fetched a beer, and unscrewed it for her.

"Well? What was that?" Philip asked after she'd taken a long drink.

"Oh," Shelby said as if she'd forgotten and was trying to remember. "I got fired."

The table exploded with concern and anger, Philip and Jaya leaning in to comfort their friend. Agatha put her palms on the table, jaw clenching until her teeth felt like they might crack. Her dad, who'd thrown down his napkin and was leaning back in his chair, made eye contact.

"Can you believe they fired her like that?" he asked Agatha quietly. "On a Sunday."

"Like *hell* they did."

There it was. That purpose she'd been missing.

CHAPTER TWENTY-SIX

Over the past week, Isha had watched a narrative form around the Paxton nomination like a chrysalis. Flipping through the news channels or the editorial pages of the major newspapers, she saw the same opinions and ideas repeated, repackaged, and often restated using the same language in the same exact word order. Part of that originated in the talking points issued by the White House to its proxies, who farmed out across the media landscape, laying out the administration's position on cable and network news shows. But part was due to the fact that the media was an echo chamber. Everyone read each other's work; everyone knew what other outlets were covering, and how. Every take became a variation on a theme, which in turn became conventional wisdom, which at last hardened into the Narrative, capital *N*, full stop.

This was especially true for major stories. Safer to move with the current. If everyone was wrong, then everyone would be wrong together, and, well, mistakes happened. The blame fell evenly on the "media" and not on any one reporter's head. But should a reporter swim against the tide and be proved wrong, then they risked being branded a hack who peddled crackpot conspiracy theories. Such a misstep could sink a career, and Isha feared being dragged out to sea just as she made port. Something far more insidious was at work with this nomination; she was absolutely sure of it. She just couldn't prove it, much less print it.

The initial coverage of Paul Paxton's nomination had been caustic at best. So many norms had been casually violated, and partisan howls for impeachment echoed across the political landscape. Surprisingly, though, the White House hadn't played defense and even leaned into the accusations of cronyism, arguing that it was precisely the president's history with Paul Paxton that had convinced Clark that the congressman was the ideal man for the job. There was no law stating that the president couldn't know his nominee, and wasn't it in some ways foolish to nominate a complete stranger to such an essential role? Abraham Lincoln had made Salmon Chase, his longtime secretary of the Treasury, the chief justice, so this wasn't without precedent. In any event, it had been more than a decade since the president and Paul Paxton had worked together. The White House's position was that any opposition to the nomination was political grandstanding, nothing more.

Day by day Isha had watched the narrative swing in the White House's favor. Not everyone was placated, but calls for the president's impeachment were softening, and an editorial in Friday's *Times* even described the decision to expand the pool of candidates beyond the judiciary as "visionary" and "necessary to the long-term health of the court." That take had been the overall conclusion of the Sunday-morning political roundtables, opinion solidifying into conventional wisdom.

Sidney Lowenstein had called a staff meeting for late Monday morning to plan the paper's coverage of the impending confirmation hearings. The White House was asking the Senate to move quickly and appeared to have the popularity, and thus the votes, to make Justice Paul Paxton a reality before the August recess. Lowenstein made a few introductory remarks and then handed things off to Roger Fitzgerald, who went around the table assigning roles and responsibilities from a legal pad. Isha had been included in the meeting, but it felt like a courtesy for breaking the Paxton story initially. Since the White House announced the nomination, Isha had felt increasingly irrelevant, frozen out of her own story. She felt let down by Fitz and betrayed by Bernard.

"Isha, I want you to dig into Donna Tomlin."

"A profile piece?" she said, making no effort to hide her frustration.

"On the chair of the Senate Judiciary Committee, yes. We haven't written many words on her since she replaced O'Brien last year. We're overdue to address that oversight. Let's circle next Sunday's edition."

It would be a major piece under her own byline and an opportunity she would have jumped at a month ago. Now it felt like she was being bought off. "So you're taking me off Paxton?"

If a groan could be inaudible, then that was the tenor of the uncomfortable silence in the conference room. Everyone had heard her theory about Paul Paxton and the president. And more than once. She knew no one on staff believed her. She knew how she sounded—the way anyone with a theory but no evidence sounded. But she couldn't help herself. The more her colleagues rolled their eyes, the harder she pushed, and the more unhinged it all sounded. To Fitz's right, Bernard raised four fingers off the table in a cautioning gesture. *Let it go,* he mouthed. Isha was well past letting anything go.

"This is ridiculous," she said with a vehemence that caught even her off guard.

"Excuse me?" Fitz said, taking off his reading glasses and looking evenly at her.

Bernard, for his part, had the defeated expression of a coach who'd drawn up the perfect play only to watch his team fumble the ball away. Lowenstein, who had a reputation as a man of few words, watched but said nothing. It wasn't his way to get involved until all other options had been exhausted.

"You heard me," she said.

"Alright," he replied. "You're in my place. What would you have us do?"

"Be a real newspaper instead of doing what we're doing now."

"Which is what, exactly?" Fitz said icily.

"Regurgitating the White House's talking points. Since when did we become free PR for this administration? At least let's dust off our critical-thinking skills. None of their messaging makes any kind of sense. Paul Paxton got added to the vetting list at the last minute, and it wasn't to 'shake up the composition of the court,'" she said to a sea of skeptical faces. "I'd find out why Felix Gallardo really left the White House."

"He took a job at Fadden and Martin," Gary Hopper, a tall, world-weary reporter with thinning hair and a walrus mustache that could best be described as ill-advised, chimed in. He and Isha had never seen eye to eye, and he'd taken her obstinacy over Paul Paxton as proof that he'd been right about her all along.

"Except he didn't interview. There's no record of him meeting with anyone in upper management. I talked to someone over there in HR who said it was as if he just appeared there one morning. No warning, no announcement."

Bernard said, "He's a high-profile figure. I'm sure they weren't anxious to broadcast his hire until the ink was dry."

"Six months ago, his ex-wife gave him an ultimatum to make this exact move. He got a divorce rather than quit the White House."

"How do you know this?" Susan Radosta asked.

"She went to college with him," Hooper explained in a dismissive tone that made Isha's connection to Felix sound suspect.

"I know Felix," Isha pressed. "There is no way he quit the White House to take a job in crisis communications at F&M. Working for Clark was his dream job."

"Maybe they threw money at him. Who knows? People change their minds all the time."

Frustrated, Isha changed tack. "What was he doing meeting with Tina Lu, Paxton's chief of staff, the week before the White House announced Paxton was being vetted?"

"Jesus Christ, Roy," Hopper said. "Maybe meeting about the announcement?"

"That would be coordinated through the White House counsel's office. And anyway, there's no indication that Paxton was on the president's radar at that point."

"So what do *you* think he was doing there?" Fitz asked.

Isha sat back in her chair with a dramatic sigh. "I don't know. That's why it's called investigative journalism, not take-their-word-for-it journalism. When did you become so toothless?"

There was a flutter in the conference room as if a dozen coal mine canaries had all sensed things taking a dangerous turn. Lowenstein was watching Fitz for his reaction.

"Okay, I want you to wait in my office," Fitz said.

"This is bullshit," she said.

"Not another word," Bernard cautioned.

For a moment all Isha saw was two men trying to silence her. She opened her mouth to say something unforgivable. But then she closed it again. Instead, she gathered up her things and left the room.

Isha went to Fitz's office as she'd been told. She sat on the edge of his couch, laptop resting on her knees, feeling like a teenager who'd been sent out of class. Not that she'd ever been to the principal's office in high school. The only time she'd gotten in trouble was when Lisa Belpanno started a fight in ninth grade. Her high school had a zero-tolerance policy for fighting, and it was an automatic suspension for everyone involved, even if that involvement was getting slapped in the back of the head and falling face-first into her own locker. Her parents had been furious with her for jeopardizing her future; asking them what she should have done differently had only made them angrier.

She'd been raised not to speak back to adults, and even though she was one now, she still struggled not to see bosses through that prism. Which meant that everything she'd said back in the conference room felt wildly out of character. As if she'd finally snapped after thirty years of biting her tongue. She didn't know how she should feel about it. Her initial reaction was mortification and an intense need to apologize, but with every minute that passed, she felt her heels digging in again. What was she apologizing for? Being in charge didn't make them right.

Fitz and Bernard came in together, finishing a conversation they'd begun in the hall. Neither addressed her immediately, which she took as a bad sign. Fitz circled around his desk and leaned over his computer to check his email. Letting her sweat before he dropped the hammer. She glanced over at Bernard, who leaned against the wall, arms folded casually. His expression was inscrutable.

"So? Am I fired?" Isha asked, tiring of the foreplay.

"What?" Fitz said, looking over his monitor at her. "No, of course you're not fired."

"I'm not?"

"No. And stop being so dramatic," Bernard said.

Fitz added on, "It wouldn't be much of a newspaper if our writers never fought for a story they believed in. Passion is essential."

"Not that I recommend pulling that stunt on a weekly basis," Bernard added.

"So I can stay on the 2001 angle?" she asked hopefully.

"No," Fitz said as if she hadn't been listening. "You will write the piece you are assigned like everyone else. We are a newspaper, and there are deadlines."

"But this story is real," she insisted.

"And you'll be ready to go to print with it next Sunday?"

"Well, no."

"Then you will write the Donna Tomlin piece for next Sunday's edition," Fitz repeated. "You understand that's how we keep the lights on?"

"And if I do make my deadline?"

"As long as you meet your responsibilities to the paper, you are free to develop leads," Bernard told her.

"Within reason," Fitz added.

"Within reason," Bernard echoed.

Isha spent the next few hours at her desk with her head down. Ostensibly she was doing background on Donna Tomlin. She put a call into her office and talked to Tomlin's chief of staff, Katherine Milbrandt. Her heart wasn't in it, but she also knew that Fitz and Bernard were right. She had nothing but conjecture to go on. Nothing that didn't have a dozen reasonable explanations, no matter what her gut told her. Even if Fitz did give her free rein, she needed a place to start. The problem with conspiracies, at least competent ones, was that they were closed loops. Unless someone was willing to talk, there was no way in. Felix wasn't returning any of her calls, and to no one's surprise, Agatha Cross hadn't reached out as she said she would. Isha was thinking about the inherent unfairness of that when her phone rang. The caller's number had been blocked.

"Isha Roy," she answered, propping the phone against her shoulder so she could keep typing.

"I have information on Paul Paxton," a woman said. Her voice sounded young, with traces of a southern accent that had been sanded down through considerable effort.

Isha stopped typing. "Who is this?"

"Have I called the right number?"

"Yes," Isha said. "Yes, you have, but I'd like to know who I'm talking to."

"You can have my name or what I know about Paul Paxton. Your choice."

Isha reached for a pen. "Tell me what you have."

When she hung up the phone, Isha went looking for Bernard. He looked up warily when she sat on the corner of his desk.

"Bern, what do you know about Paul Paxton's poker game?"

Bernard's expression softened. "I know it's been going on for twenty-five years."

"If it's still going on, is it a story?"

"He wouldn't be that reckless." Bern sounded unconvinced.

Isha raised her eyebrows. "Wouldn't he?"

"When?"

"Tonight."

Bernard stood wearily. "Alright, let's go talk to Fitz."

CHAPTER TWENTY-SEVEN

"I don't want to go in there," Shelby said and not for the first time.

Agatha understood. It wouldn't be pleasant walking back through these doors, but sometimes the hard thing was the only thing to do. This had to be done, and as much as Shelby was dreading it, she'd feel good about it later. Agatha believed that, even if she'd had to twist Shelby's arm to get her this far. Shelby was tough and just needed the right encouragement. She'd thank Agatha when it was over.

They were idling across the street from the World Justice Initiative, a nondescript building in the West End. Shelby had interned there during her master's and been hired full-time after graduation. Until last night, that was, when her boss had called to deliver the bad news—financial constraints were necessitating the elimination of several junior analyst positions. The organization was heartbroken but saw no other option but to let Shelby go. Blah, blah, blah—Agatha recognized a crock when it was served hot. Somehow the WJI had learned that Shelby had been moonlighting as an escort and needed a cover story to fire her. It was a coward's way out, and they weren't going to get away with it.

Shelby had taken the news with quiet resignation, but the devastation on her face was unmistakable. The party had broken up shortly thereafter. Agatha hadn't been nearly as circumspect. This had Cal Swinden written all over it. Retribution for not playing his game his way. Well, they would see about that.

"Let's just go home," Shelby said from behind oversize sunglasses. "It's okay."

"They can't just fire you."

"Actually, they can. I was there."

"Not like this," Agatha said with finality.

"What am I going to say to them?"

"Just let me do the talking. Do you trust me?"

"Yeah, but . . . ," Shelby answered hopelessly.

"Well, then, let's start by getting out of the car, okay?"

Everything would be fine once they got moving; the first step was always the hardest. Reluctantly, Shelby did as she was told and stood on the sidewalk, staring at her old offices like a dog realizing it had been tricked into going to the vet. Agatha took her gently by the arm and guided her across the street. Agatha was wearing her suit. *Again*, despite promising herself no more. She felt like a dilettante with her one good outfit and scuffed shoes. At least her ensemble would be new to them, and if they were looking at her shoes, then she'd messed up badly.

They went in the lobby and up to the third floor. Shelby kept her head down and her sunglasses on. Not everyone recognized her, but there was a murmur from those who did and more than one double take. Her boss's office door stood open, and he looked up from his desk when Agatha knocked. He was a tall, thin man, pale and freckled from too much time in the sun, perhaps forty, with a head of fine blond hair that fell to one side in a wave. His expression was of a man who thought he'd locked the bathroom door.

"Shelby?" he said, removing his reading glasses as if confirming his guess.

"Hi, David," Shelby said, lingering by the door.

The bruise on Shelby's face had faded, turning yellow and green, but it was unmissable. David certainly hadn't and stared at it with troubled eyes.

"Can we have a minute, David?" Agatha asked and sat down without waiting for the minute to be given.

"I'm sorry. You are?"

"Agatha Cross. I'm a friend of Shelby's."

"What can I do for you?" he asked, glancing from Agatha to Shelby and back again.

"I was sorry to hear of your financial woes. And the WJI is such a venerable organization. It's unthinkable, really."

"Yes, well. Life of a nonprofit. It's a cycle," David replied, waving one hand vaguely in a circle.

"So how many?" Agatha asked.

"How many what?"

"How many junior analysts did you have to let go so those ends would meet?"

"What?" David said, his reading glasses dipping and bowing like a conductor's baton. "That's confidential, of course."

"Mm-hmm," Agatha agreed. "Well, I hope it's more than one."

"I beg your pardon?"

"More than one junior analyst 'downsized,'" Agatha said, making exaggerated air quotes. "So that it looks good. Because if Shelby is the only one, then you're going to get murdered in the lawsuit."

"I assure you—"

"Oh, that's good. Very believable. But save the heartfelt assurances for the deposition. For now, this is just a courtesy call. You've made a real mess, David, and you need help minimizing the fallout. First, can we agree that Shelby Franklin wasn't let go to cut costs? You got clued in to what happened in Saint Thomas, and your board is allergic to scandal."

"I agree to no such thing."

"Was it Cal Swinden?" she asked.

"It was not," he replied, which Agatha took as confirmation. A random name should have produced a "Who?" But he already knew the name well enough not to be surprised and to be prepared to deny it.

"How do you think this is going to play in the media?"

"What?"

"A think tank firing a gifted young analyst from its human-trafficking desk for being human trafficked. That's quite a headline."

"That's not fair."

Agatha leaned forward, warming up to her part. "You're right. It's not fair. Human trafficking is a scourge, and the WJI does essential work advocating and pressing for policy to combat it. Now here's your chance to put your money where your mouth is and champion one of its victims. Or are the WJI's positions just performative?"

"Agatha?" Shelby said quietly from the doorway.

"We're almost there," Agatha said without looking back.

"Can I speak to David alone?"

Something in Shelby's tone made Agatha pause. This was no time for a divided front, not when they had him on the ropes. She swiveled in her seat to encourage Shelby not to lose heart and was met by Shelby's eyes, which implored her to leave.

"What are you doing?" Agatha asked.

"Please."

"Okay." Rattled, Agatha gathered herself to leave, fixing David with one last cautioning glare. "I'll be right outside."

Except Agatha didn't wait right outside; instead, she walked out to the street, where she paced up and down the sidewalk. What the hell had just happened? They'd been so close. She hadn't smoked in decades, but the old urge to hold a cigarette crept back into her fingers. To have something to do with her hands, she checked her phone. Speak of the devil, there was a missed call from Cal Swinden. She'd tried him a couple of times with no luck. Of course he would call now. She dialed him back.

"If you've been calling about the job, it's no longer on the table," he began.

"You're a real son of a bitch."

"Look, I thought about what you said. You were right."

She felt as if she'd stumbled into a conversation that was already halfway finished. She was talking about Shelby, but he was on another subject entirely. "Right about what?"

"That I don't need you for this. Just sit it out, and maybe we can do business down the road. Can you do that for me?"

"Sure," she replied cautiously.

"And as a show of good faith, our deal about Shelby stands. Does that work for you?"

"Yeah, that'll work."

"Good, I'm glad to hear it. Now just sit tight and stay tuned to this channel," he said cheerily and hung up.

Agatha stood in a daze, phone still to her ear, replaying their conversation at the cathedral. There was only one thing he could mean. Swinden was going for the photographs. Why? Because in her zeal to protect Shelby, and maybe to prove herself, Agatha had provided him a trail of gold-plated bread crumbs leading to Paul Paxton.

Before Agatha had time to digest what had just happened any further, she caught sight of Shelby coming out the front door of the WJI. Her face was locked in neutral. Agatha couldn't get a read on how things had gone inside.

"How did it go? Did you get your job back?" she asked, hurrying over.

"Yeah," Shelby said without sounding exactly enthusiastic.

"That's good, right?"

"Well, then I kind of quit."

"What? *Why?* We *had* this," Agatha said, kicking herself for agreeing to leave. This was exactly what she'd been worried about. Shelby was smart, but she was young and inexperienced. Her boss had taken advantage of that, twisted her around somehow. "Let's go back inside. We can still fix this." She started back toward the WJI. When Shelby didn't follow, Agatha took her by the arm. "Come on, let's go."

Shelby didn't budge. "Agatha. Stop. Just stop."

"What is going on with you? Why would you quit?"

"Because I don't want to work somewhere I'm not wanted."

Agatha was angry now. "Then why didn't you say something? I wasted my whole morning on this."

"I did, but you're not exactly a take-no-for-an-answer person."

That pulled Agatha up short. She'd been so caught up in beating Cal Swinden at his own game that she'd never stopped to ask Shelby what *she* wanted. Even when Agatha was trying to do some good, everything somehow managed to become all about her. Maybe because all she had ever cared about was winning. And Shelby? Shelby was just another battlefield. Agatha saw that now. Twenty years had passed, and she still hadn't learned a damn thing.

Shelby took Agatha by the hand. "I'm sorry. You've done so much for me. I didn't want to let you down. I'm sorry."

"You've got nothing to be sorry for. I shouldn't have pushed so hard."

"I really appreciate what you did. You're just kind of a lot, you know?"

Agatha smiled despite herself. That was putting it mildly. Then she asked a question that she realized she hadn't but should have. "Are you okay?"

"No, I'm pretty angry right now. But I'll be fine," she said with a wan smile and nodded back toward the WJI. "David's going to give me one hell of a letter of recommendation."

"And severance?"

"Three months."

"Well done," Agatha said with an admiring laugh. "I really am sorry. Sometimes I just get ahead of myself. Old habits."

Shelby asked if she could buy Agatha a coffee. They crossed the street and got in line.

"So what's next for Shelby Franklin?" Agatha asked after they'd ordered and found a table.

"I don't have a clue. Take a breath. Look around. Figure out where I can make a difference."

"Someone will snap you up."

"We'll see," Shelby said. "If not, I'll go back to graduate school and get my PhD. I'll figure something out."

"I imagine you will," Agatha said and squeezed her arm across the table. "Oh, by the way, turns out it wasn't Cal who talked to your boss."

"I know. That was the other part of my severance package. David gave me a name."

"Who?" Agatha would pay a lot for that name.

"My ex. Asshole. I should have seen it coming."

"Jackson?" Agatha said the name as if it were a curse word. "What are we going to do about it?"

"Nothing."

"Nothing?"

"What's to be gained?"

"But he thinks he's won."

"Yeah, so? Why would I give him a reason to think otherwise? You always ask me what I really want. Well, I want nothing to do with him. If this job is the price to have him out of my life, so be it."

Agatha sat back and smiled. The more she thought about it, the more she admired Shelby's decision. Were their places reversed, Agatha knew she'd have retaliated, escalating the situation even if it made her miserable. She'd never been one to stand on principle. Maybe now would be a good time to start. But if so, she'd need to pick some first. What should hers be?

"Sounds like you've got it figured out."

"I don't know about that, but my sister graduates high school next month. I'm going to try and talk her into moving up here. She'll need a place to live, but because of you, I have the money for that now."

"I have a spare bedroom," Agatha said, surprising even herself.

"What?"

"Upstairs in the house. I've got plenty of room. She can live there."

Shelby stood up and threw her arms around Agatha. "I don't know what to say. Thank you."

"Just until you figure things out," Agatha said, trying and failing to extricate herself from the embrace until Shelby was good and ready to let go of her.

"So what about you?" Shelby asked. "What will you do now?"

"I have a mess I need to clean up."

"Is it Cal?"

"It predates Cal, but he's involved now because of me. Can I ask a question? It's about Saint Thomas." Agatha had made a point of not asking more than was necessary about the events on board the yacht, but now she had no choice. "There was a Russian on board the yacht to meet with Dale Havitz. Did you see him?"

"No, they kept the girls away from him, and he never came up on deck," Shelby said. "But I know who he is. Havitz kept talking about him to us. Boasting, really. He's an idiot."

"Who was it?"

"Kirill Tumenov. He's an oligarch. Ex-KGB from back in the day. From what I found online, it sounded like he was stationed in East Germany and was notorious for his methods. Parlayed it into an oil and gas fortune in the nineties. The White House sanctioned him in 2020, froze all of his assets in the West. Seized everything."

"And now he wants his toys back."

"Yup, but Havitz wouldn't play ball."

So Cal was working for a Russian oligarch. That tracked from what she knew of the man—ambitious, reckless, and deeply unethical. It was playing with fire, so the potential payday must've been huge. The problem was that Cal hadn't produced results. Involving Dale Havitz had proved to be a serious miscalculation, and Saint Thomas had likely undermined Cal's credibility with his Russian master. He'd made promises and failed to deliver. What were the odds a man with Tumenov's reputation was the understanding kind? No wonder Cal was so frantic. He was scrambling for a plan B and, in desperation to make things right with his client, had set his sights on a set of twenty-year-old photographs. Agatha couldn't blame him. If the president had been willing to make Paul Paxton a Supreme Court judge to protect his secret, surely he'd be willing to unsanction one Russian oligarch. Although that would not be the end of it. The president would be permanently compromised. Tumenov would own the White House for as long as Clark remained in office. Agatha didn't like thinking about the harm it could cause, or that she would be its architect.

"Can I help?" Shelby asked.

"I don't think that's a good idea."

"Come on. There's got to be something I can do."

Agatha thought it over. "Well, actually, there is something."

"What? Tell me," Shelby said, tugging at Agatha's sleeve. "Teach me your ways."

Agatha laughed. "Will you make a call for me?"

"Sure. Who?"

"Isha Roy at the *Post*."

Shelby's phone appeared in her hand as if by magic. "What do you need me to tell her?"

Agatha laid out the bullet points and then stepped away to make a call of her own before she lost her nerve. Darius answered on the first ring.

"What up, A?"

"I have a big favor to ask." The other end of the line went quiet. "Still there?"

"I'm waiting. Let's hear it."

CHAPTER TWENTY-EIGHT

Isha fiddled with her seat belt, waiting for something newsworthy to happen. In the driver's seat sat Ralph Malone, the photographer the paper had assigned her. Ralph had been a combat photographer in his twenties but was now in his grizzled late-forties, seen-it-all phase and seemed entirely over this shit. *Shit*, in this case, being work, life, and people, though not necessarily in that order. Sitting in a parked car down the block from Paul Paxton's house with Isha apparently qualified as all three, and he sighed dramatically and often, much to Isha's delight. He was straight out of a Sidney Lumet movie and couldn't have been more perfect. It wasn't an exaggeration to say that this was the single greatest moment of her life.

That was probably why she'd overreacted when Fitz had tried to reassign her. Paul Paxton's nomination was why she'd become a journalist in the first place. How did she know that? Because sitting in a car on a dark residential street in Arlington thrilled her in a way nothing else ever had. How many hours had she spent playing stakeout in her parents' driveway? And now here she was living it. The hardest part was hiding her giddiness from Ralph, who found her enthusiasm irritating and wasn't afraid to let her know it. Isha didn't mind, even if his car did smell like the inside of a vape pen. Having her chops busted by an old-timer just added to the vibes.

"So what do you want? Pictures of his guests walking up to the house?" Ralph asked.

"At the door. Preferably after Paxton answers, so he's in the frame."

"Easy enough," Ralph said, resting his telephoto lens on the steering wheel and lining it up on Paxton's front door. He took a burst of test shots, checked the image finder, and adjusted the settings. "What's the story? This is a poker game or something?"

"Yeah."

"And that's a big deal? 'Supreme Court nominee plays poker at home.' That qualifies as news these days?" he asked with the cynicism of someone who'd taken photographs while under heavy fire.

That depended entirely on who showed up. According to Isha's anonymous source, the Paxton poker game had begun in the late nineties at the dawn of the Texas Hold'em craze. It had been going strong ever since, and once every other week, a rotating cast of friends, rivals, and colleagues would gather at the congressman's home for bourbon, cigars, cards, and backroom dealmaking. Her source had refused to identify herself, but the voice had sounded too young to be in the know, so Isha had run it all by Bernard, who knew about the game anecdotally. He said there was an unsubstantiated rumor that a major provision of Dodd-Frank had been stripped from the bill when three queens lost to a gutshot straight on the river.

They waited. Isha in anticipation, Ralph in a near-catatonic stupor.

A Tesla parked up the block. Ralph sat forward with his camera, but it was only a couple returning home from the grocery store. They unloaded their bags and disappeared into their house.

"Want me to get some pictures? We could break this story wide open: 'Virginia couple shops at Whole Foods,'" Ralph said, holding up his hands as if framing the headline for Isha.

She smirked at him humorlessly, and he went back into hibernation. They waited.

A second car, this time an Audi, turned onto the street and parked outside Paxton's house. Isha recognized the man who got out but couldn't put a name to the face. He was in Congress, but that was the best she could do. There were people in town who could name all 435 voting members. Isha wasn't one of them.

Ralph snapped pictures all the way up the walk and got a great shot of him with Paxton. Over the next half hour, Ralph got pictures of two more congressmen and a uniformed four-star general who Ralph recognized as Thomas Hughes of the Joint Chiefs. Paxton greeted each warmly at the door and invited them inside. The general seemed to turn Ralph around on the entire enterprise. The photog began muttering darkly about the depressing state of the world.

Three congressmen and a member of the Joint Chiefs—it was a good haul but lacked the knockout punch that Isha was hoping for. She had her head down, scrolling through the congressional website, hoping to ID her mystery congressman, when Ralph elbowed her. A black SUV had just parked down the street. Isha was past getting her hopes up. But then John Ridgeway, junior senator from Wisconsin, emerged from the back seat. His name she knew. Only in his first term, but his movie-star looks and easy charisma had made him an instant media darling. That wasn't the above-the-fold headline, though. That distinction belonged to Ridgeway's committee assignment. He sat on Judiciary. This little poker game had just graduated from minor indiscretion to scandalous conflict of interest. Openly socializing with a senator on the committee responsible for your confirmation hearings? Even for DC, it required a brazen arrogance bordering on sociopathy to take this kind of risk.

Ridgeway presented Paxton with a bottle of what she assumed to be a good bourbon from the way Paxton beamed. The camera shutter whirled, capturing shot after shot. Isha watched in disgust but also a kind of awe as the two men glad-handed and preened openly on the front steps without a care in the world. Was this how nature documentarians felt when they recorded an elusive species? The mating ritual of the Washington peacock in its natural habitat . . . note the colorful plumage and distinctive mating dance.

The two men finally disappeared inside. Surely that must be everyone; six was a good number for poker. She should get on the phone to Bernard, share what she'd seen . . . but something told her to wait. Bernard would tell her to come back to the office and get to work. He'd be right too. There was a ton to do before this story would be ready to print.

"What do you think?" she asked Ralph. "Call it?"

"No, you crazy? There's more." Gone was his snarky, dismissive tone, and she caught a glimpse of the man who'd gone to war without a weapon.

"Right?" There was something in the air. She could feel it too.

"Let's give it an hour. See what we see."

Ralph produced a tin of mints, inspected the contents, and popped two into his mouth. He offered the tin to Isha in what felt like an initiation ceremony. She took one and thanked him. Then they waited again. Fifteen minutes, then thirty. She didn't pay any attention to the woman on the sidewalk. Maybe Isha had assumed everyone on the guest list would be a man. But then she recognized the silver hair.

"Holy shit," she whispered.

"What?" Ralph had dozed off but was wide awake now.

"That's Agatha Cross."

"Who?" he asked but started taking pictures without waiting for more information.

Isha watched the congressman's former chief of staff go up the walk and ring the bell. Paxton answered the door. Maybe it was the distance, but Isha couldn't interpret his expression. Not a surprise, really. This was, after all, a man trained in the art of having private conversations in public.

"Are you getting all this?" she asked.

"Damn straight. What do you think they're saying?"

She wished she knew.

Then the unexpected happened. Agatha Cross turned and pointed in their direction. Paul Paxton followed her finger and frowned at what he saw. They'd been made. Isha sank down in her seat even though she knew Paxton couldn't see her in this light. Ralph paid no mind and kept on taking photographs.

Isha was so focused on the events unfolding at the congressman's door that she didn't notice the SUV parked five cars behind them. If she had, she might've recognized it as the same SUV that had been following her for the last week, and the person behind the wheel as the man who'd accidentally knocked her over at Starbucks. He'd been incredibly apologetic, though, and even helped her to pick up her things. It hadn't been a big deal at the time. These things happened.

When Agatha worked on the Hill, there'd always been rumors that she was sleeping with her boss. Congress was a boys' club, so a young, single, female chief of staff? How else had she gotten the job? Never mind that she was damn good at the work; people saw their close working relationship—the energy whenever the two were in the same room, the way they finished the other's thoughts—and assumed the congressman must be wetting his beak. It had been insulting and infuriating until Agatha had figured out how to turn it to her advantage. Then it had been insulting, infuriating, and useful. Being underestimated as the congressman's bimbo had strategic value. It meant no one saw her coming until it was too late.

But people weren't entirely wrong. There *had* been something between them. A spark. She'd loved him; she knew that now. It just hadn't been sexual. Narcissism was more like it. Meeting Paul had been like catching her reflection in the mirror for the first time. A Nietzschean shock of recognition. They were the same. Two cold-blooded sharks swimming the same murky waters, game recognizing game.

Until Paul, Agatha had kept her less-upstanding instincts more or less in check. Denny once told her that he could always spot recruits who'd only joined to have an excuse to kill someone. Paul must have recognized something similar in her, and set her loose. She'd thrived, and the decision to quit had been the hardest thing she'd ever done. But after Charlotte's death, she knew for certain that if she stayed, then there really was no bottom. Nothing she wouldn't say, nothing she wouldn't do. So long as she remained in Paul's orbit, the ends would always justify the means. Working for him was an addiction, and she'd gone halfway around the world and gotten married just to keep temptation at bay. She didn't blame Paul, though. The devil might whisper in your ear, but it was on her for listening.

It all made her a little jittery walking up to his front door. Twenty years had passed, but she vividly remembered the last time they'd seen each other. It had not been a fond farewell. Things had been said, assurances given. And veiled threats, she realized in retrospect. It had been naive of her to think that he would take her at her word when she promised to stay out of his business. And as much as it hurt, she respected his foresight to take those pictures and put her in this box. How long had he been questioning her loyalty? He'd always had a gift for sniffing out other people's weaknesses and planning accordingly. With Paul, there was always an out, always a contingency. That was what she'd most admired about him.

Well, she was clever too.

She rang the bell and took a deep breath, trying to shake off her nerves. It felt akin to stage fright. The moment before a big entrance, wondering if she would remember her lines. But then Paul opened the door—a curtain rising—and, like that, her nerves were gone.

Neither spoke immediately. It was a lot to take in. Looking in the mirror every day, it was easy to stop noticing all the little ways time was catching up with her. It was another thing entirely to see the full power of time etched into the face of someone she hadn't seen up close in years. Decades passed in the blink of an eye—the thinning hair, the paunch, the sun damage from too much time on the golf course. It made her joints ache just looking at him.

"Agatha," he said, breaking the silence between them. Despite the circumstances, he sounded neither surprised nor angry to see her. He'd never been an easy man to fluster. She'd always appreciated that about him, even if she'd been hoping for a little consternation. But, if anything, he had the weary resignation of a principal confronting a problem student for whom he harbored a soft spot and just hoped would stop getting into trouble. "Of all the doorbells, on all the streets, in all the world, you rang mine."

He meant it to be a charmingly off-the-cuff thing to say, but it snapped her back to reality. Of course he thought he was the Bogart in this situation, opposite her, the heartbreaker. Perfectly on brand for a man whose success had been built on the belief that he was the main character in any situation. She found it a whole lot less charming than she once had.

"What exactly are you doing?" she asked.

"Good to see you too."

"You're this close, Paul. This close. So why are you trying so hard to screw it up?"

"It's just a poker game."

"Oh, that's not John Ridgeway from Judiciary in there? Are you out of your mind?"

"He's a friend."

"The problem with you, Paul? You never did know when you'd won."

He smirked at her, and right then and there, she had a long-overdue epiphany about her old boss. It had never been about winning for him, but his need to demonstrate, at every turn, that the rules applied only to those foolish enough to follow them. There was a perverse kind of logic to his wanting a seat on the Supreme Court, where he would have the final say on those same rules.

"I appreciate your concern, but it's under control."

"Under control," she repeated scornfully, pointing at the Honda Accord parked down the block. "Is that what you call a *Post* reporter and photographer taking pictures of your guests?"

The smirk faded to a grave frown. Gingerly, he stepped out of the house to get a better look. "How do you know it's the *Post*?"

"Because the same reporter stopped by my house to ask questions about you."

He actually looked relieved. "Oh, that's just Isha Roy. Don't worry, I've got her covered." He reached for his cell phone and dialed the first name on his favorites' list. It rang and rang, eventually going to voicemail. For the first time, he looked irritated. "Tina, where are you?" he asked and then paused, as though her recorded greeting might answer his question. "Well, call me as soon as you get back from whatever it is you're doing. Our little friend from the *Post* turned up at the house and is taking pictures. Coordinate with the White House's man and put a lid on it. Call me back."

"Good help is so hard to find," Agatha commiserated.

"Where the hell is she?" he asked rhetorically, making another call, this one answered. "Felix, my boy, glad someone is burning the midnight oil. We have an Isha Roy situation." He quickly laid it out in broad strokes. "Tina tells me you have a relation with this woman. Any chance you can convince her to stand down?" From the look on Paul's face, the answer was no. "Well, try bartering a trade. Think of something. Is there anything the *Post* wants more? A sit-down interview, maybe. That's got to be more alluring than an innocent poker game."

Agatha turned her head. If she didn't roll her eyes soon, her head was going to twist off like a bottle top. She saw Isha Roy walking toward them. Paul hadn't noticed yet, but things were about to get real interesting. Bracing herself for impact, Agatha thought through what she would say.

Suddenly the reporter stopped in the middle of the street to answer her phone. Whatever the caller said had quite an effect, because Isha Roy turned and ran back toward her car. Isha assumed that was Paul's doing. More of his political black magic. But he seemed as surprised as Agatha.

"I wonder what that was about," Paul said.

"That wasn't you?"

"Sadly, no."

The car's headlights came on before it made a jerky three-point turn and sped away.

Paul's phone began to ring.

CHAPTER TWENTY-NINE

Sitting in the dark of the car, Isha had needed a minute to reach a decision. Should she go back to the office and write up what she had, or should she confront Paxton and Cross? That they knew she was there and continued to talk fearlessly out in the open profoundly offended her. She tried calling Bernard to get his advice, but both his cell and work phone went to voicemail.

It was Ralph who broke the deadlock. "Don't let these bastards off the hook. Challenge them. Now. Get 'em on the record before they have their stories straight."

"What if they just go inside the house and don't answer the door?" Direct confrontation had never been her strongest suit. The job had thickened her skin, but she didn't relish it the way some of her colleagues did.

"Are you kidding me?" Ralph said, grinning at the prospect. "That's the best of all possible outcomes. Then you can write that they ran away and hid. Pray they do something that stupid."

Good advice. Gathering her nerve, Isha stepped out of the car. She was halfway across the street and building up a righteous head of steam when her phone rang. It was Bernard. She hesitated to answer, afraid of her momentum seeping away, but he was the boss.

"Bern, I'm at Paxton's. Agatha Cross is on his front steps."

"That's interesting," he said, sounding anything but interested. "Is Ralph still with you?"

"Yeah, why?" she asked, confused by the question.

"Forget about poker. I've got something more important."

"More important?" She was instantly upset. "I've got two congressmen, a four-star general, and Ridgeway from Judiciary hanging out with a Supreme Court nominee. What could be more important?"

"Tina Lu is dead."

"What?" she said, but her feet were already turning back to the car.

Bernard laid it out for her. "I don't think anyone's got this yet but us. We picked it up almost by accident, so we have a head start. I'm going to text you an address. Get there now."

Isha hung up without another word and ran for the car.

Fair to say Agatha's day had not turned out how she'd expected. Of all the outcomes she'd envisioned from confronting Paul, chauffeuring him uptown hadn't made the list. She still didn't know who the call had been from, but Paul had reacted like he'd taken a bullet. All she could get out of him was that Tina Lu had been in an accident. It took a lot to rattle Paul Paxton, and seeing how pale he had turned gave her a chill. He kept muttering Tina's name under his breath, maybe hoping that the news would change if he repeated it often enough. After unceremoniously throwing out his poker guests, he asked Agatha to drive him. As if not a day had passed and she still worked for him. But who was she to say no? She was a big believer that a little well-timed chaos was the mother of opportunity. That was why she'd had Shelby tip Isha Roy off to the poker game. But this was a thousand times better. Without Tina, Paul would be on tilt, and Agatha meant to keep him there.

They drove in silence for a time, Agatha keeping one eye on the road and one on her old boss. Either he'd become too good a liar for her to know the difference anymore, or he was genuinely devastated by the news. A stray, unwanted question occurred to her: Would he have reacted the same to her own death back in the day? Agatha shook the question off like an unwanted hug and wondered what the hell was wrong with her that she still gave a damn what Paul thought about anything. She didn't, but at the same time, she did. It was infuriating, and she reminded herself what he'd done to Charlotte Haines.

Paul finally broke the silence. "It was you, wasn't it? You tipped the *Post* tonight."

She saw no reason to deny it.

"That was childish, Agatha."

"So was threatening someone who knows where the bodies are buried and doesn't have anything to lose. That was a bad play, Paul."

He found the button on his door that controlled the window and let it down a few inches. "Perhaps it was a little heavy-handed. Tina can get out over her skis when her back is up."

"Just try and keep in mind that everything I did, you did."

"You always were pithy," he said admiringly. "But *you* keep in mind who is in those pictures and who is not."

"I think of little else," she replied and eased the car to a stop.

They'd arrived at Tina Lu's building, or as close as they would get by car. The police had set up roadblocks at both ends of the road, and traffic was being diverted down side streets. Agatha leaned forward and rested her arms on top of the steering wheel. Beyond the barricade, two ambulances and a fire truck blocked the street outside the apartment building's entrance. They'd really called all units to the scene. But why two ambulances for one woman? That didn't make any sense, and her uneasy feeling redoubled. She glanced over at Paul, a shadow in her passenger seat. *What had happened here?*

Spotting a gap, Agatha made a hard U-turn and sped back the way they'd come. There was nowhere to park, at least not legally, so she pulled into an alley and killed the engine. Paul had brought a Nationals cap and put it on now, pulling it down low over his eyes. Anywhere else in the country, she'd have laughed at him for worrying about being recognized. But in this town, he was what passed for a celebrity.

They walked back to the police line, where onlookers had gathered along the tape. Some were recording on phones, hoping for something worth posting online to happen. Others speculated on what was going on. Agatha slipped up beside two men in their midtwenties with immaculately groomed beards and scrambled hair.

"What happened?" she asked.

"Lady jumped off the building," said the taller of the two.

"You don't know she jumped," the man's companion in the Golden State jersey said. "Could've fallen."

"Who falls off a building?" the first man asked, irritated by the interruption. "Seriously."

"Seen it in a parkour video on TikTok. Dudes run around the tops of buildings. Sometimes they slip."

"Bro, that woman wasn't doing parkour."

"Just saying. You don't know it was suicide."

A young woman in a sweatshirt and pajama bottoms gave the men a withering look. "She isn't dead. She landed on the fence, but she didn't die. They're trying to figure out how to get her off without killing her."

Everyone along the police line quieted and turned to stare at the black wrought-iron fence circling the building. A collective shudder shot through them as they each pictured it.

"You saw it?" Agatha said.

"I was walking Jasper." The woman gestured to the dachshund at her feet, who looked up as if to confirm her story. "It was messed up."

The crowd murmured its agreement at the truth of her assessment. It was, as she said, messed up. Agatha looked back for Paul, who had been standing right behind her. He'd taken the opportunity to vanish. Stepping out of the crowd, she spotted his red baseball cap bobbing hurriedly away down the side street. She caught up to him in the small parking lot behind Tina's apartment building.

"Where are you going?" she demanded.

"I need to get into her apartment."

"She's still alive."

He stopped and looked at the building as if he could see through it to where Tina Lu was impaled on a fence. He shook his head as if reaching a hard decision. "There's nothing I can do for her."

It suddenly all made sense. He wasn't devastated that Tina Lu was likely going to die. That wasn't why he'd gone pale. All that mattered was how it affected him. Same as it ever was. "Why? What's up there?"

He didn't answer, but his expression gave her a pretty good idea.

"The pictures?" she demanded. "Are the pictures up there?"

"Not all of them." He cautioned her with a shushing gesture and peered around the empty parking lot.

"The ones of me?"

He shrugged innocently. "It seemed like the safest place for them."

"You're killing me here." She clutched the back of her neck with both hands and looked at her feet so she didn't have to look at him. Sooner or later the police would search Tina's apartment, and then she was finished. "How do we get in?"

He held up a set of keys. "For emergencies."

"Where are the pictures in the apartment?" she asked and reached for the keys. His hand became a fist around them, and he shrank back like she might mug him. "Fine." She shrugged. "You go up there and get them. I'll wait here."

It didn't look like he was overly fond of that idea either. She could see the tiny cogs and gears of his paranoid, Swiss-watch mind turning, calculating.

"We'll go up together," he said, managing to make it sound like he was doing her a favor.

"After you," she said.

He didn't move, and this time when she reached for the keys, he let her take them.

Isha had to hand it to the police. They had the scene locked down and cordoned off. Emergency vehicles had been parked in a vee in front of the building, creating a blind to prevent anyone from recording their rescue attempt. Ralph was reduced to photographing the uniforms responsible for crowd control. A plainclothes detective emerged from between the two ambulances. Ralph called out and waved him over. To her surprise, the detective came.

"Hey, Don," Ralph said.

"Ralph. You got a smoke?" the detective asked, shaking Ralph's hand.

Ralph produced a pack from his windbreaker and didn't blink when the detective took two. The detective had to be forty, and likely had at least fifteen years on the job, but he looked as pale and shaky as a rookie on his first call.

"Bad one?" Ralph asked, holding out his lighter.

The detective cupped a hand around the flame and lit his cigarette. "Woman fell."

"From where?"

"The roof, we think," he said with a world-weary shrug. As if to say, it didn't much matter from where a person fell, only where they landed. "There's a pool area up there."

Ralph craned his neck to look at the roof, twelve stories above. "Bad way to go."

"Oh, she didn't."

"Didn't what?" Isha asked.

"Go," the detective said. "She lives. Got impaled on a fence. Still is."

"How did that not kill her?" Isha asked.

"Hell if I know. It's the craziest thing I ever saw."

"Is she conscious?"

"She's in shock, doesn't feel a thing," the detective said, taking a long drag on his cigarette. "But she's not exactly what I'd call coherent either. EMTs say there's no way to remove her without killing her.

They've called in welders to cut out that section of fence. Gonna transport it all to the hospital and let the docs figure it out. Waste of time, you ask me."

"Why?" Isha asked.

"Because she's dead. Her body just don't know it yet." The detective dropped the cigarette and stubbed it out with his shoe. "I gotta get back. Thanks for the smoke."

"Don," Ralph said by way of a goodbye.

"Ralph," the detective replied, looking in Isha's direction but saying nothing. Isha watched him until he disappeared behind an ambulance. It was strange to think that just out of sight a woman's life was ending, while for everyone else it was just an inconvenience at the end of another day. Her eyes drifted over to the police line across the street, where a crowd had gathered. Some were probably tired and inconvenienced, others excited for the story they would have to tell, while one or two were reporters angling to turn tragedy into headlines. Those were her people.

She straightened. *Is that Agatha Cross?* She elbowed Ralph, who trained his camera where she was pointing.

"Is that her?"

"I'll do you one better," Ralph said, focusing his telephoto lens. "Paul Paxton's right behind her."

Felix would be the first one to admit that he'd had better days. First, there'd been the shit show at Paul Paxton's residence. What kind of jackass throws a poker game with a sitting member of Senate Judiciary as a nominee to the Supreme Court? Felix wanted to throttle Paxton for dumping that in his lap. It reminded him of something his mother used to say about her brother, who'd struggled with drugs most of his life: you can't help someone who won't help themselves. Paxton seemed to have a different kind of addiction, one to unnecessary risks. There was nothing worse than an adrenaline junkie in politics. No, scratch that—there was nothing worse than having to cover for an adrenaline junkie in politics.

The good news was he'd gotten a heads-up from Sam, who'd been keeping tabs on Isha. The bad news? Sam knew because he'd trailed her to the congressman's front door. It wasn't the end of the world, but with all the other smoke surrounding the nomination, it wouldn't make anyone's life easier. Felix had tried to coordinate with Tina Lu to contain the situation, but she hadn't been answering her phone. Now he knew why.

Standing outside her apartment, he felt bad for some of the names he'd called her. They'd never liked each other, but no one deserved this. Not that he had the luxury of grieving for her, even if they'd been friends. He had a job to do, and she was now another fire to be put out.

"Where are you?" Felix asked into his burner phone.

"Out back behind the building."

Felix didn't know the man's real name, but he'd come to appreciate the calm professionalism of "Sam." Rely on it, even. This whole Paul Paxton situation had been slippery from the get-go, but it now felt on the verge of spinning out of control. Felix didn't know what he was supposed to do. How far was he really authorized to take things? Nothing had been clearly articulated, only hinted at in vague terms. He felt more and more like a castaway. Supposedly Steve Gilroy was his point of contact, but the chief of staff didn't want to hear from him. Felix had called for guidance on the drive over, but Gilroy hadn't picked up. Felix had hung up and screamed at the dead phone in frustration.

Pushing his way through the vultures gathered along the yellow police tape, he walked down the road that ran along the side of the building. In back was a residential parking lot that extended down a slight slope to a wall of trees that marked the edge of the property.

"Where are you?" Felix asked.

"Here."

A man stepped out of the shadow of a large recycling dumpster beside the loading dock. Felix jumped and felt his soul momentarily leave his body. He hoped that cursing and walking in circles would convince it to return.

"Sam?"

"That's right." The man beckoned him into the shadow of the loading dock.

Felix had imagined someone larger, but Sam was average height, average build. He looked to be in his forties, although there was an assured athleticism to how he carried himself. A thin sheaf of brown hair was brushed forward, ending in a small swell like a wave breaking. The sides were high and tight, which Felix sensed was less a nod to fashion and more a vestige of his background. Felix had been around enough former military operators at the White House to recognize a veteran of foreign wars. The boots were a dead giveaway. His clothes weren't stylish, but everything had been carefully chosen. He wore a loose-fitting windbreaker although there'd been no wind today at all. Felix speculated briefly about what was concealed under it.

"I thought you said we were never going to meet."

"No, I said if we met, it would mean something had gone really wrong."

"Has it?"

"Well, depends on whether you buy that the woman jumped."

Felix hadn't thought about it. Paul Paxton's chief of staff killing herself seemed like crisis enough for one night. But now that Sam said it out loud, suicide didn't vibe with the Tina Lu he knew.

"You think she was thrown? You know that for a fact?"

Sam shook his head. "Does any of this feel right to you?"

It didn't, although maybe that was down to Sam's calm and reasoned voice putting the idea in his head. "Who, then? Why?"

"No idea, but until we know different, it might be a good idea to assume we have an unknown actor in play."

"Where is Isha now?"

"She went in the back entrance a few minutes ago," Sam said and gestured past the loading dock.

That wasn't great.

"She was following Paul Paxton."

"*Paxton's* here?"

"Yeah, he had keys. He's with the same woman who showed up at his place earlier."

Sam described a woman who could only be Agatha Cross. Felix stood corrected. This might very well be the end of days. What the hell was Paxton *doing*? The only reason for him to be here would be to stand out front, attract as many cameras as possible, and weep for the loss of a beloved staffer. Instead, he was sneaking in the back like a thief. The really troubling part was that Paul knew better, which meant he had his reasons. Reasons Felix felt sure he wanted no part of but was, once again, about to be drawn into.

"Can we get in too?" Felix asked.

"The police have the lobby locked down. Maybe we can talk our way past them, but it's a risk. I don't know we want them taking your name."

"What about the loading dock?"

"Locked up tight. I can break in, but there are cameras."

"Where's that door lead?" Felix said, meaning the plain, unmarked door without a handle or a keyhole. He knew the answer, but he was playing for time. Asking pointless questions at least gave the impression he was coming up with a plan. He wasn't, but it beat standing there with a stupid look on his face.

"Fire exit," Sam answered. "No way in without a crowbar."

"Right, right."

"What do you want me to do?" Sam asked patiently, like a teacher waiting on a struggling student to do the math.

"What are my options?"

"Anything. You just have to tell me."

Anything? Why did the open-endedness of that scare Felix so badly?

CHAPTER THIRTY

Tina Lu lived in an older apartment building in Northwest that pre-dated the nineties real-estate boom. Attempts had been made to update it, but the thick burgundy carpet and ornate crown molding felt dated in a way that made Agatha nostalgic for the city of her youth.

She led Paul down a hall, past the mail room, to a bored uni-formed officer camped out on a stool like a doorman at a bar. Police and medical personnel had commandeered the lobby. They looked busy without actually being busy, and a feeling of helplessness hung in the air. Outside, a knot of EMTs stood around a makeshift tent that had been erected over a portion of the iron fence. They looked to Agatha like people with a job to do but no earthly idea how to begin. She didn't like to imagine the scene inside the tent.

Call her an optimist, but she didn't get the impression the police were treating this as a crime scene. They seemed focused on saving Tina Lu's life, which meant there was a chance that no one had been inside her apartment yet. The thought gave Agatha hope while also planting the seeds of an uneasy question. *Was* this a crime scene?

"You live here?" the officer asked, sounding disenchanted with the conversation already.

Agatha held up the keys. "Six-oh-four."

"Okay," he said as if that proved a thing. "Just do me a favor. Go straight up."

"Of course," Agatha said. "What's happening out there?"

"Woman fell. They're trying to help her."

"She's alive?" Agatha said and gripped Paul's arm as though she might faint.

Paul played his part, patting her hand reassuringly. "That's a long way down."

"That's why it will be a big help if you and your husband go straight upstairs."

"We will, Officer," Paul said in the stentorian voice that had won him reelection time and again.

Good to their word, they went directly to the elevators. Paul hit the up button while Agatha waved back to the officer, who had lost interest and gone back to his phone. When the elevator opened, Paul pressed five over and over until the doors finally closed. He hadn't volunteered Tina's apartment number, and Agatha hadn't asked. It seemed like a good idea to let him feel in charge.

They got off on Tina's floor. No cops. Another good sign, unless they were already inside the apartment, waiting. They went down the carpeted hall. Paul stopped outside 512 and pointed a finger like one of Scrooge's ghosts. Agatha put an ear to the door, but only silence answered. Moment of truth. After slipping the key into the lock, she cracked the door a few inches. It was dark inside and still resolutely quiet. She opened the door wide enough to slip across the threshold. Paul followed, reaching for the light switch.

"Leave it off," Agatha whispered. There was enough light from the street to see, and she didn't want anyone down on the street wondering why the lights in Tina Lu's apartment were suddenly on.

The front hall was empty apart from a small table, a mirror, and a row of hooks that held a light coat and an umbrella that its owner would never need again. The table was stacked with mail and a small dish with a set of keys, assorted coins, and a green dry cleaning ticket.

Since it was an older building, the living room and the cramped galley kitchen were separate. The kitchen was unusually clean, although Agatha sensed that was because it rarely saw use. The refrigerator confirmed her suspicions. It was more or less empty: a twelve-pack of LaCroix, a Brita with an inch of water at the bottom, soy milk, assorted condiments, a carton of eggs past their expiration date, and takeout from two different restaurants. Nothing in the freezer but a gel eye mask, an unopened bottle of vodka, and an ice tray with one lonely cube. Agatha filled the tray in the sink and put it back.

"What are you doing?" Paul asked.

Agatha didn't know how to explain. It could have been her kitchen twenty years ago. She'd always viewed Tina Lu as a rival but now felt a camaraderie with her successor that Paul would neither understand nor appreciate.

"Well, come on then," he said and went into the living room.

She murmured agreement but then hesitated at the door. The knife block on the kitchen counter was empty. That was odd. Puzzling over what it meant, she followed Paul, who was in the living room staring at the coffee table.

"The hell is that about?" he asked rhetorically.

All the missing knives were laid out on a glass-topped coffee table, arranged meticulously from largest to smallest, blades all facing to the right. Agatha knew a threat when she saw one. Snatching up the butcher's knife, she moved quickly through the apartment, opening closets, checking under the bed. In the bathroom, she yanked back the shower curtain and flinched, half expecting someone to leap out at her. It was empty, and she chided herself to knock it off.

Reasonably certain that they were alone, she went back to the living room, where Paul was still studying the knives as if deciphering ancient hieroglyphics. Behind him the glass door to the apartment's small balcony was open. She'd forgotten all about it, and wasn't it always the last place you looked? But the only thing out there was a small metal table and one chair, which lay on its side. Everything seemed foreboding and menacing; Agatha told herself to knock it off, since she certainly hadn't listened the first time.

"Does anything else look out of place?" she asked, hoping to nudge Paul out of his daze.

"I don't know," he said without looking up from the coffee table. "I've only been here once."

"Fine. So where are the photos? *Paul*," she said sternly, "look at me. Where are the photos?"

"Right," he said as if just now remembering why they'd come.

"Paul . . . ?" she prompted again. "Where are they?"

"In there," he said with an infuriating nonchalance and wandered off toward the bedroom.

She couldn't make sense of it at first. There was no sense of urgency to him, no acknowledgment of the danger they were in. The Paul Paxton she remembered was a decision-maker, bold and confident. This version of him seemed at a loss for what to do. Then she realized what it was. This wasn't his world. Put him in an office or a high-stakes meeting, and he was ice cold. But he'd spent thirty years fighting dirty without actually getting directly involved. He'd always had people for that. People like Darius and Tina and, of course, herself. The dirtiest of them all.

The floor of Tina's closet doubled as her laundry basket. Paul shoveled her clothes unceremoniously onto the bed. Underneath was a small black hotel safe with an electronic lock. He took a knee and punched in the combination while Agatha stood at the bedroom door, listening, the feeling of imminent danger clinging to her.

She heard Paul curse. In his hands was a stack of documents and folders that he sorted through angrily.

"They're not here," he said.

"Are you sure?"

"I've been through everything twice."

Somehow it didn't surprise her. The knives. The fall. Someone had been here for the photos. Tina Lu had traded them for her life. It hadn't been enough.

"We need to go," she said.

Paul started checking the folders again. "Give me a minute, damn it."

"They're not there. Someone took them. We have to go." This *was* a crime scene now, and it was only a matter of time before the police worked that out for themselves.

"What do you mean, 'someone took them'? Who?"

"The hell if I know. Someone who wanted them badly enough to throw your chief of staff off her balcony. Maybe if we hang around long enough, they'll come back."

She'd meant it sarcastically, but he took her exactly at her word.

"You really think so?"

"No, they're not coming back. My guess is they're on the way to collect the rest of your photos. Assuming Tina knew where they are."

"She would never do that." He seemed genuinely affronted that there might be limits on the loyalty of his people. "Maybe she jumped. You know what the job is like. It gets to people."

"You could maybe sound less excited about suicide."

"I am not," he said in a how-dare-you tone. "I'm just saying it's a possibility."

"You think she laid her kitchen knives out on the coffee table, saw a watermark, and decided to jump? That how you think it went?"

The thought of the knives seemed to shake him. "Jesus . . . ," he whispered under his breath. "You really think she talked?"

"Wouldn't you?"

"And then they threw her out the window anyway? What kind of monster would do that?"

"Paul," Agatha snapped at him. "You're blackmailing the president of the United States. We'll be lucky if there's only one monster."

That finally seemed to light a fire under him. He dumped the folders on the ground and climbed to his feet. "I have to get home."

So that was where the photos were: good to know. Wasn't a smart move to leave things a mess, though, so she stooped to gather everything up and slid it all back into the safe. The electronic lock engaged, and she scooped the dirty clothes off the bed and back into the closet. Paul asked her what she was doing, but she ignored him. There was no time for his inane questions.

Next, the knives all went back in the kitchen. She wiped them down with a Virginia Beach 10-Miler T-shirt from the dirty-clothes pile and slipped them back into the block. The extras went into the dishwasher. She made a lap around the apartment, wiping down anything she remembered them touching. Would the police dust an ice-cube tray? She decided not.

"Can we go now?" Paul asked from the entry hall.

Honestly, she was surprised he'd waited for her. Did he assume she would so easily fall back under his sway? He *was* just that arrogant. Plus, Tina Lu was gone. He would need someone to fill those shoes. That might be useful, she thought. Well, if that was the role he needed her to play, she could fit the bill. When he reached for the door, she told him to wait.

"What?" he said, pulling back his hand like the handle had given him a shock.

"Let me go first. Take a look. Someone could be out there."

"Good idea."

She opened the door and leaned halfway into the hall. Down at the far end, Isha Roy was just getting off the elevator. Agatha didn't know why she was surprised. The reporter didn't appear to have any quit in her, which, ordinarily, Agatha would have admired. Right now, though, it was a pain in her ass. Ducking back into the apartment, she told Paul to stay put.

"What's going on?" he asked.

"There's a cop. I'll get rid of him."

He nodded, profound gratitude etched into his liar's face, and took hold of her wrist. "Thank you."

Good boy, Agatha thought and gave him an adoring smile that she hoped wasn't overdoing things. "I'll be right back."

Isha stepped off the elevator and into the dimly lit hallway. This was an old building, but for the kind of rent it charged, they could have splurged for bulbs that gave off more than a single match strike of light. She'd followed Paul Paxton to the rear entrance and slipped in behind a resident. Talking her way past the police had been disappointingly easy. Isha didn't actually know where Tina Lu lived in the building, so she'd stopped off on the second floor and put in a call to Bern. He hadn't been entirely happy to hear she was in the building but relented and tracked down the apartment number with the proviso that she be careful and call if things took a turn.

She might have rolled her eyes at his warning. What was the worst that could happen? Paxton was only a congressman.

But now, up on five, her nerves were getting the best of her. She cursed Bern for putting ideas in her head. The building was just too quiet, and she was thinking twice about her decision to leave Ralph out front to take pictures. She'd assumed Tina Lu's neighbors might be out talking and consoling each other, but the hallway was deserted. This was an American city, after all; no one knew their neighbors and thought that was something to be proud about.

Paxton and Cross were nowhere to be seen, so either she'd missed them or they were inside Tina Lu's apartment. Maybe they had a set of keys? Either way, something shady was happening—she could feel it. So what now? *Be bold, knock on the door, and confront them,* a voice that sounded suspiciously like a young, cocky Robert Redford replied. Easy for him to say. It wasn't him alone in this tomb of a building. Taking a deep breath, she started down the hall toward 512. She hadn't taken more than three steps, though, when a door opened and Agatha Cross stepped out. The two women froze and stared at each other like old high school frenemies who hadn't seen each other in years. It would have been comical if Isha hadn't felt so tense. Even in the gloom, she could see Cross debating what to do. Fight or flight.

To Isha's surprise, Cross started down the hall toward her. Isha took a half step back. Agatha Cross intimidated her for reasons she couldn't articulate. But she caught herself and, setting her feet, waited for whatever might come. It wasn't what she expected.

"I'm impressed," Agatha said.

"Thanks?"

"But I need you to turn around and leave."

"Oh, I bet you do," Isha said. "You and Paxton are up to something sketchy."

"Yes, we are," Agatha agreed.

The straightforwardness of her reply knocked Isha momentarily off-balance. "What?"

"And you're going to screw everything up if you hang around right now."

"That's kind of my job."

"No, your job is to get the story."

"Is Paul Paxton in that apartment right now?"

Agatha stared hard into her eyes. "Yes."

"Well, that's my story. I'm not going anywhere."

Cross gave her a disappointed look that made Isha wonder if she knew Bern somehow. "Concerned boss checking on his chief of staff who gave him a set of keys for emergencies. Please. An intern on their first day could spin their way out of this. *Why* is he in the apartment? That's your story."

"And you're going to tell me?"

Agatha paused like a diver on a high board looking down at the water far below. "Yes. If you leave now."

"Oh, you're so full of shit. You've been dodging me from the beginning."

"How'd you end up at the congressman's house tonight?"

"I got a tip," Isha snapped back before catching Cross's meaning. "That was you?"

"That was me. And you're welcome," Agatha said with a half smile.

"What game are you playing?"

The smile vanished, replaced by a look of profound sadness. "I'm trying to fix something that's probably unfixable. Tried to avoid it. Couldn't."

"What is it?"

"You're smart. That's obvious. You know something's going on, right?"

"Obviously."

"But the thing is you can't prove any of it. You've got nothing but your gut, and your boss won't take your gut's word for it, will they?"

Isha shook her head.

"That's the problem with a conspiracy. Unless you can get someone on the inside to talk, you just wind up sounding like a crackpot."

Isha had been telling herself this for days. Agatha Cross was about the last person in the world she'd expected to sympathize. "So there is a conspiracy. How big?"

"You have no idea."

"Does it involve the president?"

Isha would have been lying if she said she didn't enjoy the surprise on Cross's face.

"Okay, maybe you do have some idea."

"So tell me," Isha pressed.

Agatha shook her off. "Here's my best offer. Leave. Now. And I'll tell you everything I know within the next forty-eight hours. Or you can stay and run with your 'congressman seen exiting apartment' story. I'm sure they'll give you the Pulitzer for that bombshell."

Isha studied Agatha's expression. She didn't want to believe a word of this, especially because she felt herself being swayed. Despite this woman's reputation, which was the kind of thing rattlesnakes told their kids to scare them. The only thing Isha knew was that she never wanted to be in a high-stakes poker game with Agatha Cross. But then again, wasn't that what this was? A gamble between a small win now versus a massive pot later?

"Help me fix this," Agatha said. "Please."

Don't be this gullible, Isha lectured herself and then opened her mouth and said, "Okay."

"Really?" Agatha said, genuinely surprised. "I thought for sure you were going to go the other way."

"So did I. Maybe I should."

"Trust me. This will put you in the pantheon."

"I swear, if you're playing me . . ."

Agatha Cross grinned at the thought. "Wouldn't that be a move? But for once, it's not. You have my word, for all that's worth. Now, please, get the hell out of here."

Isha nodded and started back toward the elevator.

"Hey, do me a favor," Cross said.

"Another?"

"Take the stairs."

CHAPTER THIRTY-ONE

"Sir . . . ?" Sam said to Felix, glancing around the side of the loading dock toward the building's rear entrance.

So far Felix had watched Paul Paxton, Agatha Cross, and Isha all go inside. None had come out, and Felix could hear the growing impatience in Sam's voice. Not insubordinate, not yet, but the unmistakable tone of a man with serious concerns about the competence of his commanding officer.

"Just give me a minute." Felix was stalling for time, and they both knew it. If he waited long enough, the decision would get made for him. The coward's way out. Felix had seen it happen at the White House. As the pressure mounted, people either made a call or became paralyzed by indecision. His impression had always been that it was better to act than stand pat. Easy advice to give when it wasn't your head on the chopping block.

"We're on a bit of a clock, sir. Minutes we don't have."

Felix looked at his phone with the vague intention of trying Steve Gilroy again. What was the point, though? Even if Gilroy did answer, which was unlikely, he wasn't going to offer anything but more doublespeak, each word carefully chosen to be vague and open to interpretation—plausible deniability in case this thing blew up in their faces. Correction: in Felix's face. In this game of hot potato, Felix would be the only one with burned hands. They wouldn't have dangled a Senate run in front of his eyes otherwise. Risk/reward.

But did he still want it? That was the question. If so, it was time for him to earn it.

He'd reached the conclusion that President Clark owed Paxton. There was no other explanation for the hoops the administration was jumping through to put an unqualified congressman with a dubious reputation on the court. But Felix had begun to wonder whether it was more than a matter of misplaced loyalty. What if Paxton had something on the president? Something that had gotten Tina Lu thrown off a building, as Sam was implying. If so, was Felix thinking too small? If protecting Paul Paxton's nomination would get Felix into the Senate, what prize could he demand if he eliminated the threat to Clark altogether?

Behind Sam, the fire door swung open. Isha stepped out into the night. She locked eyes with Felix, who felt his brain going blank.

"What are *you* doing here?" she asked, the door swinging shut with a resounding thud.

There was no good answer, although he didn't suspect she'd need one for long. Behind the question, he could hear her putting the pieces together—and too fast for his comfort.

Her eyes narrowed. "You're still working for the White House."

"I was just in the area." It sounded weak even as he said it.

Isha looked at Sam for the first time, just a quick glance, but a glimmer of recognition caused her to give him a second look. "I know him. I know you."

"Miss," Sam said gently, putting his hands up as if cautioning someone who had wandered into a minefield from taking another ill-advised step.

"The Starbucks . . . you knocked me over. Have you been following me?" Isha turned back to Felix without waiting for an answer. "Does he work for you?"

"You really need to go," Felix pleaded.

"Me? *I* need to go? Have you lost your mind? You're the one who needs to get far, far away from this."

Sam drifted back over to the edge of the loading dock to keep an eye on the roadway behind the building. His head was shaking as if he couldn't believe his ears.

Seeing that her words were having no effect on Felix, Isha took his hand and held it in both of hers.

"Please, Felix. Please. Whatever you're doing. Stop," she said, studying his face. "I'll make a deal with you. Go. Now. I'll forget I saw you here. You don't have to be a part of this. It's not too late."

Felix smiled, but he'd stopped listening. His thoughts had returned to the day he and Isha had met. Dinner at the Cottage Club; they'd argued about, of all things, the Bear Stearns bailout. The future politician and the future star reporter locked in a heated debate. He remembered Stephanie kneeing him under the table, both having that feeling when you recognize that a stranger will be in your life a long time.

In the background, Sam caught his eye. He'd slipped up behind Isha and was gesturing with his head. Something was happening around the corner, something that required Felix's immediate attention. Silently, Sam posed the big question: what to do about Isha, who realized too late that she'd lost Felix's attention. She started to turn, following his eyes. Panicked, Felix nodded to Sam even if he didn't know exactly what he was agreeing to.

Taking that as his cue, Sam slipped one arm around Isha's neck, nestling her throat against the crook of his elbow, while his other arm formed a bar behind her head. Felix recognized a choke hold from watching MMA, but he'd never seen one performed any smoother, as if Sam and Isha had practiced beforehand to get it just right. Eyes going wide, Isha struggled, but it wasn't close to a fair fight and was over almost before it began. There was only so long a person could fight without oxygen to the brain.

Felix wanted to demand what the hell Sam was doing. Pretend not to know what he'd been asked. But it was done now. What was the point of feigning innocence? Instead, he asked what was going on behind the building.

"Paxton and that woman are talking to someone."

"Who?"

"No idea," Sam said, lowering Isha gently to the ground. "What do you want me to do with her?"

Felix looked at his friend, if he could even call her that now. "Get her out of here."

Sam nodded.

"Sam—whatever your name is," Felix said. "Take her home. Leave her somewhere safe."

"Sir?" Sam asked as if he might not have heard correctly.

"Nothing happens to her."

Sam clearly didn't agree but nodded that he understood. "What are you going to do?"

"I'm going to deal with this mess."

"Alone?"

"It's my job."

———————

Agatha pressed "G" and stood slightly behind Paul so she could watch him. It was funny. She hadn't seen him in twenty years, but she still knew him. Nothing essential about him had changed other than his waistline. He still chewed his lip when he was thinking and absently kneaded the skin around his thumb when he was nervous. Up in the apartment, he'd been running on adrenaline, but now the enormity of his mess was penetrating the optimistic force field that buffered him against the vagaries of a political life. In a mere four floors, she watched his mood disintegrate like a time-lapse recording of a flower wilting and dying. It wouldn't last, but for the moment he was vulnerable.

"I'm sorry," he said around the third floor.

"For what?"

He would need to be a lot more specific.

Paul gestured to the air. "All this."

"Just shut the fuck up, Paul. Okay? Can you do that?"

"Okay," he agreed and then, because he could never not have the last word: "But I am."

Irritated, she punched the stop button, and the elevator lurched to a halt. An alarm bell began to ring.

"Why do you even want to be on the Supreme Court?" she demanded. "Can you at least answer me that?"

He seemed caught off guard, as if she were the first person to ask. "What are you talking about? Who wouldn't?"

"No, come on, I'm serious. What's the angle? Because I'm not seeing it."

"Why does there need to be an angle?"

"Because you're you."

"Sorry to disappoint," he said, managing to sound offended.

"Moving to the court takes you out of the game. You're going to be bored."

"Would you believe me if I said I'm over it?"

"No," Agatha said flatly. "Politics is your life."

"It's not what it used to be. There's no honor to it anymore—"

"Paul," she said, interrupting him. "If you want me to take you seriously, it will help if you don't use words like *honor*."

"I'm serious. The hypocrisy. The brinksmanship. The Hill is just an endless hamster wheel. Everyone's a bad actor now."

"And you liked it better when you were the only one?"

He acknowledged the point with a frown. "I just want to do something meaningful with my life, something good."

She hadn't laughed so hard in a long time. "You're blackmailing the president of the United States so you can do some good? Do I have that right?"

"Well, when you put it like that . . ."

"Like how it is?" she asked. "That's got to be about the most Paul Paxton thing I've ever heard."

"Are you about done?"

"Not as done as Tina Lu," she muttered under her breath and started the elevator moving.

In the sudden quiet, Paul muttered, "That was uncalled for."

"Was it?"

Paul punched the stop button again. The alarm filled the elevator cab. "You have something you want to say to me?"

"Yeah, I do," she said, getting into his face. "I know you gave the drugs to Charlotte."

Whatever he'd expected her to say, that hadn't been it, and the gap between expectation and reality left him momentarily vulnerable. Agatha used the opening to ask the question that had been troubling her since Darius stopped by her house. This was the only shot she'd ever get, and even so, Paul wouldn't answer. Not directly. The truth would be in his eyes, but only for a moment and only visible to someone who knew him as well as she hoped she did.

"And you knew the drugs were laced. You killed her, didn't you?"

He took his time answering her, and when he did, it was with a voice full of weary disappointment. "Is that really what you think of me?"

"You tell me what to think."

He sighed and looked her in the eyes. "Yes, I gave the drugs to Darius to give to Charlotte. That's true, and I have to live with that. But, no, I didn't know they were laced with anything."

"Swear to me."

"I didn't know. I swear."

Agatha nodded and released the stop button. The elevator shuddered back to life, plunged once more into silence.

"Are we good?" he asked.

"We're good," she said and then added, "Sorry."

He'd always loved the sound of an apology, and she needed him to have that to savor. To be distracted. Because it had been there. She'd seen it. The faintest hesitation, a tremor in his jaw. He'd murdered Charlotte Haines, and Agatha couldn't afford for him to know she knew.

The police officer side-eyed them when they stepped back into the lobby. Agatha made an excuse about it being too loud and unsettling with everything happening down on the street. They would stay at a hotel tonight, she explained.

If the officer noticed that neither of them had packed a bag, he didn't let on and only nodded sympathetically.

They went out the back. Paul strode away down the access road toward the street. Agatha planted her feet and waited. He was nearly thirty feet away before registering her absence. That was actually pretty good for him. She'd expected him to get to the corner before noticing he was alone.

"What are you doing?" he called back to her.

"Nothing," she replied.

"Well, come on. I need you to drive me back to the house."

"Call an Uber."

His head tilted a quarter inch to the side. "Are we negotiating?"

"What did you tell me my first day?"

He smiled fondly at the memory. "Everything is a negotiation."

"There's your answer."

"So what do you want?"

"For you to come *here*," she said, although she didn't want to be that close to him.

He grinned at her with something close to pride, but his feet didn't move. Seconds passed like hours. All that was missing was for a tumbleweed to roll lazily between them and an old, cracked church bell to announce high noon. She took out her keys and held them in the palm of her hand.

"Take it. I'll call a car," she said.

He closed the distance between them but didn't take the keys. This wasn't about a ride. He didn't want to go home alone, and she knew it.

"Well?" he asked petulantly.

"Why don't we start with what you want, Paul."

"Can we talk about it on the way?"

She didn't dignify that with a response.

He sighed. "You're actually going to make me say it?"

"I think we're past gray areas, don't you?"

"Fine. I need your help securing my house and recovering what was taken."

She nodded as if he'd asked for a simple favor. "But any pictures of me, when we're done? They're mine."

An SUV was rolling slowly down the access road. They stepped out of the way while Paul thought it over.

"I can live with that," he said. "As long as you get them back."

"Well, it's all academic if I can't."

"True," Paul agreed, frowning at the SUV, which had slowed to a crawl. Its headlights were in his eyes, and he put a hand in front of his face. He waved for the driver to pass. "What's this guy doing?"

Agatha realized what was happening a half second before it happened. Whoever had thrown Tina Lu off her balcony wasn't on their way to Paul's house. Why break in when you could get the owner to unlock the front door?

"Paul." Something in Agatha's voice told him the rest of the story.

"Oh crap," he said.

The headlights switched off, and both front doors opened in unison. From the driver's seat a man emerged, short of hair and short of temper, judging by the lines his scowl had chiseled into his face. Agatha didn't have time to notice anything else about him. She'd been held up at gunpoint once walking home from work after a late night on the Hill. It had scared her so badly that she hadn't slept well for a month. Eventually she'd gone to a gun range in Virginia to learn to shoot. If she demystified guns, she hoped, she wouldn't be so afraid of them. Like most things, she'd taken it to an extreme and become quite a good shot. Her handgun, however, was sitting unhelpfully in her bedside drawer.

Staring at the man's hand, she realized none of it had made any difference. Having one pointed at her still scared her to death.

"Miss Cross," the second man said in a voice as smooth and cold as Russian vodka. "It is good to see you again."

His voice was familiar, but she couldn't place it immediately. Perhaps because he was sequestered in a different memory silo and didn't belong here. The sheer impossibility was making her momentarily stupid. She forced herself to look away from the gun and across the car to the passenger side. Resting his arms on the top of the SUV and looking very much like the cat who'd filleted the canary, Sergei was watching her through hooded eyes.

She was surprised as hell, but now was not the time to sound it. "Hello again, Sergei."

He smiled approvingly and said something in Russian to his associate, who responded in agreement.

"What did he say?" she asked.

"That you have the eyes of a soldier. I agree."

"Excuse me. What is going on?" Paul said, locating his voice.

"Mr. Paxton," Sergei said, only now acknowledging him. "It is good to meet you. You will get in the car now."

"I'm not getting in anywhere."

"You can get in or crawl in, Congressman," Sergei said, nodding to his driver, who seized Paxton by the arm. To his credit, Paxton took Sergei at his word and went along meekly.

"What about me?" Agatha asked.

"It is unfortunate that you did not stay out of it as you were asked."

The way Sergei said it confirmed for Agatha how the pieces all fit together.

"Cal Swinden. Cal brought you into this."

"Well, when you made it clear that you could not deliver, it was decided a less delicate approach was best." It wasn't explicitly a confession, but Agatha knew Sergei had thrown Tina Lu off her balcony— though only after she gave him the pictures. Now he wanted the rest and didn't intend to leave Paul or her alive after he had them. He beckoned for Agatha to get in on his side and looked pleased that she came willingly.

It all made her laugh.

"What is funny?" he asked.

"Just that there are a thousand cops on the other side of this building. You'd think I'd be safer."

"Nothing is more dangerous than a false sense of security," he said consolingly and held open the back door. "I told my employer about you. Suggested he hire you."

"That's very flattering."

"Unfortunately he had reservations."

"Oh? Such as?" Not that she cared. Agatha was playing for time and hoping for a miracle that was unlikely to arrive.

"You're a woman." He sounded almost apologetic.

"No arguing with that."

"He is a man from another time and prefers the old ways."

"Speaking of false senses of security . . ." Old men had always tried to stop the world from changing even as they were on the way out of it.

"Perhaps." Sergei shrugged. "And now we are here."

Agatha got in opposite Paul, who was staring, mouth agape, at the man sitting beside him. Cal Swinden. By the look of him, Cal had had better days. One of his eyes was swollen entirely shut, and the collar of his button-down was flecked with his own blood, some of which had dried at the corner of his mouth. Even so, Cal was doing his best to maintain an illusion of composure and control, sitting, legs crossed, as if he were in his office waiting for a meeting to begin.

"You know Paul Paxton, I assume?" she said.

"By reputation," Cal said. "Actually, never been formally introduced." He offered his hand. "Cal Swinden."

Paul shook it. "I've met your wife a few times. She's very impressive."

"Ex-wife," Cal corrected.

"Oh, well, in that case, congratulations."

The two men chuckled.

"Quiet. Enough talk," Sergei snapped from the front seat like a teacher shushing an unruly busload of kids. Agatha was grateful. Dying was one thing; dying listening to their adolescent banter was quite another.

Sergei added, "Pass your phones to me."

"Where are you taking us?" Paul asked but did as he'd been told.

"Home, Mr. Paxton. Where else?" Sergei replied and said something in Russian to his driver.

The SUV started forward down the access road. They didn't get very far, though. A figure darted out from the loading dock and blocked the way. Grudgingly, the SUV stopped, and the man slapped his hands on the hood.

The driver looked to Sergei and asked something in Russian. Agatha guessed it was along the lines of "Can I please run this idiot down?" because when Sergei shook his head, the driver looked profoundly disappointed.

Sergei got out while the driver turned around slowly in his seat and fixed them with a look that needed no translation—*not a damned sound.*

That was fine. From the back, all three were straining to hear what Sergei was saying anyway. It was too muffled to pick out, but to their collective surprise, he shook hands with the man and escorted him to the back of the SUV and held the door open for him.

The man got in. The funny thing was that Agatha knew him . . . well, recognized him from the news, anyway: Felix Gallardo. He'd recently left the White House for the private sector. *Or had he?* she wondered, her natural inclination to paranoia ratcheting up a notch. She couldn't decide whether it was good or bad news that he was here.

"Hello, Congressman," Felix said. "I'm sorry about Tina Lu. She'll be missed."

"Thank you, Felix. That's good of you."

Felix looked at Cal and spoke his name as if reading it from an underwhelming menu. "Cal."

"Felix."

Then he turned to Agatha and extended his hand. "Miss Cross, why am I not surprised to find you here?"

For once her natural poker face slipped. How did he know her name? She didn't know and didn't like any of the possible answers. There was a sliver of a silver lining, though—she had an answer to whether Felix being here was good or bad for her.

It was bad, very bad.

CHAPTER THIRTY-TWO

The most surreal part of the drive was how sanguine everyone was. Paul and Cal casually hobnobbing as if they'd bumped into each other in the lobby of the Kennedy Center. Felix Gallardo climbing willingly into the SUV like it was a private shuttle to the party of the summer. No one but Agatha seemed remotely concerned by the armed Russians holding them hostage. It was an impressive act of willful ignorance that made her feel like she was losing her mind. Her anxiety dreams were like this—the feeling of hurtling down a steep slope, certain that disaster awaited at the bottom but unable to get off or to make it stop. In her dreams, though, she never saw the end of the line. She always woke first, exhausted and frustrated. It wouldn't finish that way tonight.

When they arrived, the SUV backed into Paul's driveway. Sergei ushered them into the house without making threats or even raising his voice, everything so civilized and cordial. It was impressive, really. A whole pot of frogs calmly treading water that was becoming uncomfortably hot. Agatha understood it, then. These men. They'd always been able to talk themselves out of any situation, any trouble. It had always been their gift, but now it was their Achilles' heel. They couldn't see that the rules of the game had changed. This wasn't a negotiation; it was an unconditional surrender with terms dictated at gunpoint.

Sergei gathered them all in the living room, which was still set up for poker. He quickly disabused them of any illusions about why they were there. The time for pleasantries had passed. "The pictures. Where are they?"

"What pictures?" Paul asked innocently.

It was not well received. Sergei said something in Russian, and his man disappeared into the kitchen.

Paul smiled winningly. "Why don't we sit down, talk this through?"

"Your woman told me the pictures were here. She just didn't know where."

The mention of Tina Lu had a sobering effect on Paul, who cleared his throat but then didn't seem to know what to say. Sergei's man returned with a fistful of knives and began laying them out on the green felt of the poker table with all-too-familiar precision.

Paul blanched. "Okay, that's not necessary."

"Neither is lying to me," Sergei responded.

"May I?" Cal interrupted and continued when Sergei nodded. "Paul. Look. I understand this is less than an ideal outcome for you, but I think you'll see that being agreeable now is your only hope of preventing a much worse one."

"It's not right, and you know it," Paul said without taking his eyes from the knives. "You're asking me to give up everything."

"It's the only choice now."

"Easy for you to say. And what do I get out of this?"

Sergei's head tilted toward Agatha. *Are they kidding me with this?* his world-weary eyes seemed to ask.

She raised an eyebrow. *Welcome to Washington.*

"What do you get?" Cal asked rhetorically. "You get to stay a congressman. And who knows, maybe a Supreme Court judge. It might be too late to pull the nomination."

"Really?" Paul said and looked at Felix hopefully.

"Sure," Cal said soothingly. "Isn't that right, Felix."

Felix looked unhappy to be drawn into this charade. "Well, obviously, I can't speak for the president."

"But if you had to guess."

"Yes, I'm sure the president won't want to rock the boat this late in the process. And he's always been very fond of the congressman."

Agatha had never heard a more bald-faced lie, and she'd heard some beauties in her time, most of them straight from Paul Paxton's lips. She'd have thought he'd know better, but he actually seemed to be buying it. Then again, never underestimate the persuasive power of sharp knives. A person would believe almost anything if the alternative were being carved into steaks. So she didn't blame Paul when he gave up the combination to his safe without a fight. There was no reason to drag out the inevitable. What would that accomplish except for ruining his carpet?

After a short back-and-forth in Russian, Sergei's man followed Paul to the office. He returned with a manila envelope and put it in Sergei's open hand. It felt like an awards show: *And the winner of the incriminating photographs goes to . . .*

To Sergei, judging by the Grinch's smile that spread across his normally stoic face.

"*Da. Da. Da,*" he said as he flipped through the pictures. When he was done, he went through them a second time, this time turning them, one at a time, and showing each to Felix. The others could all see and leaned in for a better look. Even Agatha, who already knew what the pictures showed but felt duty bound to not look away. The least she could do was acknowledge what she'd done. How she'd minted personal tragedy into an opportunity. Opportunity for the man who'd murdered Charlotte, as it turned out. Maybe they both deserved to die.

The first shot was of Congressman Harrison Clark and Agatha in the doorway. Agatha remembered how irritated she'd been with Charlotte. It had been a challenge to navigate the body out of the room. There'd been a lot of awkward fumbling, trying to get a good handhold. Not wanting to drop their cargo, but also not wanting to touch Charlotte more than necessary. Had she even once felt any empathy for a young woman who had lost her life? If she had, she didn't remember, and it hadn't stopped her from doing what she'd done.

"Do you understand, Mr. Gallardo? What we have on your boss," Sergei asked.

"Yes," Felix said. He looked ashen, and Agatha wondered if he'd known before now. "What are your terms?"

"My employer is Kirill Tumenov."

The name clearly meant something to Felix and Paul. Cal already knew but still flinched at its mention.

"And what does he want?" Felix asked.

"Your Treasury Department, as part of more general sanctions targeting Russian nationals, mistakenly included Mr. Tumenov on their list. His assets were frozen in error, property seized. He wishes for this grave injustice to be corrected."

"Mistakes do happen," Felix agreed. "And in return, can we expect the return of these photographs?"

"No, nothing so straightforward, I'm afraid," Sergei said. "But for doing the right thing, the president can depend on Mr. Tumenov's *enthusiastic* endorsement for a second term."

"I understand. Well, I'll deliver your message. Let me see what I can do. How should we get in touch? Through Mr. Swinden?"

"Yes, he will remain our proxy," Sergei said and fixed Cal with a look that Agatha would remember as long as she lived. "For now."

"I understand," Cal said. "Thank you."

"*Убей его,*" Sergei said, switching to Russian.

Agatha's attention had been on the photographs and then on Felix. She'd lost track of Sergei's man and hadn't noticed him slip around behind them. Neither had Paul. At least not until the belt dropped over his head and was yanked brutally tight around his throat. Paul let out a gurgling cry as he was lifted onto his toes, back arched painfully, hands flailing behind him. It was terrifying how fast his face began to turn purple.

Cal backed away. Felix took the Lord's name in vain and, when that had no obvious effect, chanted it over and over like a lost supplicant. Only Agatha took an instinctive step toward Paul, wanting to help, not knowing how. Sergei pointed his pistol at Agatha and ordered her to stop.

She put her hands up. "You don't want to do this."

"It is regrettable. I'm sorry."

Paul's arms went limp at his sides. He wasn't dead, not yet, but there wasn't much time left.

"You need him," she said quietly.

Sergei frowned at her, disappointed. They both knew she would say anything at this point.

"Clark might lose," she explained.

"What?" His expression didn't change, but he put a hand up. His man loosened the belt marginally. Paul's heels returned to the rug.

"What if he loses the next election?" Agatha said.

"He's very popular."

"So was George Bush in 1990. A lot can happen in two years. Does your boss really want to take that chance?" she asked. "Me? I wouldn't put all my eggs in one basket."

"Eggs? I don't understand. What do eggs have to do with it?"

"Figure of speech. What I mean is that even if Clark wins a second term, what does your boss get? At best, six years. And then what? A new president is elected, and Tumenov is back to square one. But a justice on the Supreme Court? You realize that's a lifetime appointment. Think of the possibilities."

Sergei pointed to the floor. The belt came away. Paul slipped gracelessly to the ground. After a moment, his hands twitched, and he took a labored breath as if his body had forgotten how. He would live but would need to wear a scarf for a few weeks.

"You are very, very good," Sergei said. "Regretfully, there is another problem."

Agatha nodded, recognizing it before he could say it. "What do I bring to the table?"

"Yes, I knew you would see my problem," Sergei said, gesturing first to Felix, then Cal, and finally Paul. "This one will be my contact with the White House. This one works for me and cares only about money. And this one wants to be a judge. But you? What do you want?"

"I just want to be left alone."

Sergei grimaced. "Those are the words of a loose end."

"The only reason I'm here at all is because I'm in some of those pictures. I just want them destroyed."

"And then you'll return to private life, never to be heard from again. Is that the fairy tale I am wandering through?"

"You don't need all of the pictures. It's the president you want, not me," Agatha said, intensely aware that Sergei's man had taken several quiet steps toward her, belt in hand.

"I don't know that I would do that even if they were mine to destroy."

"So keep them," Agatha suggested. "Incentive for me to keep quiet. I trust you with them more, anyway."

"That's very generous of you. And of course you give your word."

"I do," she said.

"Why don't we put it to your countrymen? Let them decide," Sergei suggested, turning to the group. "Do we do as she suggests and let her go? Trust her to keep her mouth shut."

The silence was profound and damning.

Agatha looked from face to face. Cal looked away, suddenly entranced by his hands. To his credit, Felix Gallardo had the courage to look her in the eyes. He'd clearly made his mind up, though, and said nothing. Finally, she came to Paul, who had recovered enough to find his feet, one hand gently massaging the livid marks at his throat. An apologetic half smile was the best he could do.

"I just saved your life, you son of a bitch."

"And I won't forget it," he croaked.

"'Thank you for your service'—is that it?"

Paul didn't have an answer but looked to Sergei and nodded.

"You're all sons of bitches," Agatha said but had to hand it to Sergei. Letting them decide her fate was a stroke of genius. It made them all culpable in her death. Coconspirators now and forever. One final blood sacrifice binding the three Americans to him. He should get a group photo with her body. It could be their annual Christmas card.

"You played a good game," Sergei said. Leave it to a man to think a compliment would make up for killing her.

"May I see my phone for a moment?" It was a Hail Mary, but a prayer was all she had left.

"I think not." Sergei chuckled but gave no orders in Russian. She felt him sizing her up, trying to spot her angle.

"Trust me. There's something you'll want to see," she said and held out her hand, not knowing whether it was an empty promise.

Reluctantly, he fished her phone out of his jacket pocket. He didn't hand it over but held up the lock screen for her to enter the passcode. It showed a dozen unread text messages from a blocked number. Agatha breathed a sigh of relief and opened the first photograph.

Credit where credit was due, Darius hadn't lost his touch. Even in the dim light behind Tina Lu's apartment building, Sergei was unmistakable. Same went for the pistol in his hand and the license plate of his vehicle. Sergei cursed and kept scrolling through the pictures, which told the story of Agatha and Paul being forced into the SUV. There was a good one of Felix, too, before the scene jumped to Paul's front yard, where everyone was herded into the house at gunpoint.

"And what do you intend to do with these pictures?" Sergei demanded, a scowl replacing his confident smile.

"Nothing. They have no value."

"No?"

"Not if I walk out of here in the next few minutes."

"You think I can't get out of the country before the FBI knows to look for me?"

"Oh, I'm sure you'll get out in one piece, Sergei. You're a survivor. But what will Kirill Tumenov think? It'll be the end of his scheme. How long until you find *your*self dying slowly on a fence somewhere?"

A murmur of protest went up from the three American men. Sergei silenced it with a look that verged on a felony. "I'm still not giving you the pictures."

"Keep them. It doesn't matter anymore."

"And you will keep your word and say nothing about my business here?"

"You didn't take my word when you had the chance, and I don't offer it twice. But if I talk, I go to jail. It's not that complicated."

"A woman of principle."

"Never been called that before."

The corner of Sergei's lip twitched but went still before Agatha could name the emotion behind it.

"Go," he said, handing her the phone. "Go, before I change my mind."

Agatha didn't wait to be asked twice. She took one last look around the room on the way out the door. Paul, Cal, and Felix watched her. Three wolves in a dark, dark wood that had believed they'd cornered their prey and couldn't comprehend how it had escaped. She smiled and made a silent promise to each of them. Out on the street, she walked hurriedly up the sidewalk. It took every ounce of self-control not to look back, expecting at any moment for that belt to loop around her neck.

A car slowed alongside her. She heard her name but kept walking.

"A. Hey, A! Agatha!"

She finally glanced over. It was Darius, trying to get her attention. Behind the wheel, Shelby waved joyfully like they hadn't seen each other in years.

Agatha let out a breath she'd been holding since the living room.

Darius waved her over. "Come on. Get in."

She did just that, climbing in the back seat, and threw her arms around the headrest and hugged him gratefully. She wasn't much of a crier, but it sounded really good right about now. It wasn't time, though. Maybe later, when this was done.

"You saved my life tonight," she said.

"Hey, I just took the pictures. Should've seen young miss drive. She's no joke."

"Not much to do in Stamps but drive too fast," Shelby said with a grin.

Agatha reached for Shelby and squeezed her arm. "Thank you."

"What happened in there?" Shelby asked.

"You don't want to know."

"But it's over?"

Not yet it wasn't. While Shelby drove them away, Agatha scrolled through her contacts and dialed Kat Milbrandt's number. It rang so long that when it finally picked up, Agatha assumed it must be voicemail.

"Agatha?" a sleepy voice answered.

"Hi, Katherine."

"Are you alright? What's going on? It's late."

"How are the confirmation hearings? Got you working hard?"

"Night and day. You know how Tomlin is. It's got to be by the book, or she's not happy."

"I have a favor to ask."

"Another one?"

"I know, I know. I'll owe you. I promise."

"What is it?"

"Does she have room on the witness list for one more?"

"It's pretty full, but yeah, probably," Katherine said, sounding confused. "Who do you have in mind?"

Agatha paused, gathering her resolve to not chicken out now. All it took was picturing Paul, Cal, and Felix, standing there like three see-no-evil monkeys while Sergei prepared to kill her. She'd made them all a promise, one she aimed to keep no matter the cost.

"Who do you have in mind?" Katherine asked a second time.

EPILOGUE

Unable to sit still, Agatha fussed in front of the mirror, trying vainly to ignore the commotion on the other side of the door. It sounded like a small army was setting up camp in Hart 216, otherwise known as the Central Hearing Facility. She smoothed her skirt and rebuttoned her jacket, thinking how ironic this all was. When she'd bought the suit to finesse a meeting with Cal Swinden, Hart 216 was the last place she'd expected to wear it. At least she was getting one more use out of it. She smirked—look at Agatha Cross, finding the bright side.

"What?" her dad asked. She hadn't smiled often lately, so his confusion was warranted.

"I paid too much for this outfit," she said. "How do I look?"

"Like my daughter," he said and stood beside her. He was wearing the suit he'd buried his wife in and had sworn not to wear again until they laid him down beside her. After thirty years, it was a little big on him, but Agatha thought he looked handsome. He'd even shaved.

She leaned against him. "Thanks for being here, Dad."

"Anytime, kiddo."

His phone vibrated with an incoming text. He glanced at the screen and smiled, showing her the message. It was Shelby asking what to get for dinner, like it was just any old Tuesday. She'd returned only yesterday from visiting her sister down in Arkansas, where they'd been finalizing plans for newly minted high school graduate Lola Arthur to move to

Washington. Agatha found it inexplicably calming to have her tenant back.

The door to the anteroom opened just wide enough for Katherine Milbrandt to slip inside. The clamor of voices followed her, rising to a roar until she shut the door behind her. She put her back to it as if a barbarian horde were ready to break it down. Was that an unfair way to characterize the Washington press corps? Agatha glanced over at Isha Roy in the corner, typing away on her laptop. No, *barbarian horde* would be harsh, but there was an uncivilized tension in the air. Whispers about Agatha's testimony had made their way around town, and opinion was bitterly divided over whether she represented a nomination bombshell or just another partisan crackpot. The president's political apparatus, headed up by Felix Gallardo, was already working overtime to paint her as the latter.

"How is it out there?" Agatha asked.

"Going to be a full house," Katherine said with a practiced smile intended to reassure. "They're almost ready for you."

She had been saying that for the better part of an hour.

"Promises, promises."

"I know," Katherine admitted. "You just have the place on edge. Lot of backroom maneuvering going on before they gavel in."

"You have a seat for my dad?"

Katherine nodded. "He'll be right behind you. Do you need anything before we get started?"

"A way out? Any chance this place has a secret tunnel?" she asked hopefully.

"No such luck." Katherine's smile was genuine this time.

"Then I guess I'm all set. Thanks for nothing."

Katherine squeezed her arm. "Okay, I'll be back for you in a few minutes."

When Katherine was gone, Agatha put her hands on her hips and stared at the floor.

Her dad put a concerned hand on her back. "You okay?"

She nodded and glanced up at Isha, who watched intently. Good to her word, Agatha had spent dozens of hours talking through the night of Charlotte Haines's death, as well as the events surrounding Tina Lu's tragic fall. Darius and Shelby had even volunteered to corroborate Isha's story on the condition that they stayed on background. Agatha had told Isha everything, and after a lifetime spent behind the scenes, she'd never felt more naked and exposed.

It had also given her time to be honest with herself about the testimony she would give today. Since walking out of that house alive, she had decided two things for certain: Paul Paxton didn't belong on the Supreme Court, and Harrison Clark was a threat to the country so long as he remained in the Oval Office. Living with the knowledge that she was responsible for both wasn't an option. Not anymore. So here she was, ready to tell the truth at long last, even if it made not one shred of difference. She was a realist. Without the photographs, it was simply her word against theirs. She was about to martyr herself for nothing.

"There are places I'd rather be," she admitted. "Never really liked being the center of attention."

Isha nodded and typed a note into the laptop perched on her knees. Her first major article on Paul Paxton would publish in conjunction with Agatha's appearance at today's hearings, but she had a lot of follow-ups in the pipeline, including a backstage account of today's hearing.

"Honey, talk to me," her dad said.

"You know this won't work, right?"

"It's going to be okay."

"I'm serious, Dad. There's no proof. I don't have the photographs. I've got nothing. Just a wild story about Russian oligarchs and the president of the United States. All they have to do is paint me as a crazy, vindictive bitch and vote to confirm Paxton anyway. It's happened before. You know it has. This was a stupid idea."

Isha had stopped typing and was watching to see if there would be an eleventh-hour twist to the tale.

John Cardiff took his daughter by both arms and faced her. "You can't control what other people will do."

"Dad," Agatha pleaded. "What do *I* do?"

"Exactly," he said, looking her in the eyes. "What *do* you do?"

An idea came to her, unbidden and unwanted—*confess*. That was what she would have to do. Confess that it had been *she* who'd given the drugs to Charlotte Haines, not Darius. Confess that she'd known the drugs were laced with poison. How? Because she'd conspired with her boss, Paul Paxton, to kill her. They'd planned it together, every step of the way. People would have to believe her then, wouldn't they? No one confessed to a crime if they were innocent. It was ironic, but to be credible, Agatha would have to commit perjury. She had to be guilty. Maybe that was how it should be.

"I don't know that I'll make it to Uncle Pat's for Christmas."

"Then I'll come to you," he said. "Wherever you are."

The door to the anteroom opened, and Katherine slipped back inside.

"It's time," she said, almost apologetically.

Agatha felt herself nodding, which led miraculously to her standing up straight. If her legs were shaking, it would just be her little secret. She checked herself in the mirror one last time and met her dad's eyes.

"Ready?" she asked.

"I'm right behind you. Lead the way."

ACKNOWLEDGMENTS

I'm not from Washington—in a city with so many transients, to be from DC means something—but my family moved here when I was a boy, and it's been home for much of my life. In high school, I saw *No Way Out* at the Uptown Theater, or perhaps I just loved the balcony so much that that's where I remember seeing everything. It's a spy thriller with a killer twist, but my strongest memory of the movie is the audience's collective groan followed by laughter as Kevin Costner eluded the bad guys via the fictional Georgetown Metro. Georgetown's conspicuous lack of a metro is a matter of DC lore and legend, so it struck us as especially funny. No one likes to see their home misrepresented.

When I began outlining *The Slate*, I wrote "No Georgetown Metros" in my notepad and underlined it. Creative license is unavoidable in fiction, so perhaps it was a fool's errand, but I set out to write a political thriller that felt true to the city and wouldn't make my friends and neighbors roll their eyes . . . at least not too often. I'll leave it for you to decide how successful I was, but should you find yourself groaning, know that that's on me and not the incredible people who agreed to read early drafts, offer suggestions and corrections, and generally steer me in the right direction.

Profound thanks to those readers for their support and giving so generously of their time and expertise—Vanessa Brimner, Steve Feldhaus, Lee Friedman, Sy Damle, Carolyn Fiddler, Corbett McKinney, Nadine Nettmann, Johnny Shaw, and Aliyah Oestreicher.

To the P&B writers' group—Joe Hart, Matt Iden, D.M. Pulley, Steve Konkoly—you're a good lot, and our Zooms made the last few years much more survivable. To paraphrase an old Steve Martin movie, I'll just say that I would rather be with you than with the finest people in the world.

My deepest thanks also to Gracie Doyle, Megha Parekh, and everyone at Thomas & Mercer. Meeting all of you changed my life, and I am forever grateful.

Writing *The Slate* also gave me the opportunity to reconnect with Ed Stackler, the wonderful editor of the Gibson Vaughn series. I'm grateful to all his guidance in rounding the book into shape.

Lastly, to David Hale Smith, my agent and friend: thanks for continuing to be a miracle worker and just generally the best.

ABOUT THE AUTHOR

Photo © 2017 Douglas Sonders

Matthew FitzSimmons is the author of the *Wall Street Journal* bestselling Gibson Vaughn series, which includes *Origami Man, Debris Line, Cold Harbor, Poisonfeather,* and *The Short Drop,* and the Constance series. Born in Illinois and raised in London, he makes his home in Washington, DC. For more information, visit him at www.matthewfitzsimmons.com.